"ARE YOU NERVOUS BEING ALONE WITH ME, JANE?"

Graham spoke softly as he held her in his arms. "You don't have to be."

"A little." She smiled up at him. "This is all so new to me."

"I feel as if I've known you forever," he admitted. "And I've been wanting to kiss you since that first day we met."

"Have you really?" Jane felt as if her breathing had stopped. Her heart was bursting with excitement, fright and happiness.

He nodded, his blue eyes holding hers. His fingers, warm and strong, cupped her face, turning it up to his. A moment later his lips settled on hers, as light as a bird's wing, then harder so her mouth slowly opened under his. . . .

ABOUT THE AUTHOR

Lynn Erickson is actually a writing team
hailing from Colorado. Molly Swanton and
Carla Peltonen became friends first and then
started writing together nearly nine years ago.
Molly handles the initial plotting, while Carla
focuses on research. They then work on alternate
chapters and "write and rewrite" till the book is
perfect. Theirs has been a fruitful collaboration;
A Perfect Gem is the seventh Superromance for
this delightful twosome.

Books by Lynn Erickson

HARLEQUIN SUPERROMANCE

HARLEQUIN INTRIGUE

Don't miss any of our special offers. Write to us at the
following address for information on our newest releases.

Harlequin Reader Service
901 Fuhrmann Blvd., P.O. Box 1397, Buffalo, NY 14240
Canadian address: P.O. Box 603,
Fort Erie, Ont. L2A 5X3

Lynn Erickson

A PERFECT GEM

Harlequin Books

TORONTO • NEW YORK • LONDON
AMSTERDAM • PARIS • SYDNEY • HAMBURG
STOCKHOLM • ATHENS • TOKYO • MILAN

Published September 1987

First printing July 1987

ISBN 0-373-70276-0

This book is dedicated to the memory of Smedley Butler, of whom it must be said his truth was even stranger than my fiction, and to Bob Duggan, the real-life Rob Dearborn and head of Executive Security International of Aspen, Colorado. I ask his forgiveness for any liberties taken with his character and thank him for his invaluable assistance.

CHAPTER ONE

JANE MANNING'S HANDS GRIPPED THE WHEEL competently as she steered into a skid that brought her dangerously close to the edge of the road. The car she drove was an old state-trooper cruiser with a beefed-up suspension and a throaty-sounding engine; in the back seat sat her passenger, a silent blond man who was bounced around as she evaded her pursuers.

"Hang on," Jane called over her shoulder to her charge, "I'm going to try something."

She downshifted, pulled out of the skid skillfully and glanced once again into her rearview mirror. One of the drivers chasing her had overcorrected his skid and slid off the road into a sagebrush-lined ditch. Good.

The ribbon of pavement lay in front of her, curving away across the dry Colorado plateau. The July sun glared into her eyes and made her back stick to the plastic seat of the car. Jane watched carefully, her eyes darting back and forth across her field of vision and then to the rearview mirror again. What else would they pull? Two cars had started out chasing her but were there more waiting in ambush behind that pile of old tires? Or would men with machine guns pop up from that ditch and shoot at her and her passenger? Would there be a barricade ahead?

There was no time to consider that, Jane thought as she weaved expertly across the roadway in order to present a difficult target. Venturing another quick glance in the mirror, she saw that the remaining car was speeding up, nudging her bumper. Jane stepped on the gas, forcing the pedal to the floor as the sound of machine-gun fire reached her ears. She drove like a demon, just on the edge of control, while sweat trickled from her brow into her eyes. Adrenaline pumped through her veins furiously and she fought the instinct to duck her head.

Okay, this was it. She jammed on the brakes, heard the squeal of tires, smelled hot rubber. The driver behind her braked violently to avoid a collision and Jane spun the wheel, screeching into a 180-degree turn, then hit the gas, leaving the other car smoking and stalled, in a ditch, half off the road.

She'd done it! Jane pulled up at the starting line of the track and got out of her car. She opened the back door and grinned widely at the tall blond man who emerged unperturbed from the back seat.

"Good work," said Rob Dearborn quietly, shaking her hand.

"I passed?" Jane asked.

Dearborn nodded in his usual unemotional way. Not a hint of the hair-raising ride he'd just been subjected to showed on his coolly placid features. He gave away nothing beyond his always carefully selected words. "You pass," was all he said.

Jane pumped his hand even harder. The other students, all men, crowded around, congratulating her. "Good driving...helluva maneuver...great control...smart move."

Jane turned to them and smiled, feeling triumph and relief and satisfaction. "Wow, what a way to pass a final exam!" she exclaimed.

Graduation was a week later. The International Security Academy of Aspen, Colorado, the most renowned bodyguard training school in the United States, always held its graduation party in the Steak Pit, an unpretentious restaurant that catered to local Aspenites. After finishing the salad, the juicy steaks, the steaming baked potatoes, everybody sat back and relaxed as Rob Dearborn, the head of the ISA, stood and gave a short speech.

Jane Manning sat with the nineteen other students and listened carefully to her teacher's words. She had been studying for almost two years: weaponry, martial arts, bomb detection, evasive driving, first aid, electronic surveillance, the psychology of criminals, followed by an intensive, two-week practical session in Aspen. This evening was the culmination of it all.

"You've learned how to use certain methods to protect yourselves and your clients," Rob Dearborn was saying. "But the use of violence is only a last resort. If you have to use your physical skills or a gun you've already failed in the principal lesson, which is staying out of trouble. When a weapon is drawn, you are committed to using it, perhaps eliminating more favorable options."

Jane listened in rapt attention. There wasn't much Rob Dearborn said that was not to the point, significant and well reasoned. Despite his laconic manner, he was a man who appeared to know something no one else was privileged to know and Jane respected him enormously. She sat straighter in her chair, proud of what she'd accomplished under his tutelage, ready to put into practice her hard-earned skills.

"The world is entering a chaotic time," Dearborn continued. His high cheekbones and air of perfect control and containment reminded one of a blond samurai warrior. "There will be crises. You *will* be needed."

Then the other teachers gave their speeches. They all had something to say: the burly ex-Secret Service agent who dealt with the field of security; the well-built, suntanned former FBI man who taught undercover skills; the India-napolis 500 racer who was in charge of evasive driving; the bearded paramedic who instructed students in first aid; and the powerful, stocky teacher of evasion techniques and client protection, who liked to play terrorist against his students.

There were awards: best marksman, best driver, best re-flexes. Jane gasped in surprise when she got an award for her achievement in Hwa Rang Do, the exacting form of Korean karate the students all had to learn from Rob him-self. She went up to collect her certificate from him while the nearly all-male audience clapped and hooted. Jane felt herself blushing with pleasure and on-the-spot embarrass-ment.

When she sat down again her father shook his head in baffled consternation. One of her older brothers, James, punched her in the biceps gently and mouthed, "Congrat-ulations, squirt."

After the presentations there was much bantering, good-natured teasing, high spirits and a few damp eyes. Jane in-troduced her father, Tom Manning, and her brothers, James and Jared, to Rob Dearborn.

"You've raised quite a girl there," said Rob with his calm smile.

"I certainly have," replied Tom Manning in his charac-teristically straightforward fashion. Nevertheless he was still shaking his head in bewilderment. For all his pride in her, Jane knew precisely what he was thinking: *my little girl, a bodyguard*?

"She'll do well," Rob commented. "I've got some peo-ple interested in her already."

"For a job?" queried Jared.

"*Of course*," said Jane, mortified. "Women make the best bodyguards."

The three male Mannings appeared skeptical.

"It's true in many cases," explained Rob, rescuing her. "Female bodyguards help a client keep a low profile. They don't *look* like bodyguards. It can be very effective."

"But she's not, you know, strong," protested James. "Not like a man."

"She's learned ways of disabling an attacker by using his own weight against him. She's quick and wiry and knows her karate. She'll manage very well," Rob assured him.

"That remains to be seen," said her father, still shaking his head.

When the evening came to a close and it was time to say goodbye, Jane felt a bit teary-eyed. Who knew when the students' paths might cross again? They had all grown so close, as people do when they are subjected to difficult, demanding times together. There had been the terrible moments of doubt when Ned, the overweight young man from Florida, nearly killed himself in the driving school; there had been the sadness and confusion of all the students when three had dropped out of the course after only two days of intense training; there had been the time when Jane herself had frozen during a well-staged terrorist attack involving two young women wheeling baby carriages.

But there had been the good times as well: the night the other students, all men, had invited Jane to go for a beer; the day they had received their black sweatshirts with the Korean karate symbol on the front and International Security Academy stenciled on the back; the time they'd all hit the bull's-eye in target practice.

And for Jane, especially, there had been Rob, who'd encouraged her when everything and everyone seemed to be against her goal of completing the bodyguard course.

"Why do you want to become a bodyguard?" Rob Dearborn had asked during her initial interview two years before.

Jane had considered the question carefully before answering. "I want something more than staying on our ranch. I want more than marriage and a family. I want to do something exciting and maybe a little dangerous. I want to *prove* myself."

Rob had nodded, understanding, and Jane had known then that she could do it. She could do anything if she set her mind to it. Maybe she felt that way because she'd been raised by her widowed father and four older brothers. There'd never been any slack for little Janey. She'd been expected to take the rough-and-tumble existence of growing up on a ranch, the wild horseback rides, the stubborn calves to rope, trees to climb, haylofts to jump out of, dares and challenges to accept. It had made her tough physically and stubborn mentally.

And yet there was nothing unfeminine about Jane. Five feet eight inches tall, she was slim in build with small breasts, a narrow waist and a compact rear end. Her nose was too small, turned up and freckled; one front tooth was not even with the other and her gaze was alarmingly level. She had green eyes, dark brows and heavy brown hair cut in an easy-to-keep pageboy style. She knew she was often described as down-to-earth, wholesome, refreshing, at best "cute." Never beautiful, sexy or glamorous. And even though Jane was twenty-six years old, she only looked eighteen.

"That's good," Rob had told her when she complained. "No one would ever suspect you of being a bodyguard. Use it to your advantage, Jane."

Two long years of hope and frustration and doubt had passed and now the course was over. Rob had said the graduates were ready to face the real world. She sure hoped he was right as she exchanged addresses and final good-byes. With her father and brothers Jane walked out of the restaurant into the cool summer night of Aspen and drew in a breath of crystal-clear mountain air.

"So now you're a bodyguard," said Jared. "You gonna *guard* our stock?"

She ignored him pointedly and climbed into the dusty station wagon for the hour and a half ride home to Rifle, Colorado, where the Manning ranch was located.

"Now, really, squirt, what're you gonna do?" asked James.

"I'll wait until Rob places me. He's always got people calling him. You heard what he said. Someone's already interested."

"What if you get a client who's *too* interested in lady bodyguards?" Jared teased.

"I'd probably punch him out," she said coolly, "and then quit."

"You'll have to leave home," said her father sadly. "No one wants a bodyguard in Rifle, I reckon. It'll be some big city feller, some sheikh or the likes."

"Maybe. But, Daddy, you knew I was going to leave sooner or later."

Her father kept driving, his strong craggy profile shadowed, his Stetson drawn down low over his brow. "I guess. But not so far away." His large work-worn hands grasped the steering wheel as if it were a tractor. "If your mother knew..."

"You know she'd want me to do what I had to, Daddy," Jane said softly. "And I have to do this."

"You can always come home, Janey, whenever..."

"I know."

She'd heard the same thing from all five members of her family for years now. Not one of them could understand her restlessness or her need to pit herself against the world. However, it was to their collective credit that they never actually tried to stop her from doing anything. They might argue, grouse, tease, even swear, but the final decision had always been Jane's and she'd never shied from making them.

Originally, she had decided to go to veterinary school in Fort Collins when she'd graduated from the University of Colorado in Boulder. Her father had grumbled halfheartedly about marriage and a home but Jane was determined, and he took it in stride, even coming to like the idea of a homegrown vet to care for the valuable rodeo stock he raised.

Then, after two years and a lot of soul-searching, she'd realized veterinary school was not for her. She needed wider vistas and more excitement. Returning home, she'd helped out with the stock, broken a few mustangs, raced quarter horses at the local fairgrounds, dated casually and had been bored silly.

One day the *Denver Post*'s front page had featured Rob Dearborn and his International Security Academy, and Jane had been hooked. "Women have edge as hired shadows," a headline had shouted. Jane had read the article then reread it. "Holy cow," she'd whispered to herself, a great hope growing in her chest and a surging excitement. She'd run out to the barn where her father had been holding his prize quarter horse stallion for the blacksmith.

"Daddy, read this!" she'd cried, waving the paper in his face. "This is for me!"

"Take it easy, Janey, you'll scare Indigo."

The yelling and arguing had begun at the dinner table that evening. "Go ahead and do it, squirt," said James, the youngest male. "Plumb insane," scoffed Jared, the joker. "You sure you want to do this?" asked Joe, the oldest and most serious of the group. Married with a young son, he'd come over for a family conference.

"I'm as sure as I'll ever be," answered Jane with assurance.

"You just need a man," said John, the second oldest. He was engaged and tended to be chauvinistic about women of late.

Jane stood up and leaned over the table. "That's about the dumbest remark anybody's made!"

"Sit down, Jane," said her father. "Now, tell me again—what do you have to do and how much will it cost?"

Jane sank down into her seat, glowering at John, and began to explain everything to her father.

Six weeks later she had been interviewed by Rob Dearborn and then enrolled in the course. Texts were mailed to her: manuals on weaponry and surveillance, the history of terrorism, criminal psychology, emergency first aid. She'd studied hard every day. Her brothers had strutted around looking smug and superior, waiting for her to give it up. Her father had watched her thoughtfully but said nothing. She knew they all wanted her to change her mind about being a bodyguard but something intractable and resolute in her wouldn't give in.

Once a week she'd driven the hour and a half up the Roaring Fork River to Aspen to take Rob's Hwa Rang Do class, which Jane found grueling yet fascinating. It was hard physically but graceful, much like the discipline of ballet. It encompassed the mind, too, for concentration was a powerful aspect of Oriental martial arts. And respect for the teacher; a bow over folded hands was required at the start and end of class.

Jane learned that Hwa Rang Do began in Korea in A.D. 540 as a form of court entertainment. *By women.* Only later was the art form taken over by men and turned to warlike use. The study of the discipline consisted of innumerable "forms"—moves, joint locks, holds and kicks in combination that could disable, immobilize, even kill an opponent. They were repeated over and over until they became instinctive. Anyone attacking a Hwa Rang Do practitioner would find himself in an instant, reflexive whirl of hands or feet that could do great damage.

A year after Jane had begun her karate training, a year in which her brothers teased her without mercy, she finally got in a stew one day and tossed James to the floor of the barn with little more than a turn of her wrist. The jeers and taunting stopped miraculously.

Rob, however, always warned against the indiscriminate use of violence—of any sort. "I haven't used Hwa Rang Do in anger in fifteen years," he told his students. Rob was a fourth-degree black belt and just watching him move was exciting. While the rest of the class struggled, grunted and sweated, Rob flicked, feinted, and struck snakelike, totally in control, moving *with* his body instead of against it.

"Your hands and feet are deadly weapons," Rob would say and when Jane watched him demonstrate a kick or a hold she knew his words were true.

Jane had passed all the tests on guns with flying colors: she would assemble and reassemble the weapons, and practice her shooting over and over until her arms were tired and then start again. She knew the feel of weapons and their capabilities but was much more comfortable without one. Rob assured her that a bodyguard did not need to carry a gun; if her client were indeed attacked, chances were things would move so quickly there would be no opportunity to use a weapon, anyway. Up close, her hands were just as effective.

Now the months and months of work were over, Jane thought, as her father drove along the dark road home to Rifle. Would she really get a job as a bodyguard? Sudden doubts assailed her. What if her client were hurt, kidnapped, or even killed? Her training had been rigorous, her dedication complete, but the responsibility now seemed awesome.

The lights of Glenwood Springs appeared in the distance, and her father turned west on Interstate 70 and followed the Colorado River toward Rifle. She wondered where she would end up working. A foreign country maybe? Someplace exotic? Would she be a nanny for some top executive's children or a guard for a political figure? Probably she'd never see a moment of action in her life; Rob had told all of his students that it was more likely that a client would break a bone, get stung by a bee or have a coronary than get kidnapped. Jane wasn't sure whether she'd prefer an uneventful career or an action-packed one.

"So, you've done it," her father said finally. "I have to admit I sure was proud of you tonight. A little puzzled maybe but proud. And scared, Janey."

"Me, too," Jane said fervently.

IT WAS VERY HOT in Rifle, Colorado, the second Sunday in July but the heat didn't stop the ranchers from gathering at the Garfield County Fairgrounds for a day of quarter horse racing. Anywhere else where the thermometer hit ninety-nine degrees, people would have worn shorts, T-shirts, maybe a sundress and sandals. Not in Rifle. From toddlers to grandparents, everyone in the shaded stands wore Levi's, Western shirts, straw cowboy hats and boots.

Jane was dressed exactly the same save for the number twenty tied over her shirt. She was riding four horses in various races that day—two young ones for neighboring ranchers, a promising mare for her father and good old Indigo, who was bound to win the half-mile open event.

She loved the excitement of racing, the thunder of the horses' hooves as they pounded at top speed around the track. Quarter horses raced short distances but they "went like hell," as the old-timers said. Two-dollar bets could be placed before each of the eight races.

"Get that girth tight," came a humor-filled voice from over Jane's shoulder as she struggled with the leather strap holding the lightweight racing saddle on.

She turned, pushed her cowboy hat back and squinted up at a suntanned, handsome man on a powerful bay horse; he was one of the race marshals. "Branch Taggart," she said, smiling. "Haven't seen you in ages."

"Too long, Jane. I hear you been learnin' to be a body-guard. Is that crazy rumor true?" His grin widened.

"Sure is, Branch. I just graduated. I'm waiting for a job right now."

Branch leaned forward in his saddle, his smile fading. The big bay sidestepped nervously. "Jane, you are kiddin' me."

She deliberately turned her back on him and continued pulling her horse's girth tight. "I'm dead serious, Branch."

"You think we could go out tonight and talk about it over a beer or two?"

She cocked her head up at him and wiped the sweat off her upper lip with a finger before answering. "Sure, why not? But don't think I'm going to listen to you haranguing me about my career."

Branch straightened, held a hand up and chuckled. "I'll try my damnedest not to," he said then kicked his horse and trotted off toward the track.

Jane leaned against the horse she was saddling and watched him go. His broad shoulders filled his denim shirt and his big brimmed straw hat was set at the correct, rakish angle. She and Branch had been seeing each other on and off ever since she'd graduated from college. He was older, about thirty-five, and very much a local. He wanted a wife, Jane knew. She liked Branch. But he was a little too predictable, too much like her father and her brothers, too much like all the men she'd met. She shrugged and turned back to her horse, gave his belly a slap to make sure he wasn't puffed up, then tightened the girth another notch.

The bugle was sounding for the first race. "That's us," Jane said to the three other riders nearby. She switched her cowboy hat for a hard hat, swung up on her horse and let her father lead her out to the track. And all the way she kept thinking: *Branch Taggart is a good catch, a good man. Why can't I be like other girls and just get married?*

Jane won her first race with ease, lost the second to a rangy gray gelding, then won again with Hazel, her father's new mare. The thrill of the race itself always filled her, moved her, but it was a fleeting thrill. After only a few moments it was over and Jane felt the heat and breathed in the dust.

The afternoon's big race was the open event in which she was riding Indigo. Branch trotted his horse over to wish her luck. Her brother, Joe, and his wife, Trish, came by with little Joey. Her father grew increasingly silent—a sign of nervousness, Jane knew.

Indigo stomped and wet patches of sweat appeared on his neck. He knew what was coming.

The bugle blew once more and Jane's heart, as always, skipped a beat. Four other riders were competing against her. The distance was just over a half mile, a long race for quarter horses.

"Ain't your horse there gettin' too old?" asked the young boy who was starting in the gate next to her.

"Not yet," Jane said and the boy laughed, unbelieving.

The gun went off, the gates sprang open and Jane crouched forward in the stirrups as Indigo burst out onto the track. His muscles gathered powerfully under her as he got into stride. "Come on, Indigo!" she shouted but he knew what to do and Jane didn't even need the crop.

They rounded the curve, all the horses bunched up and leaning into the rail. The dust spurted up under their hooves, while lather flew in specks off the horses' straining necks. Jane urged Indigo on with her hands and feet and voice, and he began to pull ahead. The horse on the inside, with the young boy astride, suddenly swerved toward Jane—deliberately? her mind flashed. But Indigo kept his stride and moved past and then there was nothing but the empty track ahead and the finish line.

Her father came running up the minute the race was over. "That kid hurt either of you?" he asked.

Jane took her hat off and swung a leg over the horse's withers, then slid to the ground. "I don't think so but we'll check Indigo out later."

"Scared me silly, that kid," said her father, taking the horse's reins.

"Me, too," breathed Jane, "but I loved it. What a thrill!"

Tom Manning looked at his daughter sourly.

"Well, I'll bet you wagered plenty on old Indigo here. Would you rather I'd pulled him up and lost?" Jane teased.

"Maybe I do."

But Jane only laughed and put an arm around her father's shoulders.

Later that evening they pulled up at the barn to unload their horses; hot, tired and dusty. Jared came out of the ranch house to help them.

"God, I need a shower," said Jane as they walked toward the house.

"Oh, I forgot to tell you," her brother began. "Rob Dearborn called earlier. He says call him at home. I wrote the number down—"

"Why didn't you *tell* me!" cried Jane.

"I just did."

She began to run. "It's about a job, I know it is!"

She dialed the number without even taking off her hat. "Oh boy, oh boy," she whispered to herself.

Rob's wife answered. "Sure, just a minute," she said to Jane's query.

"Hello, Jane," came Rob's familiar, uninflected voice. "I think we've got you a prospect."

"What? Where? When?"

"Hold on," said Rob. "It's for a courier service in New York."

"Courier service?" Jane was picturing a delivery boy on a bicycle, a Federal Express van, mailbags.

"They deliver art, gems, valuable securities, anything and everything worth stealing. Anywhere in the world."

"Oh, wow."

"They like the idea of women bodyguards and want to interview you."

"Where? When?" Jane was hopping up and down with excitement.

"They have a man who'll be in the area next Friday. He'll come to your place. I've given them all the particulars. They're very interested, Jane."

"Here? Next Friday?"

"Yes. And good luck, Jane. This is a great opportunity for you."

"Oh, thank you, Rob. Boy, am I excited! Thanks again!"

She hung up and turned to her father and brothers who had—very casually—gathered around to listen.

"I've got a job interview, you guys! For a job in New York! Oh boy! And he's coming *here* next Friday!"

"Way to go, squirt," said James and he gave her a none-too-gentle punch in the arm.

CHAPTER TWO

THE SMALL, UNOBTRUSIVE SIGN reading Norcom marked the entrance to the sprawling complex. Graham Smith pulled his sporty rental car into the drive and noted the perfectly manicured lawns; the low, trimmed bushes that butted up against the cement block plant; the blue tinted glass and sloping skylights that faced the visitors' parking lot. He pulled into a vacant spot, climbed out of the Audi and surveyed his surroundings. Silicon Valley. Aptly named, Graham thought, comparing the place with the ancient, teeming cities and silent hills of Japan from where he had just returned. Norcom was situated in the ultra-modern metropolis that covered the floor of the valley, spreading like a surrealistic set for some sci-fi flick.

Crossing the parking lot, Graham glanced around once more. Nothing was out of place. No cars had followed him too closely from the airport, no one had seemed too nervous or too studiously casual. Automatically he patted the inside pocket of his European-cut, steel-blue sport coat of slubbed silk and assured himself that the microchip was still there.

Ten grand, he mused. A lot of money. More than a year's salary for some people yet it had taken Graham less than twenty-four hours to earn it. All he'd done was visit Norcom's Tokyo production office, pick up the prototype of the chip, fly to San Francisco and make the short drive south to Silicon Valley. It meant nothing to him that the chip was top secret, revolutionary, the so-called break-through of the decade in computer science. His job was merely to deliver it. And he was nearly finished; he almost had the ten thousand earned. Everything had gone smoothly, like clockwork.

He identified himself to the security guard at Norcom and waited for clearance to enter the plant. A familiar, mild disappointment settled over him. Too many of his courier jobs went without incident and, Graham admitted to himself, an occasional hitch did add a certain interest to his work. Not that he would welcome a theft, of course, but a foiled attempt every so often...

"You may go in, Mr. Smith," said the guard, and the man handed him a badge that Graham pinned to the breast pocket of his silk jacket.

His mother, Renée, a French Canadian from Montreal, often told Graham that someday he was going to grow too cocky and outsmart himself. "You're one of those thrill seekers, *mon cher*," she'd say in her slightly accented voice. "Someone who can't sit still for a moment. You should have stayed in the foreign service, like your father. At least *he* had the common sense to know when he was well off."

But Graham hadn't wanted the life afforded him by working for the U.S. government. It had been too narrow and confining. Sure, he'd graduated from Georgetown University—like his half American, half English father, Smedley, before him—and at first he'd liked the idea of working in the foreign service.

Graham had even found his own special niche when he was transferred into security and he'd learned all the new electronic techniques used to protect Americans working for the government at home and abroad. He'd even studied martial arts under a Chinese master when he'd been stationed with the embassy in Hong Kong for two years.

He'd gleaned a lot from the foreign service, done some courier work for diplomats and liked that end of it even more. Then, when he'd found there was a real need for trained couriers in the private sector, he'd gotten the notion to quit the service and strike out on his own as a free-lance courier.

It was lucrative work, not to mention the opportunity it provided for travel and adventure. So he'd given notice to the government, advertised his skills in national newspapers and fallen into his present work effortlessly, with that deft touch and winning smile, which as Renée Smith once put it, "Could charm the money from a Scot."

If asked where he saw his life heading, Graham would have answered lightly. "Who knows? I hope it's a surprise and I sure don't agonize over it." And in that statement there was more than a little truth. He was easygoing, a charmer, a man who did not consciously seek involvement. His life-style produced misconceptions about his true self, at least where women were concerned. They seemed to view him as flighty, not the type to settle down at all. But Graham saw himself as one who had not yet found the right mate, that one person who would share his life and his need for adventure, who would neither tie him down nor make impossible demands of him.

She was out there somewhere, he knew, waiting for him, ready to accept him exactly as he was.

He was thirty-three years old, Graham thought as he greeted the receptionist at Norcom, and already he could almost retire on what he'd earned in the last three years. But he couldn't retire. What would he do for kicks then?

"Mr. Smith," the smartly dressed young woman said, "we've been expecting you. I'll buzz Dr. Laurence." She smiled. "If you'll just have a seat, I'm sure she'll be right along."

He sat in the comfortable, pastel-colored reception area and looked up idly at the skylight. It was a beautiful July day outside, sunny and pleasantly warm. At home, in New York, it would be hot and muggy, the steam rising from subway vents in the streets, hot metallic air pumping out of myriad dripping air-conditioners that studded every building, the white summer sky close and burdened with moisture.

Perhaps, he ventured to himself, there would be a message on his answering machine when he got home to his brownstone, a new job awaiting him. It was amazing how fast his reputation for integrity and speed had spread in the corporate world, how quickly one courier assignment had led to another. And all in the space of a few years.

He glanced over at the young, auburn-haired receptionist and her gaze snapped away from his instantly. Graham enjoyed her attention. He loved women, all kinds, all shapes. He adored their mannerisms, their strengths, their foibles. He liked the way their minds worked with immutable, realistic logic. He appreciated their clothes, their curves, their jewelry, their makeup, their intelligence and nurturing abilities. And, recognizing his admiration, women liked him in return.

Graham was also cognizant of the effect his uncommon good looks had on most women. He accepted it without conceit or vanity. At thirty-three he'd kept his trim, six-foot-two frame in excellent shape by practicing his martial arts and working out at a gym when he was in New York. But it wasn't just his physique that drew the interested perusal of women. It was also his unusual coloring. His hair was thick and somewhat unruly and strawberry-blond. His complexion was ruddy and healthy and his eyes very blue, a startling China-blue like his father's. He also had Smedley Smith's mouth, wide and humor-filled, and the family's hollow cheeks above a lean, narrow jaw. His nose jutted out in masculine generosity.

All in all, Graham possessed the look of an adventurer, of a man born out of his time perhaps, someone who should have been commanding a sixteenth-century galleon. As it was, he was never certain if his appearance was a gift or a hindrance. Women, although initially attracted, tended to become wary of him.

Dr. Laurence, whom Graham had never met, finally rounded a corner from behind the receptionist. She was tall—strikingly so—at least five foot ten, he guessed, and stunning, with jet-black hair falling softly to her shoulders and wide-set brown eyes that perused him confidently.

"Mr. Smith," she began, "so nice to meet you at last. It's always difficult to do business by phone, don't you think?"

"Absolutely," he replied, shaking her hand, observing the firm breasts beneath the loose white lab jacket. She was wearing heels. He drew himself up to his full height. Striking, he thought once more, and obviously smart as well. Dr. Laurence, Graham recalled, was Norcom's top research technician, a woman who had, at thirty-five, been written up in *Time* and *Scientific American* and God knew how many professional journals.

"You have our precious little baby, of course?" she asked.

"I do. Safe and sound."

"Would you follow me, please?"

She led him down a long, sterile corridor past many closed doors. Then she stopped and produced a key and opened a door that had Dr. Jeanette Laurence stenciled on it. Inside was a tidy office and on the far side of the room was another door, leading, he imagined, into the lab area of the giant plant.

Jeanette Laurence indicated a chair for Graham to sit in. "I have to admit," she said, smiling a little self-consciously, "I didn't sleep a wink last night."

"Worried about the microchip?"

She nodded. "You must understand, it's been seven years in production. And it's been in my head for ten years."

"So you developed it yourself? Impressive."

"Thank you. It's been my life's work. The chip will make computing possible for anyone. It will be easier to operate our new computer than it will be to run the simplest of typewriters." She went on to explain to Graham some of the technical breakthroughs provided by the microchip's existence but he found his interest waning. What did hold his attention was Dr. Laurence.

"And you see," she was saying, "a child of four will be able . . . Oh, listen to me, will you? You probably couldn't care less."

"Would you be angry if I said I didn't?" he admitted, his blue eyes twinkling. "In my line of work, it doesn't really matter what I carry. Just as long as I complete the job successfully."

Graham reached into his inside pocket and produced the sealed courier envelope that held the chip.

"Oh, am I glad to see this!" She smiled and breathed a sigh of relief. "Any number of computer companies would give anything to get hold of it."

"I can imagine."

"I hope you didn't have any trouble," she said.

"None. In fact, I rather expected there might be an incident. At least in Hawaii, where we stopped to refuel."

"I'll tell you, Mr. Smith, your fee was worth every penny. Within the next four years Norcom is going to lead the world market in sales with this chip."

"I'm glad to hear that. And," he added, "I'm very glad you're satisfied with my service."

"Oh, we are." She pulled open a desk drawer and produced a cashier's check made out to Graham Smith for the sum of ten thousand dollars. "I got your name through a friend in San Francisco," she remarked, handing him the check. "He works at Delmar Labs, pharmaceuticals."

"Yes, I did a job for them last year," Graham recalled.

"That's right. My friend said you were tops, too."

"Do thank him for me." Graham put the check into his coat pocket and stood. "It's been a pleasure doing business with Norcom." He held out his hand and when she shook it, Graham felt a certain reluctance on her part to let the touch end. So the good doctor had felt the attraction as well.

"You're staying in San Francisco?" she asked, her tone considerably lighter than it had been up to now.

"Actually," replied Graham, "I'd like to but I'm off on another job. Flying out tonight, in fact."

"Oh, I see."

"You live in the city?"

She shook her head. "No. Just south of it, though."

"Umm. Well," he said, opening the door and turning to give her one of his devil-may-care smiles, "if you're ever in New York . . ."

"I'll make a point of calling you."

"Goodbye, Dr. Laurence." He closed the door and strode down the hall, all the while toying with the idea of spending the night in California although he had another obligation. He lifted his hand to the security guard, shut the door to Norcom and Dr. Laurence behind him and felt a twinge of regret.

DAMN LEW RAPP, thought Graham without true malice as his flight touched down that night in Grand Junction, Colorado. How had he let Lew talk him into doing this favor? He didn't even work for Mercury officially; he'd merely taken on two or three odd jobs for Lew since last spring. He *could* have been turning down the sheets for Jeanette Laurence at that very moment. Instead, he was in some rinky-dink Western Slope city in the middle of the Rockies, having to search out a lonely motel because tomorrow he'd promised Lew that he'd conduct an interview.

Lew could have done it himself, Graham decided, as he tossed his bag onto the bed at the Holiday Inn. But Lew, the owner of Mercury Courier and Smedley Smith's old pal from the foreign service, had felt Graham's expertise was invaluable in this area whereas Lew's experience with bodyguards and security was scant.

Ordinarily, Graham would not have minded this favor. From his days in security with the foreign service he was quite familiar with the credentials necessary for a bodyguard. He would certainly look this prospect over on Lew's behalf and admittedly Rifle, Colorado, was on his way back to New York—sort of—but tonight he was tired due to a bad case of jet lag. And it *was* difficult to get Jeanette Laurence, all glorious five feet ten of her, out of his head.

The following morning sunlight streamed through the opening in the green-patterned curtains of Graham's motel room. He looked at his watch. Eight-thirty. The interview was scheduled for noon. Rifle—an appropriate name for a Western town—was, what, sixty miles or so from Grand Junction?

He picked up a rental car and ate at a roadside inn, a real cowboy joint, with wagon wheels on the rough wooden walls, oil lamps hanging from the ceiling, sawdust on the floor and waitresses in jeans, boots and Stetsons. After two cups of coffee and a man-sized breakfast, he was feeling amazingly well considering he'd been in Japan only a day and a half before.

He paid his check and rose to leave.

"You come back now, mister, real soon." The waitress smiled brightly and winked at him.

"Might just do that," replied Graham easily, affecting her accent, his blue eyes alight with devilish charm.

Swinging open the saloon-style doors and striding back into the bright sunlight, Graham patted his full stomach, hitched up his belt and, fully awake now, surveyed the sweeping country of western Colorado.

It was big and breathtakingly empty. His route to Rifle followed the gently curving Colorado River. Funny, he mused, but he'd always thought of the Colorado as a mighty white-water scenic wonder, deadly and challenging, as it thundered down deep canyons and crashed across massive boulders.

Not this section, he saw. Instead, the slow, wide river carved muddy turns in the broad valley floor. And on either side of the water, grazing land spread, rising in the far distance to mesas with their amazingly chopped-off pinnacles. Above these steep-sided and striated natural elevations was the bluest sky Graham had ever seen.

An image struck him: a knife in God's sure hand, slicing off the peaks of ancient mountains and leaving behind these huge, squat, utterly flat-topped mesas for man to wonder over eons later.

The light here had a remarkable clarity and the air was so dry that the scenery looked as if it were painted onto a blue backdrop, the shadows too precise, the colors too pure, the lines too perfect. He decided that he'd like to climb those mountains someday to see if they were real.

Graham drove, enjoying the scenery, marveling over the wild, untamed western lands. He stopped twice along the roadside and checked the map. It wouldn't be too hard to miss a town the size of Rifle. And then he thought about Lew Rapp back in New York on this hot July day, stuck in the Mercury office, pushing paper around his desk. And instead of cussing Lew for asking this favor of him, Graham laughed out loud. This was no favor, it was a bonus!

Besides, Lew had his hands full anyway. Mercury's couriers had been hit by robbers three times in the past few months and Lew was beginning to gnash his teeth. The police were getting nowhere with solving the thefts and the bonding agent and the insurance company, Lloyd's of London, were breathing hard down Lew Rapp's neck. Either the thefts ended or they'd cancel Lew's bond and his policy next year when they were up for renewal.

No wonder Lew had hired a bodyguard for his couriers last month. And since the two-year-old business was growing by the week, he needed a second guard. It was quite a responsibility for Graham to judge this prospective body-guard's suitability. Lew, of course, would make the final decision should Graham give a thumbs-up.

He had to wonder though if a young, inexperienced woman would even fit the bill. Could she handle herself in a pinch?

Rifle was everything Graham had expected and less. A few years back, during all the hype about oil shale development, Rifle property had been the hottest real estate in western Colorado but now the small, rural community sat slumbering beside the Colorado River. Oil had proven to be too expensive to extract from the shale. Rifle had boomed and then collapsed overnight. And yet, despite its run-down look, Graham liked the homey atmosphere of Rifle. It still retained a flavor of the Old West, a charm left over from the days when cattlemen had driven their herds there to the busiest stockyards west of Chicago.

At a gas station he asked directions to the Manning ranch.

"You cross the river up that road," pointed out the man, "then head east a piece."

"A piece?"

"Two, maybe three miles. Watch fer the cattle crossin' and a dirt road off to the left."

Ten minutes later Graham thought he had it all down pat. A half hour later he was hopelessly lost on a muddy, pitted washboard of a road. He stopped the rental car, got out, glanced around and scratched his head. To the north was a precariously steep mountainside, heavily wooded with tall dark spruce. To the east and west was open range-land and to the south nothing but aspen trees, more grazing land, more aspens. Not a house was in sight. Not even the river was visible.

Swell.

He got back in the car, not knowing that it had rained the previous night and certainly not realizing that his rear-wheel-drive Chevy didn't have a prayer of getting out of the muddy rut he'd stopped in. Fifteen minutes later, tired of spinning the tires, sloshing up mud and rocking back and forth, Graham climbed back out and stood shaking his head.

"Well," he said aloud, "if I have to get stuck like some stupid city dude, it may as well be in paradise."

"Got that right, pardner," came a voice from behind him.

Graham spun around. Sitting astride a big horse was a real live cowboy. "Good morning," Graham said, "glad to see you. Glad to see *anyone*."

"Bet you are." The cowpoke had been sitting casually in his saddle, arms folded over the horn, reins dangling loosely from one work-hardened hand. He straightened lazily, tipped the brim of his hat and grinned. "Need some help?"

"Sure. And I'll tell you what—if you'll climb in the car I'll do the pushing." There now, wasn't that the gentlemanly thing to offer?

"In those duds?" The cowboy eyed Graham speculatively, a taunting grin curving thin lips.

Graham looked down at his silk slacks and hundred-dollar Italian loafers. "You're absolutely right. *I'll* drive, *you* push." His blue eyes met green ones and danced in challenge.

The man laughed and dismounted, leaving his horse ground tied. "Where're you headed anyway, mister?"

From inside the car Graham called, "The Manning ranch. Know where it is?"

"Just might at that." The cowboy put a strong shoulder to the trunk of the car and braced himself.

"How far off the path am I?"

"Half mile or so." He grunted with effort as he shoved. "Back the way you came. Off to the left."

Finally the car lurched forward and Graham was able to turn it around without getting stuck again. "Thanks," he said. "I better be heading to the ranch."

"Yeah," said the cowboy, "Jane gets real angry when people aren't on time."

"Jane Manning?"

"My sister. I'm John. John Manning. Pleased to know you, Mr. Smith." He put a booted foot in the stirrup, lifted himself back into the saddle and tipped his hat again. "Be seein' you." He pulled gently on the reins and his horse loped easily over a hill and out of sight.

"I'll be damned," said Graham, grinning as he put the car into gear and headed back the way he'd come.

It was a good half-mile drive along the dirt road John Manning had told him about before Graham spotted the ranch house. The sprawling wooden structure sat in the open, surrounded by cattle-dotted rangeland. To the north of the barn and corral was wooded mountainside, thick with deep green spruce trees that rose to delineate the clear blue Colorado sky.

Now this was what he'd call heaven, Graham thought. The scene was straight out of an old John Wayne movie, promising the good life laced with adventure. He had to wonder why someone would want to leave all this, to trade in a life of real Western ranching for a job in the city.

He parked the mud-spattered Chevy near the corral and got out. A moment later he heard a screen door bang and he looked in the direction of the house. A woman was crossing the wide porch and covering the intervening ground in long-legged strides, approaching him. And in that gait of hers Graham read a number of things. Her sway, her body language, told him of purpose and confidence and strength. This was no willy-nilly farm girl out to play games.

She wore working boots and jeans and a loose green tank top tucked in beneath a wide leather belt. There was a lot of limb to her—strong yet beautifully curved arms, long nicely shaped legs, a woman's hips and buttocks—and small firm breasts, a lovely throat and an open, friendly smile.

"Hi," came a husky, feminine voice and her hand was thrust out for him to clasp. Clear green eyes—the color of emerald precisely—met his. "I'm Jane Manning and you must be Graham Smith. Please call me Jane."

Somehow he found his voice. "Graham...ah, you can call me Graham." He took her hand and felt the strength in her grasp.

"Come on inside where it's cool," she offered and he followed her across the dirt-packed ground toward the ranch house, realizing that something about this woman had just left him stammering.

She fixed them coffee in a spacious kitchen that was decades old but still cozy and serviceable. And as they were conversing—small talk, things about his flight and the drive to Rifle—all that filled Graham's head was the unexpected vision of this woman, this Jane Manning, whom he'd come to interview. She was not exactly beautiful, but her features added up to a total look that, to Graham's eyes, was *right*. He couldn't stop staring at her, studying her face, learning its secrets. She had an adorable bridge of freckles across her small, upturned nose, sparkling green eyes fringed by dark lashes, a wide curving mouth and strong teeth. Her oval face was framed by dark brown glossy hair, blunt-cut to her shoulders, bangs over her brow. She wore only a touch of makeup but it was enough.

Jane led him into a den. The dark-paneled room smelled of old leather and was furnished with Victorian antiques, mostly oak pieces. On one wall was an antelope head; on another was a snarling bear.

"You hunt?" asked Graham, putting his coffee mug down on a table.

"Not since I was a kid." Jane sat in a chair across from him. "But my brothers do."

"How many brothers?" He knew about one. Should he mention his rescuer? No, his mind answered him firmly.

"Four," she replied. "All older. Joe, the oldest," she went on, "is married now and built a place down on the south hundred. I thought you could use his old room to-night...."

"I really wasn't planning on staying."

"Suit yourself," answered Jane in a straightforward manner. Was that what he liked—her openness, the frank tilt of her chin? "If you change your mind," she added, "the offer stands."

"I'll remember that."

She rose and picked up a stack of papers from the desk, handing them to Graham. "I knew you'd want to look over my credentials," she said.

"Of course." He glanced down and began to leaf through the papers. Suddenly he looked up. "You went through the ISA?"

Jane nodded. "I sure did. I was hoping you'd heard of it."

"Everyone," he said levelly, "who's connected with any sort of security has heard of it—and of Rob Dearborn."

"Yes, I know," she said, as if reading his thoughts. "Rob has quite a reputation. He intimidates a lot of his students because of it."

"But not you?"

Jane shrugged her smooth, sun-browned shoulders. "I got along fine with him. He inspired me. In fact, we became good friends."

How *good*, Graham wondered, experiencing an unaccountable, indefinable surge of emotion.

"Oh, he was tough on me," she was saying, "but then he's tough on everyone."

"Your certificate from the academy states you passed everything with flying colors."

"I worked very hard," she said steadfastly.

"Umm," mumbled Graham, glancing back down at the papers in his hand and wondering suddenly if Jane Manning could throw him. It would be most interesting, he mused with a glint in his blue eyes, to find out. He looked up. "I'm not bad myself in the martial arts."

"I studied Korean Hwa Rang Do," she explained. "Are you familiar with it?"

"Hwa Rang Do," he said, then coughed behind a hand to gain time. "Oh, sure."

"Would you like more coffee?"

"Thanks."

She left him momentarily and Graham took the opportunity to gather his thoughts. Jane was certainly qualified as a bodyguard even if she only looked eighteen. And Lew specifically wanted another woman because they were so difficult to spot in a crowd....

"Here's your coffee." Jane sat down. "I should tell you, I'm trained in weapons but I prefer my hands. I never liked guns."

"Nasty things, aren't they?"

"And I can do evasive driving, work with electronic surveillance..."

"You are definitely a most impressive woman, Jane," Graham said.

She hesitated and gave him an anxious look. "I'm being pushy," she admitted. "I'm sorry. But I really do want this job, Mr...Graham, and I'll do whatever it takes to convince you I'm your person."

"Of course." There it was again, that self-confidence, the open manner, the honesty. How refreshing! "You have to understand, though, I'm only conducting a preliminary interview. Mr. Rapp will be making the final decision."

"Oh." She sounded disappointed.

"I don't actually work for Mercury Courier." He felt he ought to explain. "I'm a free-lance courier. Lew Rapp is a very old friend of my family and I'm doing him a favor."

"I assume, though, that you're familiar with body-guarding and security?"

Aha! She was challenging *him* now. "Very much so," replied Graham. "I was with the foreign service for a few years, attached to security. I did some bodyguarding myself."

"Oh," she said, obviously relieved that he was qualified to judge her capabilities.

It was Graham's turn to go on the offensive; this was an unusual game to be playing with a woman and he was finding it quite enjoyable. "I have a few more questions," he began. "For instance, I'd like to know what made you decide on this particular profession."

"Well," said Jane, "I was looking for something special to do, something exciting and different. I graduated from the University of Colorado, then I went to veterinary school in Fort Collins. But I found out that it wasn't for me. Then I came home for a while and helped out around here. I was, you know, sort of waiting, biding my time. I knew there was something out there for me to do. When I heard about the ISA I knew what it was."

Graham cleared his throat. "It is a bit odd for a woman—"

She laughed charmingly. "Well, at least you're polite about it." She leaned forward and spoke earnestly. "Rob explained it. Psychologically, all of his students are thrill seekers. But I want to channel my need for excitement productively."

"Most commendable," murmured Graham, watching her mouth and the way her lips curved. How could a woman who'd done everything she'd done look so damn young and innocent? "You realize," he continued, catching her gaze, "it will mean leaving Colorado for a long time."

"You mean seeing the world?" Her eyes sparkled. "I can hardly wait. I've got an itch to see things, to go places."

"To have some adventures."

"Oh, you bet. Lots of them."

"I understand." A woman of his own mind.

"There you are, Jane," came a gruff voice from the doorway. "Am I interrupting?"

On the threshold stood a white-haired man of about sixty. He was tall and a bit stooped, wiry, his face browned and weathered from years on the range. He had to be Jane's father.

She stood. "Daddy, this is Graham Smith. Graham, my father, Tom Manning."

"How do you do?" said Graham, rising, shaking the man's hand.

"I do just fine, young man. Question is, what sort of employment are you offering my girl here?"

"Daddy!"

Graham's visit was growing more interesting by the minute. And he couldn't help himself, he liked Tom Manning's approach. Hell, if Graham ever had a daughter he'd be just as concerned about her welfare. The truth was—and he should tell her father—that if it were up to Graham, he'd say Jane could have a shot at the job. Of course, the final decision was not up to him but Lew.

"I like knowing the people my children associate themselves with," Tom was explaining in that same frank manner as Jane's. "I trust you're staying the night?"

"Well, I . . ."

"Daddy," Jane said, "Mr. Smith has to be on his way."

"Of course," interrupted Graham, "I *could* take an extra night." He'd been planning to fly straight to Norfolk to spend the weekend at his dad's place on the beach in North Carolina, do some work on their thirty-five-year-old sailboat, the *Renée*, but the invitation to stay at the Manning ranch was extremely tempting. He'd been traveling a lot this past week. It was a Friday, after all. The country here was certainly captivating. And so, he admitted to himself, was Jane Manning.

"Now sit back down there, Mr. Smith," said Tom Manning, "and tell me how you got so confounded lost and stuck so bad my boy had to push your car out of the mud."

"What?" asked Jane, her dark brow arched.

"Well, you see," Graham began, "it was like this...."

CHAPTER THREE

JANE MADE HIM A SANDWICH from the leftover pot roast for lunch. It had lots of mayonnaise and horseradish, the way he liked it. And an ice-cold beer. She sat at the kitchen table with him while he ate, her chin resting on her hand, letting Graham get a delectable view of her emerald-green eyes and soft lips.

The sight almost took his appetite away. Almost.

"You drove from Grand Junction this morning?" she was asking and he had to force himself to concentrate on her words.

"Uh, yes. I've never been there before. To tell you the truth, I never *heard* of Grand Junction before."

She shrugged. "I'm not surprised. Did you come from New York for this interview?"

"No. I was on the West Coast after doing a job in Japan, so it was almost on my way."

"Japan." She said it breathlessly in that throaty voice of hers, longingly. "What kind of job?"

He should have been wary or irritated at her frank curiosity but he wasn't; it was too genuine.

"I had to pick up an electronic component and deliver it to a Silicon Valley firm."

"For Mercury Courier?"

"No, it was a free-lance job."

She seemed disappointed. "Does Mercury do jobs like that?" she asked hopefully.

"Sure, Mercury does anything they're asked. Once, Lew told me, a courier had to deliver a very valuable parrot. It squawked curses all the way across the country in the airplane."

She threw her head back and laughed, so that her long graceful throat showed, her eyes crinkled and he could see that she had one crooked tooth in front that was much more attractive than the perfection of a movie star's smile. It was absolutely endearing. Graham decided he was going to tell her a lot more funny stories.

"I *love* it," she said.

"Well—" Graham stopped munching on the sandwich and looked her right in the eye, serious suddenly "—there's danger in this line of work, you know. It isn't all squawking parrots."

Her eyes met his in total understanding. No fear, no naive bravado, no nutty self-destructive urge peered from their emerald depths. "I know," she said calmly. "I hope you didn't get the impression I'm only out for thrills. I've been taught to avoid danger at all costs." She hesitated, as if weighing something in her mind, but obviously decided to go ahead and say it. "I *want* this job. I know I can do it. I just want a chance to prove myself."

Perfect. She was perfect. Every reaction was precisely right. Graham would have hired her on the spot but, of course, it was not up to him. Nevertheless, he'd recommend her as highly as he could. And then he wondered if his desire to see more of Jane Manning was coloring his judgment. Because he *did* want to see more of her and he'd sure hate to make the trek out to Rifle, Colorado, for a date every Saturday night.

He changed the subject to one that was safer. "I really didn't thank your brother John properly for pushing me out of the mud."

"Was he insufferable?" she asked with a grin. "John loves to put dudes on." She looked startled then added hastily, "I mean, not that you're a dude, exactly."

It was Graham's turn to laugh. "But that's what I am!"

She eyed him carefully. "You don't look like a dude, except for your clothes, that is. But I'll bet Jared's your size and I'm sure you could borrow a pair of his jeans, that is . . . if you're staying."

Did she want him to stay? An odd, melting warmth suffused Graham's midsection. "Stay? Well, I just might at that."

"Good," she said firmly, as if it were all settled.

FIVE BIG STRONG MEN filed into the dining room at 6:00 p.m. sharp, each of them scrutinizing Graham with decided suspicion and curiosity.

Jane introduced them. John grinned widely as he took Graham's hand. "See you made it," he quipped.

Joe, the oldest, shook Graham's hand, too. "Just on my way home," he explained, "but I wanted to meet you before I went."

James, the youngest, full of fun and easygoing, greeted him next. He was followed by Jared. Yes, he was about Graham's size. Thirty-three waist, thirty-four inseam, forty-two chest, Graham guessed. Well-worn jeans and scuffed, low-heeled boots and a line on his forehead dividing the white skin above from the suntan below.

Tom Manning gave Graham a sharp look. "So, you're staying," he remarked.

It took all of Graham's considerable charm and courage to smile and act unconcerned. He felt like a mouse under the paws of a family of cats. Would they eat him for dinner or let him go?

"Hot out, isn't it?" he asked, resolutely cheerful. He had the distinct feeling that Jane Manning would view with disparagement any man who could not stand up to her menfolk.

"Normal," said Tom. "Can't air-condition the range."

"Daddy," admonished Jane.

There was a middle-aged woman who came in to do the cooking, a gaunt, sour-looking lady who appeared tough enough to handle the Manning clan with one hand busy stirring the chili pot.

Joe left, tipping his hat to Graham. The rest sat down at the heavy, claw-footed oak table. Jane led Graham to a seat next to hers and whispered to him, "Don't mind Daddy. He's overprotective."

"Hey, no problem," Graham whispered back. Overprotective, he thought. Did that mean emotionally or physically?

The meal began with chili. Scorching and spicy. Then a thick beefsteak, a mound of salad and biscuits still hot from the oven. Apple pie for dessert. Jane ate a respectable amount of food but nothing like her brothers, and Graham had to admit he did justice to the meal, too.

A chipped enamel pot of very strong coffee was placed in the center of the table and everyone sipped the brew from heavy mugs. No decaf for the Mannings!

"So," Tom Manning began, "you're interviewing my daughter here for a bodyguard job in a company called Mercury Courier. Is that correct?"

"Yes, sir." Good Lord, Graham hadn't called anyone "sir" since Boy Scout camp!

"Tell me something about this company."

So Graham told them all about Lew Rapp, what the company did and what Jane's duties would be. At one point he wondered who was interviewing whom here.

"Why do these couriers need bodyguards?" asked Tom.

"Mercury Courier is a licensed, bonded and insured company. In order to keep the insurance and the bond, bodyguards are being required as of this year. You know about the insurance crisis, I suppose."

"We aren't that ignorant," said Jared.

"Of course not," Graham amended hastily.

"So there's danger of these couriers actually being waylaid," Tom concluded with narrowed eyes.

"It's a precaution, Mr. Manning, like carrying an extra gallon of gas in your car. You'd probably never need it." He wondered what kind of a look Tom Manning would shoot him from those faded eyes if Graham told him about the holdups the Mercury couriers had experienced lately.

"Come on, Daddy, let's not badger poor Graham," interjected Jane. She turned to Jared. "I wondered if Graham could borrow your jeans and boots for the evening. You look to be the same size."

"Sure. You gonna ride, Smith?"

"I have ridden . . ." Graham started to say.

"We got this gentle ol' pony," James said, a devilish grin on his face, "that'd be perfect for you."

Graham groaned inwardly. Setup. The gentle ol' pony would turn out to be a raging stallion with fire coming out of its nostrils and a notorious dislike for Eastern dudes. How did he get himself into these situations?

Jane was looking at him, waiting for his answer, trying to hide a smile.

"Hell," said Graham unflinchingly, "I'd love to ride your nice old pony."

He changed into a clean pair of Jared's jeans and donned the pointy-toed, fancy-stitched boots. His hand-sewn French shirt looked a bit out of place but he rolled up the sleeves and unbuttoned the collar. Glancing into the mir-

ror, he undid another button for that sporty look. Not bad.
Jared's well-worn pants fit him just fine. All he lacked was
a Stetson with a sweat-stained band but, he supposed, he'd
have to earn that.

He emerged from Joe's room, the guest room now, feeling somewhat foolish and out of place, but how could he
have known what he was getting himself into when he'd
told Lew he'd interview Jane Manning? No one had mentioned the gentle ol' pony or all these rather *large* Western
fellas....

And, as if the Manning men weren't enough to intimi-
date just about anyone, there was yet another male in the
crowd that greeted Graham. This one was blondish, tall,
very tall, maybe weighing two hundred pounds—about
thirty-five or so and all solid, range-riding muscle. He was
a good-looking guy with a big white smile and laughing
blue eyes that were as clear as the sky. Who was he? And
where had Jane gone? The sound of running water and the
rattle of dishes in the kitchen told him she'd temporarily
abandoned him.

"This is Branch Taggart," Jane's father said, striding
across the living room to make the introductions. "Branch
here is a friend of Jane's ... from way back. How long has
it been, Jane?" he called out.

First the challenge of the ride on the horse and now this:
Jane's *friend*. Tom Manning seemed to be throwing every
curve he could at Graham. Was it to divert Graham's attention from Jane? The jealous-overprotective-father routine? Or was Graham merely supersensitive at present, too
aware of Jane, too anxious to be one of the guys, to impress the very pretty lady?

"Pleased to meet you, Smith," said Taggart, clamping
Graham's hand with the relentless pressure of a bulldog's
jaws.

"My pleasure," replied Graham in a silky voice as his knuckles turned white.

"Hear you've come to interview Jane for a job in New York."

"That's right."

Jane emerged from the kitchen and handed Taggart a can of beer, then stood looking up at the two men, her head cocked slightly, her thumbs hooked in her jean pockets. Was she enjoying this? A million questions batted around in Graham's head. Was this big blond hulking cowboy really Jane's boyfriend—her lover? Of course a woman as attractive as Jane *should* have a lover, shouldn't she? After all, thought Graham darkly, why *wouldn't* she have someone tall and strong and cocky who'd come over to meet the dude from New York? Especially since that dude might take his lady away to the city. It was only to be expected, but blast it, Graham was getting darn tired of Branch Taggart and he'd only just met the man!

"The boys tell me you're a courier," Taggart was saying. "Odd job, isn't it?"

"Branch," began Jane in her husky voice.

"No, that's all right," Graham interjected with a whole lot more charm than he was feeling. "A lot of people are curious about my line of work."

"What does a courier do?"

"Oh, this and that."

"They deliver parrots," said Jane as her cheeks dimpled with a smile.

"Parrots?"

Graham grinned. "An inside joke."

"I see." Branch popped the top of his beer and took a long swig, his blue eyes meeting Graham's over the top of the can. "You going for a ride or something?" He eyed

Graham's outfit long and speculatively, his lip curling at one corner.

"He's gonna give Pard a workout, right, Smith?" said James from where he sat straddling a wooden chair, twirling his Stetson on one finger.

"Pard, eh? Thought you fellas put him out to pasture a long while back. Sure you can handle the old boy, Smith?"

"Why, sure I can, Branch. At least I can give it a try, can't I?"

"Don't see why not."

And wouldn't you just love it, Taggart, if I end up on my butt in the dust. He tried his best not to, but Graham glanced at Jane in spite of himself, to catch her reactions. Now, in the movies, anyway, the gal would stand up for the poor, unsuspecting Eastern dude who'd been roped into this situation by a bunch of slaphappy cowpokes. But evidently not Miss Manning here. She stood not three feet from him, rocking back on her boot heels, smiling, not in the least troubled. Of course, the Westerns Graham had seen took place in an age long past, when women stayed home, cooked and had babies. Somehow he could not see Jane landing the part.

"It's gonna get dark soon," John said, rising from his chair. "You staying for the ride, Branch, or did you just come over to drink a beer and sweet-talk my sister?"

"Hey, John." Jane narrowed her eyes at her brother but Branch merely laughed good-naturedly.

"Always did like your cold brew, John. And now that you mention it, I wouldn't miss Smith's ride for anything."

"Go and have your fun," said Jane then. "I think I'll finish up in the kitchen." She did, however, walk Graham to the door ahead of the others. "You know you don't have to go through with this."

"Why, Miss Manning," Graham murmured, leaning toward her, "I didn't know you cared."

"It's your funeral." She smiled and pushed open the door for him and the men, all six of them now, filed out and sauntered toward the corral.

Graham wondered, as the evening sun struck distant peaks and gold touched the tips of dark spruce trees, if Jane had stayed behind in the kitchen out of necessity or because she was embarrassed to see Graham make a fool of himself. At any rate, even though he missed her already, even though he'd much rather watch Branch Taggart bite the dust as opposed to himself, he was just as glad she wasn't going to see him fail Bronco Busting 101. *Especially* in front of her friend here.

Pard stood in the corral, head hanging down. He was a thick-necked, pale-colored Appaloosa who looked as harmless as a lamb. It was only when John bridled and saddled Pard that he came alive. His ears perked forward, his eyes grew bright, his neck arched, his big body seemed to radiate excitement.

"You get on the left side," Taggart said helpfully.

"Why, thanks for the tip," Graham answered. He gathered the reins and swung up into the deep-seated Western saddle. Pard stood stock-still for a moment and Graham just had time to notice that the Mannings and Taggart all ducked under the corral fence—*oh hell*—when he felt Pard gather himself, take the bit in his teeth, put his head down and go on a rampage.

The horse jumped stiff-legged, landed hard, twisted, and leaped again. Dust rose in a choking cloud and somewhere Graham heard a voice yell, "Ride 'em, cowboy!"

Then the ground came up very hard and he was sitting in the middle of the corral, shaken to the core, while Pard stood eyeing him.

Graham slowly got to his feet and slapped dust off Jared's jeans.

"Guess Pard is feelin' his oats," said James, mock-apologetically. "You want to try another horse?"

"No way. I'll stick with Pard here. That was the most fun I've had since I did a belly flop from the twelve-meter diving board, fellas."

Limping slightly, Graham approached the now docile horse and mounted again. This time he kept a tight rein and a hold on the pommel. Pard humped his back and gave a jolting jump or two; then he kicked out his hind legs but this time his bucking lacked its original enthusiasm. Graham was beginning to enjoy himself.

And then Jane was there, an arm hooked over the corral rail, Taggart by her side. "Did they really give you *Pard*?" she called to him. "Those creeps!"

"Oh, he's a great piece of horseflesh," Graham called back. "There's more to him than meets the eye!"

By then Pard had settled down to a bone-rattling gallop around the corral and Graham was feeling much better. He was glad Jane hadn't seen him bite the dust. He pulled Pard up into a trot then a walk, then kicked him into a lope, neck-reined him into a figure-eight loop around the enclosure, stopped him, backed him up, and spun him around on his hind feet.

"Well-trained horse you got here," he said casually to the men's carefully expressionless faces.

"Thanks," choked out John finally.

"Well, I'll be damned," he heard Branch Taggart say.

Jane looked triumphant, as if she were responsible for Graham's skill. She slapped John on the shoulder and bubbled over with laughter. John looked shamefaced, then a grin split his lips and he was laughing, too, and soon all four of the Manning men were guffawing and pounding one another on the back. Only one of the group was still unsmiling—Branch. Of course, Graham knew, he'd just won a round in front of Taggart's lady—a very uncool thing to have done. Nevertheless, Graham was feeling as pleased with himself as a high school kid who'd just scored a touchdown in front of the prettiest cheerleader in the squad—the girl who was going steady with the quarterback.

"I gotta hand it to you," Branch said as he strode over to Graham, "that was a nice ride."

"Lucky," put in Graham—the true gentleman.

"Skilled." And he put his hand out and shook Graham's; this time there were no white knuckles. "Well, glad to have met you, Smith. I gotta be getting along here, early call tomorrow. You know how us ranchers are."

"Sure."

"Walk me to the pickup?" he asked, turning to Jane, and Graham tried to look busy with Pard's reins.

They were gone a long time. Five minutes, at least. It seemed like an hour to Graham as he stood alongside the men talking horseflesh and the like. And he really hadn't the slightest notion what they were chatting about because all he could see from across the corral was Jane standing near the mud-spattered pickup and Branch, leaning casually against the driver's door, his head bent close to her shell-pink ear. What were they saying, exactly? Making a date for next Saturday night? Getting engaged? A knot twisted in Graham's stomach and he felt hot and dizzy suddenly. Must have been the hair-raising ride.

"And when you hit the dust there, pardner," John was saying, "I thought for sure it was all over!"

Somehow Jane was beside him. Graham didn't have to look; he could simply feel her presence there, smell her scent—fragrant, clean, as fresh as a mountain meadow full of bluebells and primroses.

"Taggart leave?" asked Jared.

Jane nodded and looked down at her hands for a moment.

"Haven't seen him around for a while," John put in artlessly.

"We haven't been going out for ages, if it's any of your business."

"You don't have to go and get all huffy like that. I only asked—"

"Kids," Tom Manning warned, "that'll do."

"Come on." Jane turned to Graham and smiled.

"Let's leave these guys to their practical jokes and go for a ride. I'll show you some of the rodeo stock."

"Sounds great," he said, relishing in the knowledge that Jane and Branch had not been seeing each other in some time. He waited while she saddled up a fine-looking black stallion she called Indigo and they set out across the wide irrigated fields toward the distant rise of gray-brown buttes. The sun was dipping to the west, the air was dry and warm and scented with sagebrush, the shadows were growing long.

"You *can* ride," she said after a while. "Those guys are going to hurt someone one day with their stunts."

"I have to confess I've never ridden a horse like Pard. I've just done some fox hunting in Virginia when I was stationed in Washington."

"Pard's an ugly old thing but he was a champion cow horse in his day. I think he enjoys his times in the spotlight more than my brothers do."

"Do all male visitors undergo the same test?" asked Graham, enjoying the easy rhythm of the horse, the scenery, the woman riding by his side, especially the woman.

Slim, lithe, strong, she was a natural rider, an athlete whose body always moved in balance, without wasted movement. A woman whose eyes met his forthrightly, with no coy games, who seemed totally in command of her life, who knew what she wanted.

"Only the ones they think can take it."

"I'm flattered."

"And they're impressed. What else do you do well, Graham Smith?"

"I'm an excellent cook," he said. "I speak fluent French. I'm good at my job."

She waited.

"Actually, I swam in school and ran track. I did a four-and-a-half-minute mile once. Oh, and I sail a bit."

"A bit?"

"Well, I crewed in the America's Cup one year," he admitted.

"Anything else?" She was smiling.

"A game of tennis now and then."

"Now and then?"

"Well," he allowed reluctantly, "I was in the quarter finals of the juniors at the U.S. Open years ago."

"I see."

"And you?"

"My accomplishments hardly compare. I ride, I can rope. I can throw a calf and brand it, give it a shot, neuter it."

"Ouch," Graham winced.

Jane gave him a quick, humorous sidelong glance. "I jog a few miles from time to time. I race quarter horses. Just hometown stuff. Indigo here won a race last week." She patted his shiny black neck and Graham wished she was caressing him so lovingly.

"And then there's the stuff I learned at ISA. But you've seen all that on my application."

"You're quite a woman, Jane Manning," he said sincerely.

"And you're quite a man, Mr. Smith." She laughed, then touched her heels to Indigo's sides and took off across the range, scattering cattle, a graceful figure on the flying black horse.

Graham watched her for a minute, enjoying the sight, then he kicked Pard into a canter. "We better catch up, old boy. I've got a feeling that a lady like that could leave us in the dust."

After the ride he and Jane put the tack away and let the horses go out onto the fields to graze.

"Thank you for the ride," Graham said, meaning every word of it.

"Wouldn't you show me the Empire State Building," she asked playfully, "if I were in New York?"

"Without a moment's hesitation." He was aware of the warm pungent smell of horses, cattle, oiled leather and the nose-prickling aroma of sweet alfalfa hay. His muscles were sore and strained and he'd lay odds he had a black and blue mark on one hip but he felt good—cleanly, physically tired.

The setting sun hovered on the horizon, big and orange, and its rays reached across the earth to enter the huge double-door opening of the barn. In its gilt light swallows swooped, insects buzzed, dust motes hung like tiny golden snowflakes. And within the glow Jane walked, unselfconscious and full of grace, a woman with an inner beauty and strength that Graham found novel, intriguing, exciting.

The sun brushed her skin with gold dust, touched her small nose and strong cheekbones and dark lashes as Graham would have liked to touch them: softly, delicately, reverently.

"Nice night, isn't it?" he remarked inanely, just to hear her husky voice.

"It always is in the summer," she replied.

They walked on toward the lighted ranch house. She wore jeans that fit her slim hips like a second skin. Graham could see her long flank muscles working as she moved. Wonderful. His head whirled.

He'd woken that morning one man and now he felt like a whole different person. He noticed things more acutely: the feel of the warm air against his face, the sound of horses snorting and stamping off in the dark, the scent of Jane Manning's smooth, tan skin.

The darkness hid her expression but he knew she must be feeling the strength of his emotions. She *must* feel them. He'd kiss her in a minute if it weren't for the fact that he was supposed to be there on business. Hah, business! And, of course, there were still four big Manning men waiting in the house—and Joe probably not far off.

Come to think of it, there had been something between him and Jane from the first moment. A certain tension, a constant pulse of attraction. And one totally unlike what he'd felt for any woman before.

Something special.

He'd just have to convince Lew to hire her. Not that he'd be doing either Lew or Jane a disservice. And then he could see Jane often. He'd love to take her out on the *Renée*...

What was he thinking? Jane Manning might not get the job, she might not *want* the job—although she'd said she did. He might never see her again. The thought was sobering, like a dash of cold water in the face. Never see Jane again? Unthinkable.

The house was full of light and talk. Joe had come over with his wife, Trish, and their son, Joey. It was a family gathering, complete with a whiskey bottle, cigars and bowls of popcorn.

"Heard you rode Pard," Joe said, rising and holding his big hand out to Graham.

"I tried."

"Did more than that," John put in. "He put ol' Pard through his paces."

The atmosphere had definitely lightened. Graham guessed he'd passed his test. Somehow that made him feel good, which was ridiculous. Why should he care if this family accepted him?

Jane took Joey from his mother's arms and cuddled him. "Oh, he's grown since last week! And he's getting hair." She nuzzled his fat cheek.

A crazy picture popped into Graham's head: Jane holding a baby, but he had strawberry-blond hair. It was *his* baby and hers and they were—he snapped the image off as if it were a television program he didn't like. What was the matter with him?

"Come on, Graham," Tom was saying. "Set yourself down and have a drink. Cigar?"

"Sure, thanks," he answered automatically. The whiskey was old and mellow and went straight to his head. The cigar made him slightly dizzy. He felt himself sinking into the leather armchair in which he sat as if he'd never be able to get up again. He was content to sit there forever listening to ranch talk, admiring the huge beams and stone fireplace and Navaho rugs of the ranch house's living room, watching Jane's face change expression, watching her slender neck and brown arms and gorgeous strong legs. And that adorable crooked tooth . . .

"You look sort of sleepy," Jane finally said to him.

His heart thumped and he forced a dopey smile onto his lips. "I guess I am. I feel like something hit me over the head. It must be the altitude."

Graham had recovered some of his self-possession by the next morning. He'd slept like a log and woken up with the fleeting memory of a dream about Jane, something about trying to hold her hand to convince her of a terribly important fact but he'd been on Pard who'd been bucking and her hand kept slipping out of his grasp.

The Manning men were already gone but the littered breakfast table attested to the fact that they'd been there—in force.

"Good morning," called Jane from the kitchen.

Graham nodded briskly but he still remembered the feel of her hand in his dream. "Morning, Jane."

She looked glorious. Jeans and a white shirt rolled up at the sleeves. A wide leather belt with a silver buckle around her slim waist. Lovely swinging, shiny brown hair. Her hands were small and square and capable, with short fingernails. The freckles on her nose were charming.

"Eggs?" she asked.

"If it's no trouble."

She had a cup of coffee while he ate. "I stayed behind to see you off. The boys want me up on the plateau to help them with some calves later."

"You didn't have to wait."

"Why, sure I did. I couldn't let you get off all by yourself."

"Well, I'm glad you did."

She smiled. She liked him, he thought happily. But how *much* did she like him?

He collected his bag after breakfast and started out to his muddy car. Jane walked at his side.

"So," she said in a straightforward manner, "what do you think? What are my chances of getting this job?" No fawning, no false modesty, no beating around the bush. This woman knew her own worth. "Do I measure up?"

Graham looked at her for a long moment, wanting to memorize her features, knowing he would see her again. "Lew will want to interview you, of course. I'm sure you'll be hearing from him soon. But on *my* yardstick you measure up just fine."

She held out her hand. Her grip was warm and firm. Her touch made his stomach roll over deliciously. And when Graham got into his car and started it, he knew he'd held her hand just a touch too long.

And Jane Manning knew it, too.

CHAPTER FOUR

THE FOLLOWING WEDNESDAY, Jane's flight made its approach to La Guardia and she finally had her first glimpse of Manhattan. As the plane banked, she pressed her nose to the glass and gazed at the sprawling city below her. The Statue of Liberty stood tall and majestic amidst the many ships and boats dotting the Hudson River. Beyond that were the twin towers of the World Trade Center, the Empire State Building, the lushness of Central Park. The buildings, packed close, piled up, new and strange and yet so wonderfully familiar, filled her vision and seemed to stretch to the horizon and beyond.

"Your seat belt, please," came the stewardess's reminder and Jane buckled up, feeling her stomach twinge with excitement and trepidation.

She was here at last, eager and prepared and yet nervous about whatever challenge the city and her new life offered. In her purse was the address of the Gramercy Park Hotel on Lexington Avenue, the street number of Mercury Courier and fifteen hundred dollars in traveler's checks. There was no return ticket to Denver, however. Jane was going to get this job or else. Optimism sprang in her heart as the plane's landing gear thumped down onto the runway.

Her first impression, oddly enough, was of the hot damp air of the East coast, which hit her in the face when she emerged from the terminal. It was funny, Jane decided, as her bus carried her into the heart of Manhattan, but all her preconceived notions of New York had been wrong. It wasn't sophisticated, sleek and glossy, not at first glance. Nor was it dirty, criminal and brutal, as she'd heard. New York was made up of individuals and there seemed to be no norm, only exceptions. The variety dazed her. On one street corner stood a pasty-skinned woman carrying two big shopping bags wearing all black: black shoes, black textured hose, black dress, even a black floppy hat. In the oppressive July heat no less. And there were foreigners from everywhere dressed in saris or robes or odd European styles. Businessmen, gorgeous women, students with huge Afro hairstyles, poets, actors, shoppers, orthodox Jews in black hats and beards. Fat women who sweated and screamed at pale children, writers, artists, messenger boys on bicycles, bums asleep on benches.

New York.

Everywhere Jane looked there was a person with a new eccentricity, a mark of uniqueness. A mark of being a New Yorker. Would she look that way after a while? Jane glanced down at her neat outfit and grimaced. Well, she certainly wouldn't fool anybody yet. And, she noticed, she was too tanned. Everyone she saw had a distinct city pallor.

Then she couldn't help recalling that Graham Smith had been ruddy and healthy looking. Idly she wondered where he was at that exact moment. In the city? Off on an assignment somewhere in the world? All the way to New York on the airplane Jane had imagined that Graham would be at the airport to meet her. It was a silly, impossible notion but one she couldn't dismiss. She'd imagined him standing in the terminal, waiting for her, his strawberry-blond hair a little unruly, an expensive summer-weight sport coat hanging loosely, carelessly, off his broad shoulders, his blue eyes dancing, welcoming her.

Of course, it had merely been a pleasant fantasy. He'd no idea that Jane had arrived that day. Heavens, her appointment with Mr. Rapp wasn't even till Friday.

Jane glanced out the bus window again. New York, she was here at last, she mused, her heart beating just a little faster as she craned her neck and looked up, not even able to see the tops of all the skyscrapers. And then, on a whim, on an impish impulse, Jane turned to the businessman seated next to her. He was rocking back and forth with the motion of the bus, his eyes half closed, an expression of utter boredom on his face.

"It's a far cry from Rifle," she said with a smile, guessing that this obvious New York native had never before been spoken to by a complete stranger on a bus.

"Pardon me?"

"It's not much like Rifle, Colorado, I said."

"Rifle?" He looked alarmed then very concerned then a bit dazed, but by the time they'd sat chatting for a half hour in the heavy city traffic, Jane had his card—he was a dress designer who worked in the garment district—and had promised to look for his labels at Macy's.

And who said New Yorkers were unfriendly?

SAFELY OUT OF THE AFTERNOON HEAT and checked into her air-conditioned room in the Gramercy Park, Jane glanced at her watch: 3:00 p.m. Plenty of time to explore—or shop. She opened her suitcase and eyed her clothes, then stood back with her hands on her hips. They were all wrong. Her summer slacks had no pleats and were hopelessly too wide in the leg; her skirts were two inches longer than she'd seen the nicely dressed women on the street wearing; her two dresses, left over from college days, were just plain out.

And the A-line khaki skirt and Hawaiian-print camp shirt she'd worn on the flight made her look fifteen.

How did a person find Bloomingdale's?

Jane took the subway uptown from her hotel, which was on 21st and Lexington. The desk clerk had told her that the train was a safe bet at this hour and would actually stop in the basement of Bloomingdale's. Unbelievable! The subway was already crowded with commuters so she stood, marveling at the new sights and smells, feeling the damp closeness, hearing the unearthly roar of the train, holding onto the swinging handle over her head and rocking back and forth with the car's motion, knocking companionably into other passengers. On one side of her stood a well-dressed Arab businessman whose dark eyes never left her. On the other side was a Puerto Rican boy in a baseball outfit. Seated at knee level was a transvestite whom she tried not to stare at but whose matching red pumps and red purse were hard to ignore. He had on twice the makeup she did! Jane tore her gaze away and looked up at the graffiti.

She had fifteen hundred dollars, Jane thought, as she pushed her way through the throng and out the doors to exit at Bloomingdale's basement. How much could she afford to spend and still be able to eat until payday?

A couple hundred. She could afford that much. Sure, why not?

Up the escalators, into the air-conditioned levels she went, strolling past elegant displays of every imaginable designer. Anne Klein, Halston, Christian Dior, Gucci, Ungaro. So many clothes! Jane wanted everything she saw. But the price tags! Her two hundred dollars wouldn't even buy her one outfit. Finally she did find a few summer-sales racks and bought a pair of white linen slacks—with pleats—for seventeen dollars. *Smart buy.* She patted herself on the back mentally.

Jane took the escalator up again. There had to be more sale racks, probably scattered all over the store. She felt dreadfully out of place in her provincial outfit among the beautifully attired shoppers with their fashionable dresses, wide belts, scarves and glittering jewelry. And how *did* they walk on those high heels?

At last Jane found a dress. It was jade-green and white and had a full skirt—wide green belt included. The bodice had a double-breasted overlay with big buttons, and the sleeves were elbow length and cuffed. She knew she looked good in it and her white pumps would go fine.

Oh gosh, that multicolored scarf over there. How much was it? Twenty-five dollars? Oh well... She signed another traveler's check, got her change and figured she could spend another ninety dollars. She found a beige, below-the-knee skirt for twenty-eight and a soft yellow cotton top with a scoop neck and short sleeves. The brightly colored scarf would go beautifully.

Down one escalator. Why, she hadn't even seen this part of Bloomingdale's. There was nothing she could afford here, though. Down again. Oh my, what exquisite perfumes. She was in cosmetics. Miles of makeup were dramatically spotlighted, set off by smoky-black mirrors behind every display. Nearby stood counter after counter of sparkling jewelry. What heaven!

"Hello," said the saleslady behind the Elizabeth Arden counter, "have you smelled our new fragrance today? Here, let me dab a little on your wrist. Isn't that lovely? What pretty skin tones you have."

"Thank you," mumbled Jane.

"But you've been in the sun a great deal. I wonder, are you wearing the right protection?"

"I use a sunscreen...."

"With alcohol, I'll bet." The saleslady's red, glossy lips parted in concern. "Could I show you a product that will bring back the elasticity in your skin while protecting it at the same time?"

"Well . . ."

Jane let her apply the whole gamut. Astringent, moisturizer, base, blusher, three colors of eyeshadow blended expertly to highlight her "lovely green eyes," two shades of peachy lipstick, eyeliner, dabs of goo to soften those tiny lines at the corners of her eyes, smoky brown mascara. Oh, my gosh, her reflection in the mirror was certainly . . . well, amazing!

"What do you think?" asked the bejeweled saleslady.

"I, ah, it certainly is different."

"I'm glad you're pleased. A change in cosmetics can alter one's whole outlook, can't it?"

"That's the truth," replied Jane.

"Would you like me to write this up?"

"Oh." Jane thought quickly. She'd bet all these products would run a hundred dollars. "Well, tell me how much it would come to."

Five minutes later Jane had her answer. "That will be $378." The woman smiled again pleasantly. "Plus tax." Jane swallowed hard. She escaped the Elizabeth Arden counter finally, minus fifty-odd dollars, with a blusher and a lipstick and a night cream.

She fell into bed that night full from a Chinese meal, her new clothes hung carefully in the closet, night cream smoothed sparingly on her face and delicious guilt curling in her belly.

The following day she called home and told her father all about her impressions of New York. "The sirens go all day and night," she said, trying to remember the quiet of the ranch, trying to relate, to grasp her two divergent lives.

Before her interview the next day, she had plenty of time to explore the city. She visited Times Square, marveling at the crowds, walked through Greenwich Village, took subways all over because she couldn't resist exploring. She strolled by the Plaza Hotel, read the menu in the window and decided tea would cost her twenty dollars. She avoided the department stores like the plague.

Friday morning she put on her new jade and white dress, more makeup than usual, sprayed her hair until it looked full and luxurious, and took a cab to the offices of Mercury Courier. It was exactly 8:58 when she took in a lungful of sooty, heavy summer air, pushed open the door to the four-story building and marched in.

"Good morning, you must be Jane Manning," said the receptionist who had been typing away at an astounding speed considering the length of her purple nails. And she was chewing gum as fast as she typed.

"Yes," replied Jane, feeling nervous perspiration bead her upper lip. "I'm supposed to see Mr. Rapp. At nine," she added needlessly.

"Why don't you sit over there a sec and I'll see if he's off the phone. By the way," said the girl, "I'm Donna. Donna Lippman." She swiveled in her chair and checked the blinking light on the telephone console. "He's still talking away...." Donna shrugged. "Want some coffee?"

"Do you have a glass of water?"

"Sure."

Jane glanced around the office. It was old, Victorian. The windows were big and the walls were papered and there was dark oak trim around the high ceiling. From the reception area Jane spotted several doors down a dim corridor. There were polished wooden steps leading upstairs and no elevator that she could see. The building must have been a house once, or had apartments, and been converted into an office.

"Like the place?" asked Donna, returning with the glass.

"Oh yes. It's very comfortable-looking."

"Lew bought the building three years ago and did some renovations. It used to be a house. All the couriers have their own offices."

"How many couriers are there?"

"Five right now. Well, four really, but Norma has an office, too."

"Norma?"

"Norma Stedman. She's the other bodyguard. An ex-cop. She's really something, a tough old broad." Donna turned in her chair again to check the console. "He's still talking. Sorry."

Jane couldn't help liking Donna. The girl had a heavy Brooklyn accent, dark brown twinkling eyes and was probably four or five years younger than Jane. She had black frizzy hair to her shoulders, a tiny little nose and painted mouth, long fingers with bright purple nails, clothes straight out of a punk shop in the Village—lots of purples, blacks, drapes and folds and tons of silver jewelry.

And then, as Donna continued to ignore her typing, Jane couldn't stop the question from coming to her lips. "Is Mr. Smith around?"

"Quicksilver?" Donna grinned knowingly.

"Excuse me?" said Jane.

"We call him Quicksilver around the office. He's the real elusive type, you know, hard to pin down."

"Oh," Jane replied. "Is he here?" she repeated casually.

Donna shook her head, her long silver earrings swinging. "No. Haven't seen him for a couple of weeks. He doesn't really work here much, just does odd jobs for Lew. You know, he and Lew go way back. I think he and Graham's dad are old friends or something.''

"Well, well, hello!'' came a loud, heavily accented voice from the front door. "And who do we have here?'' If forced to put a label to his accent, Jane would have chosen Russian.

"This is Jane Manning,'' Donna said. The man was huge, at least two hundred and thirty pounds, all solid muscle, with a short dark crew cut. The buttons of his tan suit strained across his chest. "Jane is interviewing for the other bodyguard spot,'' Donna was explaining. "Jane, meet Lukas Yurchenko, one of our couriers.''

"Pleasure to meet you, Jane,'' he said, holding out a beefy hand, his ridiculously small blue eyes gobbling her up.

Jane took his hand and felt the crushing pressure of challenge as his grip ground the ring she wore into her fingers. "Nice to meet you,'' she replied sweetly, her back stiffening. How rude, she thought, he wanted her to wince. Well, she wouldn't.

"Oh,'' said Donna, "Lew's free at last. I'll take you on up, Jane.''

Lukas Yurchenko released her hand. "You have a telephone number?'' he asked bluntly, the tone of his voice uncomfortably demanding.

"No,'' said Jane, taken aback.

"An address?''

"No.''

"Then how am I going to take you out?''

It was her turn to smile. "You aren't.'' Behind her she could hear Donna's chuckle.

Lew Rapp couldn't have been kinder. He had a fatherly image, the type of man whom everyone would warm to and trust instantly. He was on the short side, overweight, with graying hair combed over a large bald spot on the crown of his head. He had soft brown eyes, a genuine smile and an easygoing manner. The perspiration finally dried on Jane's upper lip.

"Graham recommended you highly," he was telling Jane in his second-story office. "And he went on at length about what a good time you and your family showed him."

He talked to Jane for an hour. They discussed her background and compared it to life in the city; they chatted about current world affairs and the amount of violence going on in America and in the center of Paris. He spoke openly of Jane's youthful appearance and how he was pleased because she would be highly unlikely to be pegged as a bodyguard.

"Do your couriers ever run into trouble?" she asked.

"I wish I could say no," he replied, his gray brows drawing together. He sat back in his leather chair and folded his arms across his chest. "Mercury is three years old now," he told her. "And up until last April we never had a robbery. But since then my couriers have been hit four times." He frowned. "I'm afraid, the robberies were successful, too. I hired my first bodyguard in June. That's Norma Stedman. But Norma can't be everywhere at once and two weeks ago, Peter, one of my couriers, was robbed crossing town with some jewelry from a safe-deposit box."

"That's awful."

Lew Rapp nodded. "I couldn't agree more, young lady. And it's going to stop. I haven't put my life's blood into this business to see it go under because of some thugs."

"Mr. Rapp," Jane ventured carefully. "My training is quite extensive and I'm sure hoping that you'll give me a shot at this job." Had she been too forward, too pushy?

"Well, Miss Manning—Jane," he said, "I intend to do just that."

"You do!"

"Yes. Starting Monday, in fact. I hope you came prepared to stay."

"I'm all set," breathed Jane, elated, not even trying to control her joy and relief.

"I think you'll fit in just fine," Lew said, "and Donna can introduce you around and show you the ropes on Monday. I won't give you an assignment, though, for a few days. I think you should get to know the men and spend some time with Norma. She's got twenty years' experience with the NYPD, the New York police, and she can fill you in on the routes the couriers use, the airlines we take, all those details." He stood, came around the desk and shook Jane's hand firmly. "Welcome aboard, Jane Manning."

"Thank you," she said brightly, "I'll do a good job for you, Mr. Rapp."

The weekend was filled with more sight-seeing and some shopping as Jane would be on the payroll starting Monday. She sampled the good food in the neighborhood restaurants near Gramercy Park. She even caught a matinee of *Chorus Girl*, which Jane adored.

Her weekend also brought moments of musing. Where was Graham Smith? she couldn't help wondering. He had gotten to her. And yet Jane was quite aware that a man as attractive and compelling as Graham Smith—Quicksilver—must have dozens of ladies drooling over him. Even if she did see him again, it was highly unlikely he'd ask her out. Yet there had been something between them—a spark. And a woman could hope, couldn't she?

New York City grew on Jane. She loved the bag lady at the corner of 20th and Third Avenue, the wino who slept on the second bench in from the west entrance to Gramercy Park, the vendors in Union Square and the weirdos in Washington Square. She chalked up the miles on foot and her blisters grew apace but nothing daunted Jane Manning, soon-to-be official bodyguard at Mercury Courier.

On Monday, Donna helped Jane get settled in. She took her up to the fourth floor, to a cubbyhole of an office. "It's weensy in here, and stuffy, but at least it's a place of your own."

"It's great," said Jane, turning around in the six-by-eight space, wondering if it hadn't once been a walk-in closet.

"Lew keeps saying he's going to have a window put in but you may have to bug him about it. At least there's a desk and a phone."

The desk was simply a piece of painted wood jutting out from one wall. The chair was serviceable; there was a burgundy metal wastebasket.

"Maybe a few posters or something," said Donna, "on this wall." She stood with her weight on one high heel, cocking her head, a small white hand on her chin. "And a fishbowl, a plant or two. Y'know?"

"I'm sure it can be fixed up just fine." Jane didn't mind the tiny, stark space one bit; it was *hers*.

"You got a place to live yet?" asked Donna.

Jane shook her head. "I checked the newspapers all weekend but the prices..."

"I know. You could try the Barbizon."

"The what?"

"It's a woman's hotel. Uptown, eastside on 63rd and Lexington. It's clean and safe and affordable. Tell you what, I'll go downstairs and give them a call. If they have space, you maybe could go and look at it during lunch." Donna smacked her chewing gum.

The morning sped by. Jane was introduced to the couriers who were not out on assignment. There was Peter Lerner, a handsome blond man in his midthirties, tall, lanky, bearded. He was friendly and mild mannered, welcoming Jane into the crew with a very attractive white smile. She was reintroduced to Lukas, the Russian—Donna said he'd been in the KGB and had defected—and to yet another courier, Rick Como, a short, stocky Italian with a mournful countenance who asked Jane, "Just how old are you, anyway?"

She knew her youthful appearance came as somewhat of a shock to the employees at Mercury. They thought she looked too innocent and too inexperienced to be taken for real. And yet Jane didn't mind, recalling Rob Dearborn's comment: "Your appearance is your best asset. It will give you the edge every time."

Jane's first impression of Norma Stedman was one of size. The woman was in her late forties, tall, large boned. She must have weighed a good solid hundred and seventy pounds but it was all muscle. Her features were also big and severe. Her hair, which she kept trimmed short was steel-gray. There was nothing motherly about Norma and yet Jane felt the older woman taking her under her wing immediately.

"I spent twenty years in the city with the police," she told Jane, "and there're a few things I've learned that I'd be more than happy to share with you."

"I'm all ears," Jane replied with gratitude.

"Good. I was afraid you'd be one of those uppity young women who thought she knew everything." Norma was straightforward and honest. Jane liked her from the word go.

At noon the sound of Donna's high heels on the steps ʃched Jane in her little office. "Oh," Donna breathed, "there you are. Listen, I called the Barbizon and they have a room available starting Wednesday. Want me to take you over and have a look-see?"

"Now?"

"No better time than the present, honey."

They rode the bus uptown, Donna with her ready tongue chatting the whole way, leaving Jane with a wealth of knowledge. "Norma's okay. She scares me, though. Big woman, isn't she? But you gotta give her credit, she's got an invalid husband she's been supporting since the sixties. Industrial accident, I think." Donna pulled a fresh stick of gum out of her big purse and Jane thought that from then on, whenever and wherever she smelled Juicy Fruit, she'd think of Donna Lippman.

"And that Lukas, what a god-awful oaf!"

Jane said nothing to that remark.

"Do you like Rick?" Donna asked as they stepped off the bus.

"I barely know him."

"I think he's sexy with those sad Italian eyes. Solid, you know. Of course Peter is a dreamboat, isn't he? Tall, blond and, oh, that beard! Umm..." Donna pushed open the door to the hotel and charged in. "Of course, Peter has a steady. He would."

Jane was pleased with the hotel. It was no luxury spot but it appeared to be clean and the price was certainly right. She was shown a room and told the clerk she'd take the next one coming up.

"It'll save you spending so much at the Gramercy," Donna said. "Where'd y'say you were from? Aspen?"

Jane shook her head. "Rifle. It's sixty miles from the ski resort. A ranching community."

"You're a cowgirl? Wow!"

"No," Jane said with a laugh, "I'm a bodyguard."

They ate at a deli near the Barbizon. Jane, at her new friend's urging, had corned beef on rye. "*Real* rye," Donna emphasized, "not like that phony stuff they have in New Jersey."

"Oh," commented Jane, lost.

On the bus back to Mercury, Donna told her about her boyfriend, Frank. "He's a long-distance truck driver. He owns his own rig, too. Cost him a hundred thousand."

"He must be rich," Jane said.

"Oh no. I should have said the *bank* owns the rig. Frank's lucky to meet his monthly payments. What with the highway taxes and the cost of diesel fuel these days." On and on she went. "You'll have to meet him, Jane. He's absolutely gorgeous! Maybe we could double-date sometime. Frank's got this friend who rides with him. Harve. He's real sexy. Maybe not so smart but a good-looker. Of course, you wouldn't have to marry him!" Donna giggled.

"I haven't met the fourth courier," Jane remarked in an attempt to change the subject.

"Oh, that's Kelly. Kelly McCall. He's on a job today. I heard he was taking documents to a Philadelphia court. A murder trial or something."

"That's interesting. Doesn't he need a bodyguard?"

"Naw. It's not a Mafia trial or anything like that."

"Oh," said Jane, "I get it."

"But you'll have lots of work. Norma hasn't been able to cover all the routes. And you know we've been robbed four times this summer. Lew is going to lose his insurance, I hear."

"Oh, no!"

Donna shook her head. "It's so sad. The police have gotten nowhere with the robberies. Not a clue. Lew thinks it could be an inside job," the girl stated matter-of-factly.

"A what?"

"You know—" she popped her gum "—someone who works at Mercury."

"One of the couriers?" asked Jane, aghast.

"Could be. Someone is giving out information. Can you imagine? The creep. Why, Lew is the sweetest man I know and I hope whoever is doing it gets busted and rots in jail!"

"Amen."

"So you think you might like to meet Harve?"

"Well, I, uh, would like to get settled some first."

"Sure." Donna shrugged, chewing. "Maybe next week."

"That would be better."

By Wednesday, Jane was itching for an assignment, but for all of Lew's fatherly friendliness, she decided it was best not to push too hard. He'd send her along with one of the couriers when *he* thought she was ready.

"No sense sticking your neck out too soon," advised Norma at lunch that day.

From Jane's tiny office, where she spent her time looking over maps of the routes used by couriers and some past job reports, she found she could hear the front door below opening and closing, its sound made possible by the echoing wooden steps. Jane couldn't help listening, imagining that the comings and goings below were clients or the couriers returning from jobs. But sometimes she found herself imagining that Graham Smith's self-assured footfalls were among those she could hear on the steps. It wasn't like Jane to spend so much time thinking about a man, trying to recall his features, the breadth of his shoulders or the color of his eyes.

She wanted to ask Donna a dozen times if he'd called or come in to see Lew but Donna was such an awful gossip. No, she couldn't ask her. Once had been enough.

But where *was* he?

Jane finally met Donna's boyfriend, Frank Hansen, that afternoon when he returned from a run to Florida and stopped at the office to pick Donna up.

"Jane," exclaimed the secretary as she gathered up her purse to leave, "meet Frank."

He was big and blond and rumpled, very macho-looking. He was chewing tobacco.

"Nice to meet you. I've heard so much about you," Jane said graciously.

Sitting on the edge of the reception desk in his big work boots and faded T-shirt, he nodded at Jane and mumbled something.

"How was your trip?" Donna was asking him.

"Lousy. The I-95 was so crowded with old fogies driving back from Miami I had to crawl. How the hell can I make a buck if it takes me an extra day to haul a load 'cause of some old . . ." and he swore nastily.

Jane cringed.

"Poor baby," cooed Donna, who was obviously, uncritically mad about him.

"And the speed limits—ridiculous," he groused. "I got a ticket from those—" he swore again "—cops in Georgia."

There was a brutal aura surrounding Frank Hansen and Jane took an immediate dislike to the man. What on earth did Donna see in him? It was definitely time for Jane to make her exit. "Well, see you around," she said politely.

"Yeah, sure."

"Oh, is Harve waiting in the car?" Donna asked.

Frank nodded without enthusiasm.

Jane turned and glanced out of the tall, old-fashioned window. Sitting in a beat-up '72 Ford, double-parked, was a large dark man, with lots of chest hair showing above the neck of his shirt. He had a beetle brow and thick arms, she could see, but his face was essentially turned away so Jane was unable to tell much more.

"Wanna come out and meet Harve?" Donna was asking hopefully.

"Well, I . . . I promised I'd call my father after work," Jane lied. "You know, he worries."

"Oh. Well, maybe tomorrow then."

"Sure, maybe," replied Jane, wondering how she was going to get out of that one. "I guess I better get on up to my office and put some files away. See you." She disappeared up the stairs, relieved to get away from Frank's uncomfortable presence, wondering, once more, what a sharp girl like Donna could see in a man like that.

The last days of July slipped away. The heat in the city was unbearable in the beginning of August, the humidity reaching close to ninety-five percent some days. Jane found that she had to shower often, twice a day anyway, to stand it. It seemed like she was grimy all the time from the soot that hung in the thick city air. The police reported an increase in domestic violence those early August days and Jane stayed in her Barbizon room at night.

It wasn't all that bad, though. Norma had her over to dinner one evening and Lew finally allowed Jane to bodyguard—locally only—until she got the hang of it.

Her very first assignment was to guard Peter Lerner while he took the plans of a revolutionary new hull design to the docks of the New York Yacht Club.

"The new hull is for a boat that'll race in the America's Cup," Peter told her.

"The design is *that* valuable?" asked Jane as she drove carefully through the heavy city traffic, keeping a watchful eye on things.

"You bet. Wait till you see the dock area. It's got more security than Fort Knox."

Then there was an assignment in which she and Peter transported artwork from Manhattan to Westport, Connecticut, and another job with Kelly McCall, who was in his fifties and could have been Lew's brother, carrying the contents of an elderly woman's safe-deposit box from one New York bank to another. Jane's jobs went, thankfully, without incident. Norma's, thus far, did too.

Only once more did Jane allow herself to ask Donna about Graham. "Oh," she said casually one afternoon, "have you seen Quicksilver lately?"

Donna shook her head. "Not a word. It's funny, too, because he usually calls on Lew every couple of weeks or so."

"Oh, well," said Jane, feigning disinterest, "I'm sure he'll come around sometime."

At night in her hotel room Jane allowed herself to think about Graham. She recalled him with utter clarity yet there were huge, empty gaps in her memory. Had his nose been straight or hooked? Was he as tall as she remembered? Was his voice as pleasantly modulated? Good Lord, was he married? No, she decided, he wasn't. Had Jane imagined his interest in her?

She was dying to see him again, to test her feelings for him. How would he feel about her in this different environment? Would he even notice her here in New York, his home?

Impatience ate at her sometimes when she thought of Graham. She'd known him less than a day, a ridiculously short time. He'd probably forgotten her but, darn it, she wanted to know if he had or not!

At Mercury she found herself listening automatically for the downstairs door to open and each time it did, her heart gave a little expectant jump. It could be him, it could be Graham. But it never was. At the Barbizon she leaped every time the phone rang, then had to take a deep breath and wait for the second ring in case it was Graham and she would appear too anxious. It was, however, either her father or Donna or Norma Stedman when it did ring, which wasn't often.

Graham Smith, Quicksilver, where are you? she asked the darkness at three in the morning or the watery sun at eight as she descended into the bowels of the city to catch the subway to work or the green, green grass in Central Park as she jogged in the awful humidity.

And then one day she was coming down the stairs at work and there he was. Tall, devilishly handsome, his strawberry-blond hair catching the golden summer light from the high window as he leaned over Donna's desk chatting.

Jane froze for a moment and then he looked up and noticed her. She was struck dumb by his presence, just as she feared she would be. There was something more to this man than just good looks. There was some indefinable magic in his blue eyes, in the insouciant tilt of his lips, in that delightfully expressive face that was so full of unspoken promise.

"Well, hello, Jane Manning." He stood up straight and grinned at her.

"Hi." She found her legs again and walked down the steps to take his hand. Oh, yes, indeed, it was still there, that current between them; it was in the warmth of his touch, in the way his fingers closed over hers, possessive somehow, yet smooth as silk and gentle.

"Long time no see," he was saying as he gazed into her eyes. "You'll have to fill me in on everything, how you like the city, et cetera."

"Sure," said Jane, releasing his hand, glad she'd worn her best dress that day and done her hair. What did he *really* think of her, though? Did he find her out of place in the sophistication of Manhattan? Did she still measure up?

"I've got to see Lew for a few minutes," he said then. "Do you think we might have lunch?"

Jane was about to say yes when Donna's voice stopped her. "Don't forget you have to go to Jersey City with Lukas at eleven-thirty, Jane."

"Oh," replied Jane, momentarily flustered, "I guess I can't make it for lunch today, Graham. I'm sorry."

He grinned, his deep, mellow voice echoing pleasantly. "So am I. But we'll do it another time."

"You're in the city for a while?" she ventured.

"Could be. Never know."

"You ready to go, lady?" came Lukas's voice from the head of the staircase.

"Oh, yes, anytime," replied Jane, tearing her gaze away from Graham reluctantly.

"I'll see you, then." Graham began to head up the steps and she watched his form until he was out of sight. She'd forgotten what a great physique he had. Those long, muscled legs, a nice rear end, the tapered hips beneath the white linen sport coat, and his easy, confident carriage made for one hell of a package.

Jane stood staring after him like a lovesick puppy, feeling as if it would almost have been better if he had not come back into her life at all.

How much time had they spent together? Two minutes? And his promise of lunch—had it been just words, polite bantering? Perhaps she should have pinned him down. "What *day* do you want to have lunch, Graham?"

But really, who could pin down a man with a name like Quicksilver?

CHAPTER FIVE

WHEN JANE LEFT THE OFFICE that afternoon Donna was standing on the curb in front of the building waiting for Frank to pick her up.

"See you tomorrow," Donna said brightly, snapping her gum. "Boy, it sure looks like rain. Hope this heat spell is over soon. Gawd, it makes my hair frizz up like cotton candy!"

"I love your hair. Mine just goes straighter in the humidity."

"Say, maybe Harve'll be along. I mean, you want to meet him? We were going out for pizza."

"Ah, gee, thanks, Donna, but I, uh, have a date."

"Oh, neat! Who?"

"Oh, you don't know him. Someone from, uh, Denver."

"Well, have fun." Then she stretched up to her tiptoes and waved a purple-tipped hand. "Oh, there's Frank!"

This time he picked her up on a monstrous black and chrome motorcycle, a Harley-Davidson. It didn't faze Donna; she merely hiked up her skirt and swung a leg over the seat. She waved goodbye as Frank revved his machine up and lurched forward into the one-way traffic but Frank himself hadn't even turned his head. Well, thought Jane in relief, at least Harve hadn't been along.

She took the subway uptown. By now she was so used to the urine odor that permeated the stations she didn't even wrinkle her nose. And she read the want ads as she stood swaying, not even hearing the clickity-clack racket of the train. The usual places were for rent: co-op on Park Avenue $1,500 per month; studio in the Village, good lighting, $950 per month; shotgun apartment in Germantown, $1,200. She folded the paper up in disgust. How would she ever find a decent, affordable place to live?

When Jane emerged from the stuffy, echoing tunnel she felt a breeze lift her hair and there was a muted rumble of thunder. Astonishing. It was the first fresh air she'd felt since arriving in New York. The leaves on the trees in front of a gray stone building fluttered weakly. Poor trees. They were encased in concrete—and their roots? Did their roots stretch down to the subways and sewers underground?

Then Jane saw that the sky had turned dark gray, lightning flashed behind a building, and when she rounded the corner to her hotel a real wind buffeted her, sending grit and dust and a few stray papers ricocheting off her. It *was* going to rain.

By the time she got up to her room the first drops were splattering on the hot sidewalks, sending up that tarry wet pavement smell, and people were rushing for cover and windshield wipers began swishing in the rush-hour traffic. Jane threw open her window and breathed in the fresh air, getting her face wet in the process. She thought of the afternoon thundershowers at home on the ranch, of the black thunderheads boiling up from the west, releasing their burden, then moving on to leave the land refreshed, the air cleansed, the sky a perfect blue. And she and her brothers, so often caught out in the rain, would have to race for the barn. "Me first!" James would always scream, bent low over his horse's neck, his horse flying over the ground, throwing clods of mud up from its hooves.

A momentary nostalgia flooded her. Then she pulled her head in and sighed. Memories were good but she'd always have them and right now she had to experience a new existence, a new city, unfamiliar people and different feelings. Then, some day, she'd probably feel nostalgic about *this* period of her life.

And, oh, how exciting New York was! It breathed, it shook with life. It rattled and honked and screeched. It smelled wonderful and horrible. It presented enough weird sights in a day to fill *Ripley's Believe It or Not*. And every neighborhood was different—Wall Street, Fifth Avenue, Washington Square, Chinatown, the Village, the Palisades. Each one was a city in microcosm, with its own smells and noises and sights and customs. New York.

Jane sat on her bed and listened to the rain and the thunder. Out there was the whole city waiting for her to explore it. It was teeming with people, promising adventures, beckoning. On the other hand, she wasn't foolhardy. To go out alone—in the pouring rain... Maybe she'd wait until the storm let up and then grab a bite to eat at the deli down the street. Or she could go to a movie, except that men in shabby trench coats had a way of sitting next to her in the theaters. It wasn't that she was afraid of them, it was just unpleasant. If she had her own place she could do so much more....

She lay back, kicked her shoes off and put her arms behind her head. Graham. Quicksilver. The thought of him came into her mind unbidden. Had he really meant that lunch invitation? Or had he known she was busy? Was he just being polite. He *had* liked her back in Rifle, she knew he had. But this was his home ground and here he was in control whereas there he'd been at a disadvantage. Actually, not really so much at a disadvantage. He'd handled things pretty darn well. She smiled to herself at the thought of Graham on Pard. Well, at least he had a sense of humor. And a long lean hard body and bright blue eyes and that firm, narrow jaw and—

The phone rang. Her father? Donna with Harve panting in the background?

"Hello?"

"Jane?"

She sat bolt upright, speechless for a heartbeat of time. She'd conjured him up in her mind and this was a phantom voice.

"Jane Manning?"

"Yes," she said breathlessly, "I'm here."

"Oh, you sound funny. This is Graham."

"Oh, I . . . I just ran up the stairs."

"Listen, I've been thinking of you a lot. I wish I'd been in town when you arrived but I was off on a job. There's this crazy writer in England . . . well, you don't want to hear about it. So, can we get together this evening?"

"I'd love to." Her heart thudded against her ribs.

"I *did* say I'd show you the Empire State Building, as I recall." His voice promised fun and she could picture him standing insouciantly—where?—someplace elegant, talking to her. "Donna told me you're at the Barbizon. Right?"

"Yes."

"I'll pick you up at 6:30. Is that okay with you?"

She glanced at her watch: 5:35. Oh my, her hair! "It's fine. Great."

"Good. See you soon."

"See you, Graham."

Jane gave herself a minute to dance around the room in her stocking feet. She grinned to herself and whistled a tune and twirled on the gold-and-brown patterned carpet. Then she stopped, gasped, and looked at her watch: 5:45!

It took her twenty minutes to wash her hair, then blow-dry it. Darn! And her hair was straight as a stick. Pulling on her white pants—thank heavens she'd bought them—buttoning the yellow blouse, she raced around her room like a madwoman. More deodorant. She'd sweat in this heat. Was the Empire State Building air-conditioned?

Then a little blush, the expensive stuff from Blooming-dale's. Mascara, but her eyes kept blinking and she smeared it. Six-fifteen. Would he be late? Sandals or the beige heels? Would they be walking much?

At 6:20 she had to stop and pat her face dry. It was still raining and thundering out. What kind of jacket should she wear? She didn't own a raincoat. He'd think her a hick. No raincoat!

Then a thought struck her—would he call up or expect her to meet him in the lobby? Should she wait in her room, dancing with impatience, or appear to be too eager and go down to the lobby?

Oh, damn, this was all so new, so difficult. At home Branch just drove up in his pickup truck and she hopped in and they went to Tilly's Café or the local Elks lodge or a movie in Glenwood Springs.

She waited until 6:35, then couldn't sit still another second. Riding down in the elevator she had a moment of panic. What if he called her room and she didn't answer and he left?

The elevator doors swished open and she stepped out. A flash of lightning illuminated the dim lobby for a split second. She looked for Graham's tall figure. Was he there yet? The front door opened and let in a gust of air, a spattering of raindrops, and he was striding across the lobby toward her, a broad smile on his face, the shoulders of his exqui-sitely cut sport coat dark with rain.

"Jane? Sorry I was late. Couldn't find a place to park."
He gave her a rueful expression. "It's raining like crazy and
I don't have my raincoat."

"Neither do I," she admitted.

"It's good to see you again," he said then, his eyes resting on her face.

"You, too." She gave a nervous little laugh. "It's different."

"You mean New York? Sure, but I'm the same and I'll
bet you are, too." He took her hand; his was wet but it
didn't matter. "Let's go. Hungry? Thirsty? I'll take you
anywhere you want. This is my town and I want to show it
to you."

Graham's car was double-parked. They ducked their
heads and ran. It was a little red Porsche, its hazard lights
blinking while a policeman stood next to it calmly writing
up a ticket as the rain cascaded off his yellow slicker.

"Officer, please," Graham said. "This is my fiancée and
she just arrived in New York. You wouldn't want her to get
the wrong impression, would you?" And he pulled Jane
close while they both got wetter and wetter. "Come on, give
me a break. I'll never do it again, officer." He bent his head
to Jane. "Will I, honey?"

"No, certainly not," she told the policeman solemnly.

The officer stopped writing and peered at them from
under the brim of his dripping hood. "Okay, buddy, I'll
make it a warning this time."

"Thanks, officer, really," Jane said, smiling. Graham
chimed in with, "We appreciate it, I'll never do it again."

"It was entirely my fault," Jane added. "I took too long
getting ready. Thank you ever so much."

Graham held the door of the car while Jane slid in, still
smiling at the policeman, then he ran around to the other
side, got in and pulled out into the traffic. He started

laughing at the first stoplight. "That down-home charm'll do it every time! Jane, you were terrific. I owe you one."

"No problem. Next time, though, tell the guy I'm your sister or something." She was laughing too and trying to wipe the rain off her face without smearing her mascara. All that frantic getting ready and she was soaked, her hair hanging in ratty strands, her linen pants creased, her blouse sticking to her.

"My sister? Hey, lady, there's no way on earth he could have mistaken you for my sister."

There was no answer to that remark. She got her comb out of her purse and tried to do something with her hair. While she pulled and tugged at the wet snarls, she could feel his gaze slide from her profile down to her clinging wet blouse. Why was it that a mere glance could be as intimate, as sensual as a caress?

Finally the traffic light turned green, and she saw him turn his attention back to the road.

"Sorry you got drenched," he said.

"Oh, well, I've been wet before. At least it's a relief from the heat."

"You're a good sport, Jane." He weaved through the traffic and turned onto a side street. "First we're going to get something to eat and dry off, then we'll go up to the Empire State Building like I promised. The rain's letting up and I know it'll stop by then. Is that okay with you?"

"Sounds wonderful." Actually, Jane didn't care where they went. It was exciting enough to be with Graham. He moved, it seemed, from one adventure to another and she was dying to see what would happen next.

He took her to a little northern Italian place in Chelsea on Ninth Avenue. They sat at a tiny table in a dark corner with a candle stuck in a Chianti bottle for light. The waiter had a dirty apron and a thick accent but the food was marvelous. Jane never remembered exactly what it was because she was so aware of Graham, so involved in their conversation, so bombarded with sights and sounds and smells.

"So, how is the Big Apple treating you?" Graham asked, sipping his wine, his blue eyes dancing in the candlelight.

"Wonderful. I love it. And Lew is great and so is my job," she replied enthusiastically. "This city is so, so *exciting*." Then she hesitated. Did she sound like a hick? Too easily impressed? But, what the heck, she *was* impressed. Why try to act otherwise?

But he was smiling at her without condescension. "I love to hear you talk. You've got just the slightest Western accent, did you know that?"

She put her head to one side and said, deadpan, "Funny, I thought everyone *here* had a funny accent, Graham."

He burst out laughing.

Jane leaned forward and asked him, more seriously, "Graham, tell me the truth. Just how much did you have to do with getting me this job?"

"As much as I could manage," he said frankly.

"Why?"

"Two reasons. I thought you could do the job and I wanted to see you again."

"You did?"

"What do you think I'm doing right now, Jane?" he asked, grinning.

"Seeing me," she said quietly.

"Now, tell me about yourself," Graham coaxed. "Everything before you decided to become a bodyguard."

"Gosh, that's boring."

"Not to me. I'm insatiably curious, you know, like the baby elephant in the *Jungle Book*."

"And look what happened to him. Didn't he get his nose stretched out by a crocodile?"

"Ah yes, but that was all for the best—for elephants, anyway."

Jane looked at him and sipped her wine. He was fun. Witty, sharp, handsome. Full of knowledge and experience and good at so many things. What was he doing with a girl like her—from Rifle? He must have his pick of hundreds of women. Or did she provide variety? And yet there was this feeling she got from him. "Vibes" they were called. He liked her, he really did. Maybe more than just *like* but she shied from putting it into words. And she felt the same. Oh yes, she *liked* Graham Smith a lot.

"Well," he said. "I'm waiting with bated breath."

So she told him about her mother dying when she was ten, about being raised on the ranch by her father and four brothers. About being dissatisfied, in limbo, until she read about the ISA and how women make good bodyguards. "Then I knew what I wanted to do. Like one of those light bulbs you see in cartoons. You know, *eureka*!"

"And are you still glad you did it?"

"I sure am." She nodded resolutely. "Now it's your turn."

"You positive you want to hear? It's not very interesting."

"That's my line. Go ahead, tell me everything. I'm another elephant's child."

She ate while he talked. He spoke well and used his hands a lot. His voice was smooth and deep, his accent nonspecifically East Coast. He described things well. His upbringing had been in various European cities where his father had been posted as a consul for the foreign service. "That's where he met Lew, who also worked for the service for years. They go way back. And that's why my

French is so good. I went to a lycée in Paris for a while. And besides my mother is French Canadian and used to speak it at home." He told her about foreign studies at Georgetown University, a year of law school and two years with the foreign service. She felt as if she was beginning to know the elusive Quicksilver, as if those gaping holes in her knowledge of him were filling in.

"You've had a pretty exciting life," Jane said.

He shrugged. "It's all what you're used to. To me your ranch is about as exciting as I've seen. And you *raced* quarter horses?"

"I was raised on a horse. That's not the least bit interesting."

But Graham leaned forward over the little table and said in a soft, caressing voice, "I love to watch you eat."

Jane's hand stopped, her fork halfway to her mouth. "What?"

"You're beautiful when you eat."

She put her fork down and stared at him. "When I *eat*?"

"You enjoy your food. And your mouth is pretty. And you have some tomato sauce on your chin."

Quickly Jane raised her napkin to wipe her chin off. She felt herself blushing. "That's mean, Graham."

"I like a natural woman. You look great even when you're wet."

"Or covered with tomato sauce?"

"Then too."

"Graham . . ."

"Yes?" he asked, mock-innocently.

When they had finished dinner and left the restaurant, it was still light out and the rain had stopped. "See?" said Graham, "I told you it would stop raining."

"Are we really going to the Empire State Building?"

He took her hand as they started out and she shivered with delight at his touch. "Yes, we are. It's open till late. And the view really is spectacular."

"The Empire State Building," mused Jane. "I never thought..."

Graham pulled her hand up to his mouth and kissed her fingers lightly. "Ah, but one never knows what life holds, does one?"

She felt her insides grow warm and ticklish and glowing. "No," she agreed softly.

She felt as if she were—what was that awful cliché?— being swept off her feet. A strong current was sweeping her along; it was wild and exciting and irresistible. It was Graham and it was happening too fast. She couldn't think; he wouldn't let her. She was scared and thrilled and full of a breathless, warm, melting sensation.

Graham Smith, the logical part of her mind told her, was a rogue, an adventurer, a man who took the world by the tail and shook it. He went at things so aggressively that she wondered if he ever took the time to stop and evaluate, to really figure out what he wanted from life.

Another part of her was fascinated by his dynamism and sense of humor, by the softness of his voice and the genuine caring he emanated and the way he could make Jane feel as if she were the only female on earth. His spirit matched hers in some ways; they were both people who wanted more from life than a steady job or security or a nice house. They both wanted some kind of stimulation, something different.

They walked to the Empire State Building. Its silhouette was so familiar it seemed as if Jane must have been there before—the grand decorative lines, the way it climbed from its base in irregular steps to the sky, its upper layers smaller than the ones below lifting in perfect symmetry to the needlelike spire. And it was elegant inside, in the ornate, Art Deco fashion of the thirties. What struck Jane was the fact that it was, after all, an office building, a place where people came to work every day.

The elevators rose so quickly Jane couldn't believe they were up to the eighty-sixth floor. She even had to pop her ears.

They walked around the observation platform while Graham pointed out various landmarks. The atmosphere was cool and hazy and she could barely make out Central Park up to the north or the World Trade Center to the south. But the city itself was stretched out at her feet, miles upon miles of gray thrusting buildings, arrow-straight avenues, the green of trees and parks, the rivers, the tiny ant-like cars crawling endlessly along the streets. It was a beautiful sight.

"It's so big," breathed Jane.

"London's bigger and Mexico City and Tokyo, I think."

"But they're not like . . . not like *this*."

"No, they're not. There's only one New York."

"Oh, Graham, thank you for this. I never realized. I mean, being down there—" she pointed "—you don't get the full picture."

It was windy on the eighty-sixth floor. Jane's slacks and blouse flattened against her and her hair blew into her eyes. The sun was setting off beyond New Jersey but the haze made it appear to be merely a yellow glow. So different from the diamond-bright clear Colorado sky where the sun shone in all its glory.

"Had enough?" he finally asked. "I'm afraid it's going to rain again."

By the time they left the building it was pouring.

"Want to get a taxi?" Graham suggested. "My car's pretty far away."

But they got wetter standing at the curb waiting for an empty cab than if they'd walked.

"Damn!" Graham yelled, shaking his fist at the hundreds of suddenly filled taxis, "you can't ever get a cab when you need one in this town!"

They finally walked, splashing through oily puddles, half running, laughing like two children whose mothers had told them not to get wet. Graham gave her his jacket but it was already so damp it didn't do much good. Still, she liked the feel of it and it smelled faintly of him.

Once they reached his Porsche and clambered inside, the windows promptly steamed up. Jane took her handkerchief and wiped at them while he drove. "That's two," she warned playfully. "Where are we going now?"

"To get dry," he said lightly and her heart bounded in her chest.

"Where?" she asked.

Graham was looking straight ahead. "To my place." He hesitated. "That is, if you want to." His voice was carefully noncommittal, as if he were allowing her the chance to back out gracefully. And she knew she could back out. Graham would never pressure her; he wanted her to go with him but if she declined he wouldn't argue.

Jane realized suddenly what his invitation signified. They were two adults. They liked each other and there was something profound between them, an undeniable affinity. They needed to learn more about each other, much more. They needed to explore their feelings, and if that led to an intimate expression of their love, so be it. If she said yes now there would be no turning back, no playing coy games. As an adult Jane owed him that much. And if she said no Graham would, as an adult, take her home.

Panic seized her momentarily. It was too soon. The city was overwhelming her, and Graham... It was all too much.

And yet, strong and definite, there was this bond between them. It had flared into being the moment they'd met and was blazing stronger with each second. It was real and important and unique in her experience.

"I'd love to," she said clearly and Graham broke into a broad smile, turned downtown on the Avenue of the Americas and stepped on the gas.

His apartment was on 10th Street close to the heart of Greenwich Village in a very nice neighborhood, a brownstone that was surprisingly charming and substantial for a single man, Jane thought. Graham parked in a nearby underground garage and while he walked around to open her door, Jane had another moment of apprehension. What was she doing?

But then he was holding his hand out and smiling, and she knew that she and Graham could have something very good, very special together. Jane drew in a deep breath, took hold of his hand and they walked to the street and then up the steps to the shiny dark-green door.

It was still raining and the thunder seemed to be reverberating off the buildings of Lower Manhattan. Jane shivered a little in her wet clothes.

"Well, here we are," said Graham, opening his door.

Jane stepped in and looked around. The foyer led into a living room that had a gleaming parquet floor, an Aubusson rug and several upholstered chairs and a couch done in floral patterns. There were gilt-framed mirrors and a few very large, very ornately framed oil paintings on the walls. Wainscoting, painted white, covered the bottom half of the walls and above that they were done in a deep forest green. There were green velvet drapes, a marble-topped sideboard and a finely carved mantel on the far side of the room.

"It's lovely," said Jane.

"Thank you. My decorator is very inexpensive, though."

"Your decorator?"

"My mother. It's old family stuff."

"Oh. Well, she did a marvelous job."

"I'll tell her."

"Does she live in New York?"

A shadow passed over his face, Jane thought. "No, in Montreal."

Of course, he'd said she was French Canadian.

"Now, let's see. You need to get dry. Follow me." He led her upstairs to his bedroom. It was plainer than the downstairs—a double bed, a serviceable dresser, a rocking chair. Maybe his mother had run out of "old family stuff." He took a blue terry cloth robe from the closet. "Put this on and we'll dry your clothes."

"What about you?" she asked.

"Ladies first."

She changed into his robe and, barefoot, carried her blouse and pants downstairs. "Your turn," she said. "Do you have a dryer? I'll just put these in..."

"Right through there." He pointed toward the kitchen. "And I'll be back in a minute."

When he returned he wore jeans and a white polo shirt that emphasized his lean physique.

"Tea?" he asked. "Or coffee? Or maybe a bit of brandy to warm you up?"

"Nothing, thanks. I'm fine." She was a little constrained with him now. What should she do next? She wondered if he felt awkward, too, or if he was used to entertaining women in his apartment.

She walked to a window and pulled back the heavy fabric. The rain streamed down the glass endlessly, making the street outside and the buildings waver. The city lights were merely globes of diffused brightness. She sensed Graham coming up behind her.

"Are you nervous being alone with me, Jane?"

She turned to face him. "A little. This is all real new to me."

"I feel like I've known you forever," he said softly. "I can't imagine not knowing you." Then he put a hand out and touched her cheek. "You know, I've been wanting to kiss you since that day in Rifle. Did you know that?"

"No," she whispered. Her breath came too quickly and her heart was bursting with excitement and fright and happiness. "Did you really?"

He nodded, his blue eyes holding hers, mesmerizing her. His other hand reached out and she could feel his fingers, warm and strong, cupping her face, turning it up to his. She closed her eyes and his lips came down over hers, at first gently, as light as a bird's wing, then harder so that her mouth opened under his.

Her arms went around his neck and she pressed herself against his body. Her blood sang, her senses quivered with the wonder of his nearness. His lips felt familiar, as if she'd known them before, as if she hadn't just met this man. She breathed in his scent as his breath mingled with hers.

He pulled back and looked at her. "That was even better than I thought it would be," he said.

Jane searched his face. It reflected pleasure and a kind of quiet awe. She sighed and laid her head against his chest. His arms tightened around her and he kissed the top of her head.

"I can't believe I'm here, I can't believe I met you," murmured Jane.

"I know what you mean." He tilted her face up and studied her so long she began to feel uncomfortable.

"Is something wrong?" she asked.

"No . . . I just wondered about . . . well . . ."

"What?" she asked, puzzled, leaning back in his arms.

"Gosh, I feel like a fool asking. But I was wondering about you and . . . Branch Taggart."

"Oh."

"Look, it's none of my business, I know, but he seemed to know you real well and . . ."

She looked down and smiled to herself. "Don't worry about Branch. It's long since over."

"You sure?"

"I've known Branch for years and he'd like to think there was something between us. But there never really was. At least, there sure isn't anymore."

"I'm very glad to hear that."

"Now, should I ask you about any of your lady friends?" she queried teasingly.

"No. Besides, there isn't one as big and strong as Branch. You don't have to worry about a thing." His blue eyes were laughing at her again and she felt happy and excited and nervous. Her pulse thumped and leaped and she could feel his hands on her waist. When his mouth covered hers once more, she gave in to the feel of his lips on hers, his smell, his touch, the moist, velvety feel of his tongue. Delight raced through her body in shivery waves. She sighed when he pulled away.

"You're not regretting this, are you?" he asked softly, his lips moving in her hair.

"No," she said into his chest.

"I don't think you're afraid of anything or anyone," he said. "I love that in you."

She raised her head. "You don't find it . . . intimidating? Lots of men would. Lots of men *have*."

He laughed. "Hell, no, Jane. I like a woman who knows her own mind."

She leaned back in his arms and asked soberly, "What's happening, Graham? I mean, what's really happening between us?"

"Something special," he answered just as solemnly, his mouth coming down over hers once again.

Upstairs in his bedroom he pulled the blue robe off her shoulders and kissed the skin he uncovered. "So beautiful," he murmured. Jane wanted to tell him she wasn't really beautiful at all but it didn't matter, not as long as Graham thought she was.

Then she helped him off with his clothes and gasped at the wonder of his nude body. He was a remarkable piece of work—long and lean, broad shouldered, with strong legs and sinewy arms. He was gentle and fierce, a practiced lover, a man who knew how to please a woman. His hands found all the secret places on her body and made them tingle in response.

He pulled back the covers on his bed and Jane saw that his sheets were a leopard-spotted pattern. She giggled and ran her hand down his bare flank. "Sexy," she whispered into his ear as they fell onto the bed together.

"Yeah, me Tarzan, you Jane," he growled, biting at her earlobe. Then he stopped and looked at her as she lay under him. "You *Jane*, get it?"

She started to laugh, burying her face in his neck. "How original!"

"Any man said that to you before, I'll break his neck," Graham murmured into her ear.

She could feel his hardness against her belly and the sensation filled her with warmth. She closed her eyes and pulled him close. "Oh, God, kiss me."

His tongue savored her mouth, his breath mingled with hers, his hands stroked her back and hips and buttocks, the inside of her thighs. Jane squirmed with pleasure, the heat building within her. Small cries came from her and he whispered quick, panting questions. "Here? Oh, yes," and "Slow, my darling," and "Is that good, is that it?"

She was ready; she wanted to feel him inside her, wanted to be one with him. "Now," she urged, "Graham, quickly!" and he took her almost harshly, stabbing swiftly and sure, filling her until she cried out.

Jane had never before felt the intensity of this joining. Graham fit her perfectly, molded to her body, touched all the right places. Her senses expanded and she seemed to float with him above everything. The world receded and there was only the two of them, alone, rocking, filled with the same pure, electrifying jolts of sensation that drove them both onward. Then she felt him grow rigid, bigger, within her and he groaned and she felt the same heat burst within her.

Jane was aware only of her breath, rasping in and out, the sweat that beaded her forehead and Graham's weight on her. It seemed to her that she'd come back from a distant place, a place where feelings were stronger, reality more real, sensations more pure.

"Jane," she heard Graham say, "Janey, my Janey. Ah, girl, you've done me in."

She put a hand on his thick, wavy hair and felt the lassitude that held her. "I hope it isn't permanent," she breathed.

"God, so do I," he said fervently then laughed. "You're wonderful. I love an uninhibited woman. There's even more to you than I suspected, Jane Manning."

She smiled into the darkness. "Was I disgraceful?"

"Delightfully so. Noisy as the devil."

"Graham, you're embarrassing me."

But he only rolled aside and flung an arm across her bare stomach. "I must be getting old," he teased.

Her head fit perfectly into the hollow between his neck and shoulder, his other arm went around her. Jane had never felt so content in her life. She slowly trailed her fingertips across his chest.

"That was special, wasn't it?" she finally asked. "I mean, it's not just my imagination, is it?"

His arm tightened around her. He thought for a minute and she was afraid that he'd tell her it had been ordinary. But he said softly, "It wasn't your imagination, Janey."

And she snuggled up to him, happy, and breathed in his scent and listened to his heartbeat until she fell asleep.

CHAPTER SIX

"TEN MILLION IN DIAMONDS," Lew was saying to Graham. "Our biggest job to date."

"A lot of money," Graham remarked distractedly, unable to concentrate on their conversation about the diamond delivery Lew wanted him to make. Between the prospect of a trip to Amsterdam, not to mention his large fee, Graham should have been all ears. But it was all he could do to pay attention.

There was a jetlike roar running through his head and a heavy pounding in his heart. His raw silk shirt caressed his skin and he felt an idiotic smile trying to curve his lips. It was almost as if he were coming down with the flu but it was a wonderful illness because he knew there was a sure, instantaneous cure: Jane.

"Detective Sorello says it's only a matter of time before the police nab the robbers." Lew stood and walked to the window in his office. "But I don't have the time to wait for the police, Graham. One more substantial loss and Lloyd's will never renew my policy. If they drop Mercury, no bonding or insurance company will touch us."

"It's bad, Lew, I know. I'm sure there's a way, though...." *Come on, Graham,* he told himself, *pay attention.* It certainly wasn't as if it were the first time he'd been with a woman. Hell, he'd had plenty of experience! But there had never been a woman like Jane Manning.

He sat in front of Lew Rapp's desk and images of Jane flew around in his head like butterflies—her husky voice like sweet music in his ear, her satin-smooth peachy skin, her small capable hands that drove him wild. They had both been wild, a fine wildness. He wondered if it had been as good for her as it had been for him.

Where was she now? In the office, out on an assignment? *Where are you, my adorable Janey?*

"Graham, are you listening?"

"Oh, yeah, sure I am, Lew. You were talking about my handling this job coming up in September. In, uh, Amsterdam. Yeah. That's right."

"Are you okay, son?"

"Oh, I'm fine. Better than ever, in fact."

"You could have fooled me."

Lew Rapp had known Graham's father before Graham had been born. Lew and Smedley had gone through foreign service training together and over the years, in their various postings, they'd kept in touch. Graham had known Lew since both the older men had been stationed at the American Embassy in London twenty years before. Lew was like an uncle to Graham, a beloved family friend, and he was in trouble. At the moment, Graham wished Lew had retired like his own father because he was having a terrible time concentrating on Lew's troubles.

Graham straightened his shoulders and with great effort, cleared his head. "I'll be glad to pick up those diamonds, Lew. No problem. And I promise you, they'll be perfectly safe with me."

"I hate to ask," Lew said. "I've got four top men here who could handle it. Especially if Norma went along. But I don't know if one of them is setting up these thefts. *Someone* in this office is."

"It does look that way," Graham agreed.

"The thieves seem to know exactly where my couriers will be. They're even *waiting* for them. And, of course, no one who's been guarded by Norma has been hit. It's got to be an inside leak."

"Must be," Graham mused.

"Another thing," Lew continued, "the crooks have only gone after stuff that's easy to fence like jewelry, cash, securities. It's a nightmare."

"I'll say. And I suppose if it isn't one of the couriers himself, someone here has friends on the outside doing the dirty work for him."

"Detective Sorello is sure of it."

Graham frowned. "Has he tried lie detector tests?"

"Not yet. But everyone is willing."

"Anyone too willing?"

Lew shook his head. "Sorello tried that ploy. It didn't work. Unfortunately," he added, "those tests are far from foolproof, anyway."

Graham sat lost in thought for a few minutes. "I've got an idea," he stated finally, "and if you don't like it, just say so. But I think maybe we could kill two birds with one stone."

"How's that?"

"I pick up the diamonds, like we talked about, and at the same time we nab the thieves."

"Easy to say," Lew said in a doubtful voice.

"Now wait a minute. It's not as crazy as it sounds." Graham sat forward in his chair eagerly. There was a glint in his blue eyes.

"I don't like that look..."

"Listen. Suppose you *don't* try to keep this diamond shipment under wraps around the office. Suppose you let, say, Donna know about it. Now we all know Donna is an ace gossip and before you could blink the whole Mercury crew would know about the diamonds. Hell, they'd probably know my flight number!''

"What's your point? My God, Graham, that would be like handing out an invitation for someone to steal them."

Graham grinned wickedly. "Exactly."

"You mean . . . lure them deliberately?"

"Yup. Right into a trap."

"I see . . . but what about actually catching the thieves? I mean, my God, what if the diamonds *did* get stolen?"

"Have some faith, Lew!" He laughed, looking cocksure. "I haven't been twiddling my thumbs and sitting on my butt these last few years. And I'll have Norma with me. Between us these would-be robbers will be lucky to get off with jail terms. Hey, how can we fail?"

"Oh, sure. Sounds great sitting here. But what about the danger to you and Norma?"

Graham leaned back in his chair, crossing one foot over the other knee and folding his hands behind his head. "The odds are with us, Lew. You know my training. And Norma's as well."

"But you can't carry guns to Amsterdam."

"I detest guns. They're for thugs and amateurs. And besides, even if your thieves were dumb enough to try to follow us carrying weapons, which I seriously doubt with the tight airport security nowadays, they'd still have to get close enough to take the diamonds and then we'd collar them. In that situation, the hands are far more effective than any weapon."

"I just don't know." Lew frowned. "The whole thing gives me a whopping case of indigestion."

"Look, why use my services at all if you don't take full advantage? Do you want to go on getting hit and lose everything?"

"Certainly not."

"But that's exactly what might happen. Say we keep the shipment hush-hush and I bring the stones back to New York safely; eventually, whoever is behind these thefts is going to strike again. The difference is, you won't know where or when or who. Listen," he urged, "let's nab them *now*. When the element of surprise is on our side for a change."

Lew paced to the window and back to his desk. Finally he put both hands on the smooth, polished surface and leaned toward Graham. "All right, I'll go for it. Logically I know you're right but I sure don't like the idea of using my best friend's boy like this."

"Dad would insist you do. He trusts me. He knows I can handle myself, Lew."

"Oh, damn," said Lew abruptly. "We've got a problem."

Graham raised a curious brow.

"The Picassos."

"What Picassos?"

"Peter and Norma are picking up a real valuable set of Picasso sketches at the National Gallery in Washington and delivering them to the Met here in New York. It would make a perfect hit and it's the biggest thing I have coming up between now and the diamond job. If those Picassos get ripped off I'm in real trouble."

"When is this planned for?"

"A week from this coming Monday. I'm positive the word is already out around the office."

"Picassos would make a good hit," Graham agreed. "There're dozens of collectors who'd pay plenty to hang them in a private gallery. Some of them just about advertise in the *New York Times*!"

"*You* could get them. If you honestly think there could be a theft attempt, and if you want to handle it."

"Done. I'll drive on down to North Carolina the Friday before. Spend the weekend at the beach with Dad. No problem." Then suddenly Graham cocked an eyebrow. "Norma. Would she be upset if she's taken off the job?"

"Unfortunately the insurance company would insist on you having a bodyguard for this one."

"Well, I can't take Norma down to the beach for the weekend. Somehow I can't see her and Dad..."

"She prefers not to work weekends, anyway. Because of her husband. He's in a wheelchair and it's hard for him to get out."

"So, no Norma." Graham's blue eyes brightened and he hit his fist into his hand. "Hey! I'll take Jane!"

Graham left Lew's office ten minutes later. He was glad he wouldn't be going to D.C. with Norma. Not that he didn't appreciate Norma's experience but the old battle-ax made it plain she didn't like him. For some unknown reason she had always eyed him speculatively when he was around her. It was clear that she disapproved of him but for the life of him Graham didn't know just why.

He and Lew had compromised finally, Lew insisting that they lessen the possibility of the priceless sketches being stolen by spreading word around Mercury that the job had been canceled. Graham had argued that they should try to catch the thieves this time but Lew had been adamant: "I don't want to risk it, not with Jane going in Norma's place. She's still pretty inexperienced."

Only Graham and Jane would be privy to the knowledge and Lew would prefer—as Donna and Jane seemed friendly—that Jane not really know about the job until after they left New York. Graham, who had been itching at first to get a shot at the thieves, was forced to agree. Then, too, Lew was right: Jane was relatively new to the job and to put her in danger, on purpose, was pushing things.

He went upstairs to Jane's office, eager to see her but she wasn't in. Once more he wondered where she was.

THE SUN WAS OUT in New Jersey; steam was rising up from the Garden State Parkway as Jane and Rick drove. It had been raining in Atlantic City where they'd gone to pick up packets of new playing cards—cards, Rick Como told her, that the casino owners thought might have been tampered with.

"How could someone mark brand-new playing cards?" asked Jane from the driver's seat. "They're still sealed, for heaven's sake."

"I suspect the owners of the casino figure it was done in the factory. Maybe a factory worker was in league with someone on the outside, a gambler, and they're running a scam on the card tables."

"What people won't do to make a buck," observed Jane, shaking her head.

The pickup in Atlantic City had gone without a hitch. But the casino had warned Rick that there could be an attempt made to grab the packages of cards and destroy them. Rick's job was to deliver the cards to an independent forensic expert who'd been hired by the casino to check for fingerprints. Should there have been tampering, it wouldn't be too difficult to lift a set of fingerprints from the cards and nail the cheaters.

Jane was quite aware of her duties. She remained vigilant for a car trailing them or for an out-of-place vehicle when they stopped at the toll booth to pay their ticket. She had great respect for her ability to outrun a pursuing car, however, and felt confident as she drove through the marshy flats of northern New Jersey.

"You're a good driver," commented Rick.

"Thanks, I took an evasive driving course and it must have helped some."

"Evasive driving. Sounds dangerous."

"It can be." She smiled. "But I thought it was kind of exciting."

"You're quite an unusual lady, Miss Manning."

Jane colored a little and said nothing.

The forensic man had a small office in the city, downtown near the docks on the west side of Manhattan. Jane pulled up in front of the nondescript building and turned the car off. This was, in her judgment, the most dangerous part of the job. Anyone could be waiting for them—in that alley or behind that pile of garbage, in any of the parked cars along the curb, in a store across the street. She was ready, all senses on the alert, her muscles ready to react to any subliminal signals she might get from an abnormal presence.

She checked the area carefully, then stepped out of the car and locked her door. Blast it, her hands were a little shaky. Rick waited for her all-clear sign. It was 4:00 p.m. The street wasn't very crowded and no one looked out of context in the normal flow of people.

Satisfied, Jane motioned to Rick who unlocked his door, stepped out and headed quickly to the entrance of the building where he moved aside to allow her to go in first.

"Just in case," she said crisply, watchful for the slightest movement ahead of her on the stairs. The halls in the old building were dark—too dark, Jane decided—moving up a flight of stairs, still ahead of Rick. At the top of the steps she scanned the dim corridor. There were several doors, all closed, and she walked slowly down the hall until she found the one they were looking for. In another five minutes they were leaving the building, the job done, but that keyed-up sense of danger still held Jane in its grip.

"I'm always glad when I make a delivery," said Rick as he got back in the car. "Especially lately. You just never know when someone's going to jump out at you. I was one of the couriers robbed back in June," he added. "I'll tell you, it was goddamned scary!"

"Did you have a chance to stop them?"

"No way! I was alone and one of the men waved a gun under my nose."

"You did the sensible thing," Jane declared. "Nothing is worth getting killed over."

"You can say that again. And another thing—" he looked over at her in earnest "—I'm real glad to have you along today."

"My pleasure." She put the car in gear, headed down the street and wondered if Rick noticed that her hands had finally stopped shaking.

"WHEN IS SHE DUE BACK?" Graham was asking Donna.

"About five, I guess." Donna put a fresh stick of gum in her mouth. "She went to Atlantic City with Rick."

"Oh?" Was there anything Donna didn't know?

"Yeah. To a casino there. They were picking up some marked cards, taking them to a guy over on Eighth."

"Interesting."

"Oh, well, we have lots of exciting cases here. Maybe not as big-time as you do, though." She smiled and winked at him. "When are you going to quit traipsing around the world on your own and settle down?"

"Why, Donna, I didn't know you were interested." He shot her a rakish grin.

"I've got a boyfriend, Mr. Quicksilver. And besides, you are definitely not the stable kind. A girl would have to go through hell trying to get you to the altar!"

"Yes," said Graham, winking, "but wouldn't it be fun?"

He left a note for Jane.

Dear Jane,
I'm cooking in tonight. If you're free how about eight o'clock? If you'll recall, I'm a dynamite cook. Please come.

Love, Graham.

It was a dozen blocks or so farther downtown to his apartment. Graham usually walked, as he loved the city and the crowds and the unique pulse of New York. Besides, he kept his Porsche in a rented garage because to leave it on the street—even for the few minutes he'd spent with Lew—was a sure way to lose his hubcaps at the very least.

He whistled a nameless tune as he walked the street in long, easy strides, his hands in the pockets of his linen jacket, a smile curving his lips.

What to cook for Jane? It never occurred to him that she might not come. He was sure Jane wanted to be with him as much as he did with her. They fit together, as if some unknown hand had molded two bodies decades ago for the single purpose of their eventual, inevitable union.

What a grand scheme life was!

He shopped at a neighborhood market, a small, cramped store with ceiling-to-floor shelves loaded with every imaginable item, pyramids of fresh fruits and vegetables, foreign specialties and a great butcher section. Safeway had nothing on Alfredo's market.

While he picked over the fresh vegetables he put Jane from his thoughts momentarily and mused over the plan he'd presented to Lew. It was a sound idea. And with Norma along in Amsterdam—forget that their time together would no doubt be uncomfortable—they were sure to thwart Lew's robbers. How could any crooks resist the temptation of grabbing ten million in diamonds? It would be a cinch to fence them. Of course, the fence would take a big cut, at least sixty percent or better, but diamonds were essentially untraceable and the thieves would come away with well over a couple of million. They *had* to try for the stones, didn't they?

"Good evening, Mr. Smith," said Alfredo, grinning his stained, uneven smile, his white butcher's jacket smeared with the day's labors. "I have nice fresh tomatoes today. Picked in Jersey this morning. You want some?"

"Sure, pick me out three."

"I have no seen you for a while, Mr. Smith. You been away? The heat is bad this summer, yes?"

"Terrible," agreed Graham when in reality he hadn't actually noticed it. He guessed his thoughts had been too consumed with other matters. Matters like Jane, for instance.

"How about finding me a nice plump chicken?" asked Graham. "Real fresh."

"I got just the one for you."

Carrying his grocery bag, Graham took the steps up to his place by twos. He felt great, like a new man, one who had the world at his feet. It was, he supposed, all due to Jane.

He put his groceries away and got out the good linen and china, then went to shower and change. His body still damp, he slipped on a clean pair of pearl-gray linen trousers and a loose, blue cotton shirt, which he rolled up at the sleeves, then went to the kitchen to start the dinner. In the background the stereo was playing classical music at the moment. As he deftly sliced the tomatoes, he wondered if Jane liked that kind of music. He'd have to ask her, maybe take her to the Kennedy Center one night. Then, after a late supper...

Graham's pot simmered away on the stove while a glass of white wine sat half empty on the tile countertop. He glanced at the time: 8:00 p.m. Surely if Jane had other plans she'd have called him by now. So she must be on her way. The evening's scenario filled his thoughts. They'd dine by candlelight, talk for a while. He'd have to ask her about spending the following weekend at his dad's place but how could she refuse him when they had to be in Washington that Monday, anyway? Of course, *she* didn't know that yet.

Jane. What a stroke of luck—or fate—that they'd met. Jane, with those long legs and nice curves, those clear green eyes with the dark lashes, the bridge of freckles across her nose, those beautiful soft lips. And that slightly uneven tooth. Could Jane be the one he was waiting for? Was he actually falling for the girl from Rifle, Colorado? What told a man that he'd met his lifelong mate? Sure, Graham loved dozens of things about Jane; he adored the way she moved, lithely and with self-assurance. And her honesty appealed to him. There was no fear whatsoever in Graham that she might someday turn into a nag. Not Jane. But how was he supposed to know that she was the one?

Again he glanced at the clock: 8:10. Maybe he'd been too overconfident in expecting her to come over.

At 8:12 the door buzzer sounded. Graham rose quickly from his chair and felt his heart begin a heavy, pleasant rhythm.

CHAPTER SEVEN

THE NOTE WAS TAPED to Jane's office door. Donna, she thought. Who else? She scanned the paper, smiled to herself, then read it again slowly, savoring each word, trying to read between the lines, noting Graham's slapdash slanted writing. She plunked herself down in her office chair and wiggled her feet out of her shoes while she reread his note, lost in thought, remembering. Then she jerked back into the present and checked the time. Oh boy, almost seven!

Should she call him right now and ask if she could come over early, just as she was? But, after all, she didn't know him *that* well. Besides she felt grubby after the long day in the car. She wanted to be fresh and clean and fragrant for Graham.

She took the subway to her hotel and raced around her room getting ready. He was waiting for her in his venerable old brownstone, chilling wine perhaps or tossing a salad. How would it be between them now, after they'd made love? Would they be awkward and uncomfortable with each other? No, she thought, shaking her head. What had happened between them was natural and wonderful.

She ran out to the busy corner to hail a taxi, hopping with impatience as one after another flew by with fares inside. Eventually one stopped at her frantic waving. "I swear," she said to the cabbie, "I was ready to throw myself in front of the next cab that didn't stop."

"Lady, you get a ticket for that kinda stunt," was all he replied as he headed downtown, jerking forward, slamming on the brakes, mumbling at other drivers, rolling through red lights.

But Jane didn't notice. A familiar excitement gripped her. Graham. Her knees felt weak at the thought of his lovemaking. She'd put aside those notions for the day because her job allowed for no distractions but now she was free to think about him, to recall the feel of his lips and every word he'd said and how he looked. She dared say the words to herself: *I love Graham Smith,* but then quickly retreated from them. How could she love a man she'd only known for a few days? Love had to grow and there hadn't been the time for that. But there could be. Why not? And if he turned out to be other than lovable, well then, she'd count their affair as experience and keep looking. But she couldn't imagine finding a man as stimulating, as gorgeous, as fascinating as Graham Smith.

When the taxi pulled up in front of his brownstone, Jane paid the driver and got out. She was nervous all of a sudden. This dating game was unsettling, and she didn't really know Graham well enough to feel at ease. There was the green door just up those stairs, the windows with their heavy green drapes. And Graham.

Had she dressed properly? It seemed in New York that you could wear anything under the sun but there was still a certain, intangible big city flair to women's fashions. Even the teenyboppers in their jeans and sweatshirts had that *look*. She'd worn her tan skirt and an emerald-green crocheted top with a V neck. The back of her neck felt damp in the overcast, muggy weather and she thought maybe she looked small-townish and gauche.

Oh well. Jane squared her shoulders and climbed the stairs. He'd asked her to dinner so he must want to see her.

She used the brass knocker and the door opened almost instantly.

"Janey," he said and her breath caught in her throat. She'd forgotten how handsome he was, how strikingly fair and tall and bursting with vigor. He pulled her in and kissed her on the mouth, hard. "I thought you'd never get here."

"We were late getting in," she said breathlessly, remembering once again the night they'd shared, the naked skin, the moans and touching, the intimacy. She knew she was blushing and she saw in Graham's laughing blue gaze that he remembered every vivid detail only too well.

He held her away from him and studied her face. "It went all right? The job, I mean?"

"Oh, yes, no problems."

"Good. Come in. I'm starving. How about you? Wine?"

Jane wrinkled her nose and sniffed the air. "Mmm, that sure smells heavenly."

"Chicken cacciatore. Old family recipe." He laughed as he poured her a glass of wine. "Actually it's out of the *Single Man's Cookbook*."

He led the way into the living room and they sat down on the sofa. "We'll eat in a minute," he said. "I want to hear all about your day. You were with Rick, right?"

"Yes, Rick. He's very nice. He told me about his son's braces and his daughter's bad grades. We drove to Atlantic City, we drove back. Routine."

"In this business routine means success. Remember that, Janey."

He'd set the dining table beautifully: Waterford crystal, fine English bone china, white linen tablecloth and napkins, brass candlesticks with tall white candles.

"Graham, you went to so much trouble," Jane protested.

"I'm only trying to impress you. Next time it's paper plates on your lap, lady."

He lit the candles and turned the lights down. A recording of a jazz quartet played mellow rhythms in the background. A slice of delicate green honeydew garnished with dark red, rolled-up prosciutto sat on a glass plate before her.

"This is wonderful," she said, leaning across the table and putting her hand over his. "I do appreciate it."

He turned his hand, grasped her fingers and lifted them to his lips, kissing each one in turn. "My pleasure, Janey," he murmured, holding her gaze.

Jane's stomach flip-flopped and her skin felt hot all over. "Let me go or we'll never get to eat," she whispered.

He grinned, gave her hand another quick kiss and released it. "Dig in," he said and picked up his fork.

They talked ceaselessly, making very slow going of the dinner. There was so much to catch up on. It almost made Jane mad that there was an enormous amount of Graham's past that she still didn't know about.

"Foreign affairs?" she asked at one point. "That must have been interesting."

"I *thought* it was going to be interesting. You see, I wanted to be a spy and I figured that was the way to do it."

"So why aren't you a spy?"

"I found out it was too much trouble. You have to lie a lot. I hate to lie."

"Me, too." She went on cutting up her chicken breast with its tangy sauce. "Umm, this is good."

Graham chewed some pasta and swallowed. "So what was it like going to the University of Colorado?"

"Fun. It's a party school. But I learned a lot. I loved fine arts and history."

"Then you went to vet school?"

"I love animals, too."

"A Renaissance woman."

"Hardly. I'm a ranch girl." She emptied her wineglass.

"More?" He poured without waiting for her answer, filling her glass with a sparkling dry Italian red wine.

Jane wondered how many women he'd had over to dinner, how many women he'd wined and dined and bedded on the leopard-spotted sheets. She felt no jealousy, merely a keen curiosity. The knowledge would help define Graham Smith, but if she asked he might get the wrong idea.

"Do you date a lot of women?" she inquired carefully.

"I told you there was nothing to worry about, remember? I *have* dated a lot of women. Right now I'm not interested in anyone but you."

"Graham..." she began.

"Hey, that's no line. I mean it. I hate games, Janey."

She smiled tenderly. "I believe you."

"Good. What about you? You must have been the belle of Rifle."

She shrugged. "There was really never anyone serious, aside from Branch, and even that petered out. In college there were a few, you know, the usual. I guess I was practicing."

"For what?"

"For you." She watched as his expression softened. She wanted to touch him, to hold him close and feel his heat and his strength.

"Jane..." he started to say but the phone rang. "Damn."

"Go on. I'll still be here when you get back."

She couldn't help but hear his side of the conversation. "Dad, how are you?" It was obviously his father calling.

He paused as if listening. "No, I can't make it this weekend. Next weekend, for sure. I'll drive down Friday."

Jane idly watched Graham's tapered back in his blue shirt. She wanted to walk up behind him and press her body all along the whole length of him. "Yeah, no problem, it's convenient," he was saying. "Oh, did that carburetor come in yet? Great. Maybe I'll get a chance to put it in the boat. Then we can do some fishing."

He had a boat. Where? Oh yes, his father lived on the shore in North, or was it South, Carolina?

"Dad, think you could clean the old place up a bit?" He paused. "Well, because I'm thinking of bringing a guest down with me."

Jane's ears perked. A guest? Who?

"Yes, female." He sounded exasperated. "I think you'll like her a lot, Dad." Then Graham laughed. "Okay, good. See you next Friday. Late afternoon probably. Bye."

Graham came back to the table and sat down across from Jane. "You'll come, won't you?" he asked.

"What?"

"You'll come down to my father's. Please. Next weekend."

"You mean that was *me* you were talking about?"

"Who else?"

"You want me to go down to your father's with you for the weekend?"

He grinned. "Chicken?"

"Well, no but . . . are you sure?"

"Are *you*?"

"I'd love to."

"Fantastic. More wine?" he asked, holding up the bottle.

"Sure. I'm off tomorrow. Did I hear you say you have a boat?"

"Yes. Actually it's my dad's but I use it more than he does now. It's an old wooden job, named the *Renée*."

"*Renée*," mused Jane.

"That's my mother's name. The boat was built for their honeymoon over thirty-five years ago. It's a beautiful thing. No fiberglass hulls in those days."

"A boat," Jane said with a sigh. "I've always wanted to go out on the ocean."

"We will, okay?"

"Oh, Graham, that'll be great. You're sure your father won't mind?"

"Janey, sweetheart, he'll adore you. Don't worry."

"Well, you met my family, so I guess it's my turn," she said, laughing.

"I wish you could meet Mom, too," he went on, wistfully, Jane thought. "But she's up in Montreal."

"Are they...divorced?"

Graham sighed. "No, not yet. They're separated. I may as well explain it all. They split up about a year ago, after Dad retired. They were driving each other crazy. I guess they both sort of had middle-age crises."

"Oh, that's too bad. After all those years together."

"Yes. Well, anyway, they're trying separation. I guess they're both at fault although I tend to side with Dad, maybe because I'm a man. But Mom tried to make him over. She'd been trying for thirty years but when he retired and started doing just what he wanted she went sort of nuts. She made him so miserable—and herself." He paused to drink some wine then swirled the ruby liquid in the glass and stared at it thoughtfully. "Women always seem to make men over, don't they?"

"What do you mean?"

"They want men to work harder or not work so hard. To eat less or drink less or dress better or help more in the house. Whatever. It's always something. A woman marries a man because she loves him, or says she does, then proceeds to make him over.''

''Now wait a minute,'' said Jane quickly. ''You're generalizing. A lot of women think their men don't need making over and a lot more know it's a waste of time to try.''

''Really?''

''I mean, sure, people will argue. You'd argue with anyone you lived with long enough. Take my brothers, for instance. Holy cow, did we argue! And don't think men don't try to make their wives over just as much. Why, there's this one poor lady in Rifle who got breast implants because her dear hubby liked big boobs!''

''Holy Toledo, Janey, I didn't mean to get you going...''

''Well, you did. Sorry. I think maybe you're a little sensitive on the subject.''

''Maybe.''

''Really, I'm sorry.'' She tried to smile. ''Did we just have an argument?''

''Sort of. A mild difference of opinion, anyway.''

''Oh, my. You're upset about your folks and I start preaching.'' She sat back in her seat and fiddled with her napkin. ''Sometimes I have an awful big mouth.''

''I love your mouth.''

''Are you going to say things like that in front of your father?'' she asked, smiling with relief that he wasn't angry.

''Maybe. Would you mind?''

''I'd be embarrassed.''

''Listen, Smedley—''

''*Smedley*?''

''That's my dad's name, Smedley. His father was Smedley, too. It's an old Quaker name. Anyway, I was going to say, Smedley is a bit eccentric. Operates on his own wavelength, so to speak. A brilliant man, mind you, but he's a free spirit. He probably wouldn't notice if I grabbed you and kissed you right in front of him. He'd just ask something like, 'Why do you suppose people put their lips together to show affection? Now, dogs are much more sensible. They...'"

Jane started giggling. "Stop," she said, "I'm afraid of what you might say."

"And you'd have a right to be. How about a safer subject: dessert. I've made brandied fruit with whipped cream."

"Sounds absolutely delectable. But first I have to use the bathroom. I'll be right back."

"It's upstairs, on the..."

"I remember," she said, feeling flushed.

"Oh, sure."

Was it the wine that was making Jane feel so warm, so full of anticipation, so absolutely relaxed? But she hadn't had that much. She made her way up the stairs to the bathroom. The mirror showed a face she almost didn't recognize—bright-eyed, pink-cheeked, lips curved with a lazy, secret kind of smile. She fluffed her hair, washed her hands and stepped out into the hall. Curiosity nudged her to peek into the half-open door across from Graham's bedroom.

There was a dark wooden four-poster bed with a mauve-and-white patterned spread, a dressing table with filigree boxes, gilt brushes, bottles and tubes and flowered china containers. Very feminine. She couldn't resist—the closet door was ajar. Inside were several clear plastic garment bags of women's clothes and one containing a full-length dark brown fur coat.

A woman lived in that room. Or *had* lived in that room. It still smelled faintly of lavender and mothballs and expensive perfume.

Jane withheld judgment carefully. She found Graham humming a tune, serving up the brandied fruit into cut glass bowls. He lifted his head at her appearance. "Just in time. There's espresso, too."

"Graham, whose room is that across from yours?" The question came out more forcefully than she intended, and she was afraid she sounded demanding and strident—and nosy.

He stopped what he was doing, the spoon in his hand suspended in midair, dripping brandy. His eyes crinkled up in mirth. "Would you believe a live-in maid?"

"No."

"Smart girl." He put the spoon down and approached her. "My God, Janey, this is the first crack in your unflappable aplomb I've seen. Should I believe my eyes?"

"Graham, I just . . ."

"You're jealous," he said, softly, wonderingly.

"I just . . ."

"I can't bear your suffering. Alas! I must confess . . ."

"Graham, I'm not jealous, just curious. Whoever it is she sure has darn good taste."

"It's my mother's room, the famed Renée."

"Oh."

"She comes to shop and likes her surroundings—shall we say—compatible. It's very handy for her."

"I'm sorry I'm so nosy."

"Janey, I have nothing to hide. Ask me whatever you want. Ask away. God, you're wonderful. You really weren't jealous." He came closer and smiled down at her. "I'd grab you and kiss you right this second but my hands are all sticky from the fruit."

Jane took one of his hands and deliberately, slowly, turned it over and licked the sweet syrup off one finger. Then another. Their eyes met and she could see that his were filled with heat, with need, mirroring her own. Then she was in his arms, breathing in his scent, feeling the hard strength of him, tasting the nectar of his mouth.

"Do you still want dessert?" he finally breathed in her ear.

"Later," she whispered back.

She slid her hands under his shirt and kneaded the taut muscles of his back. Graham was pulling her top over her head and then kissing her neck and her shoulder, tickling her unbearably until gooseflesh appeared all over her skin.

"Upstairs," Graham said in a strangled voice.

They started toward the staircase but stopped on the way to kiss, to clutch at warm, bare skin, to breathe in each other's scent. Jane's skirt fell by a table, her shoes were kicked off at the bottom step. Graham's shirt was thrown over the banister.

"I can't wait," he said and when Jane laughed softly, he swooped her up in his arms and started up the stairs, bumping into the wall in his haste.

"I'm too heavy, put me down," she protested, hanging onto him.

"No, you're not. You're light as a feather." But he was gasping, stumbling up the stairs.

"You're crazy, we'll both fall down the steps!"

"You're not being romantic, Janey," he panted.

"Graham, put me down. I promise to be romantic." Laughter bubbled up in her as she ducked her head away from the wall.

"Okay." They were halfway up the stairs, both nearly naked. It struck Jane so funny she buried her face in his chest and shook with merriment.

"It's not nice to laugh at me," Graham pointed out as he settled her on her feet.

"Sorry," she replied.

"Come on then, walk if you're so damn heavy." He took her hand and pulled her along to his room.

They stopped once more at the foot of his bed and Jane undid his pants so that they slid to the floor. "Umm, you're gorgeous," she whispered, kissing his face, his neck, his hard chest, nibbling at his skin with gentle little bites.

The leopard-patterned sheets awaited them. They lay facing each other, locked together, mouth to mouth, hip to hip. His hardness ground into Jane as she stroked his thick hair and kneaded his shoulder. Her breath came faster in exquisite anticipation. Then Graham bent his head and kissed one breast. His tongue found her nipple, his mouth closed over it and he sucked gently. An electric shock of pleasure shot through Jane and she moaned and pulled his head nearer.

"Now," she breathed, "please, now," and he rose over her and entered her swiftly, filled her, pulled back slowly, then filled her again. She moved under him, meeting his thrusts, her hands urgent on his back and his buttocks, her cries mingling with his harsh breathing.

They climbed together, slowly and sensuously, then more quickly and harder, rocking as one entity; they were a match, fitting together in utmost perfection, striving in unison for release.

When it came Jane cried out and shuddered with the powerful ecstasy of it and she felt Graham deep in her, sharing the glory with her, giving, receiving, adoring her with his body.

"Oh," she said breathlessly a moment later but then there was nothing else to say, no words with which to express her pleasure, her wonder.

Graham lay over her, supported on his elbows. "Is that all—*oh*?"

"That's all. I haven't energy for anything else."

Silently he traced her eyebrow with one finger, then moved down her nose, around her lips, feather-light, sweetly, reverently. She nibbled at his finger and sighed deeply.

"Happy?" he asked.

"Totally."

His finger kept sketching the lines of her face: jaw, forehead, ears, eyebrows again. "You're absolutely lovely," he said.

"You're prejudiced," she murmured.

"Of course. Would you want me any other way?"

"I'd want you any old way," Jane said into the darkness, turning toward him once again.

CHAPTER EIGHT

"WHAT, EXACTLY," ASKED JANE, "are these Outer Banks that your father lives on?"

Graham glanced over at her, smiled, then moved his eyes back to the country road that followed the coast of North Carolina. "Basically, it's a ninety-mile long sandbar. Only about a mile wide, though. The Atlantic is to the east, and there's a scattering of sounds, or bays, to the west."

"Oh," said Jane. "A far cry from Rifle, Colorado." The top was down on Graham's red Porsche and the hot summer sun of the South was beating down on her head and shoulders. It was a steamy heat the likes of which Jane had never felt before, a fierce, wet heat laced with salt from the ocean. She could even taste the salt on her lips and her body felt sluggish and covered with a fine sheen of moisture, as if she'd just bathed. No wonder the North had been first to industrialize while the South had lazed the long summer days away in slow self-indulgence.

They'd driven down from New York through New Jersey to the squat peninsula dividing Chesapeake Bay from the Atlantic Ocean, taken the twenty-one-mile long Chesapeake Bay Bridge-Tunnel from Cape Charles back onto the mainland of Virginia and kept the sports car pointed south along the farm-dotted coast.

Jane had done her best to listen to Graham as he gave her a guided tour from the hustle and bustle of the North into the ageless serenity of the South. From time to time one of his hands would leave the leather steering wheel and he'd indicate a landmark. "Over there across from the bay is Norfolk, where all the big naval carriers come in," he'd say and she would follow the direction of his hand, unable to see anything but the strength of his muscled forearm and its crisp blond curling hairs. She could shut her eyes and almost feel that arm encircling her, drawing her close, pressing her naked body to his.

Every move Graham made as he drove isolated itself in her mind. She'd never noticed how strong his neck was or that his shoulders beneath the light green polo shirt were wide and square. And his thighs as he braked or used the clutch—they were long and tapered and powerful looking.

"About ten more miles and we'll cross a bridge and be on the Outer Banks," Graham explained. "You'll love it there. Everyone does."

"I love anything different," she said cheerfully, blotting her damp brow with her wrist. "But, Lord, this heat!"

Graham, however, didn't seem one bit bothered. He'd kept the top down the whole way—an eight-hour drive—and his strawberry-blond hair had blown into a mass of wind-beaten strands. His forehead was burned a deep reddish brown, and his cheeks and nose, even though he'd already had a tan, were seared as well. Only his eyes, because he wore aviator-style sunglasses, had been spared. Of course, she could have asked him to put the top up, but he was enjoying himself so much and, she had to admit, so was she.

The road, which had been flanked by cornfields, hog farms, stands of pines and oaks, maples and magnolias, finally opened up to marshland and there was the bridge of which Graham had spoken, arching up gracefully over a sparkling bay. And beyond, the Outer Banks.

"It *smells* like an ocean," Jane said.

"Of course!" He laughed good-naturedly. "Have you ever seen the Atlantic before?"

She smiled. "Only through some buildings."

The moment the Porsche sped onto the bridge, Jane felt an immediate, welcome drop in the temperature. Maybe she'd survive the heat after all. And then with a swish of tires they were on the barrier island, flying past the reeds lining the bay, cresting a sandy hill. And there, spread majestically before her was the deep blue Atlantic as far as she could see to the north and south, the sun sparkling off distant whitecaps, lines and lines of them that disappeared over the curve of the eastern horizon.

"It's beautiful," she murmured.

"I know," he agreed. "I fell in love with it the very first time I came down here."

"When was that?"

"Fifteen years ago or so. When my parents built their house as a vacation home."

"How long has your dad lived here year-round?"

"Close to four years now, I guess. Since retiring from the service."

"It's so . . . so remote," said Jane, feeling the wild quality of her surroundings as Graham turned onto a broken beach road and raced along the coast. She could only see the ocean now and again as there were sand dunes covered with sea oats barring her vision and a house or two, some even built on stilts.

"I take it there are floods here," she said.

"Sure. Especially during a hurricane but a good strong nor'easter can bring the waves in as well. It's the time of year for them. Maybe we'll brew one up for you and *then* you'll get a sight of wild ocean."

"No thanks."

He gave Jane the Cook's tour. "There's quite a story behind those sand dunes. Back in the forties the Army Corps of Engineers used bulldozers to form them but maintaining them proved to be too expensive, so now the natives just let the waves do their damage. The locals down here kind of shrug their shoulders at most everything. Especially the sea. They've learned you can't tame it so they let the ocean do its worst, then get out their shovels and rebuild all over again."

"Sounds like a lot of work."

"Maybe. But there's no fighting nature, Jane. Better to let it take its course." He glanced at her slyly out of the corner of his eye. "You know, like us."

"Is that what it is with us," she asked archly, "simply Mother Nature?"

His right hand left the steering wheel and reached out to stroke her knee lightly while his eyes stayed on the road. "Janey, sweetheart, I can't even begin to tell you how much more I feel for you. Of course, the nature stuff isn't half bad," he teased, "for lapses in conversation."

"You're awful."

"I'm not, you know I'm not. As a matter of fact, I distinctly remember you calling me wonderful. Now, when was it? Wait a sec, I'll get it in a minute." He gave her a quick grin.

"Stop teasing, Graham." But Jane couldn't help the heat from flushing her cheeks nor could she stop her heart from pounding against her ribs. There was something special about Graham Smith, something she found difficult to put into words. He possessed a unique hunger to really live, to enjoy each moment no matter what. It was a kind of drive, a physical thing. His craving to see and do everything, to take the world by the tail and shake it reminded Jane of traits she'd seen in a lot of rodeo-circuit cowboys; they just kept moving, kept challenging their surroundings, pushing their limits.

And yet, she thought, as he pulled into a long sandy driveway, Graham did not scare her with his zest for life. Rather, it drew her, compelled her to find out what he was all about. To live life with him.

Sitting atop a dune was a silvering, wood-framed house that had rather a strange shape. "Your dad's?" asked Jane.

He nodded, downshifting in the sand, sliding around a curve and kicking up gravel. "It's supposed to look like a ship's prow. Does, if you're on the beach side and looking up at it."

"I like it," she stated.

"And I hope you like Dad, too. Although, like I warned you, he's a bit offbeat and takes some getting used to."

She wondered just how weird his father was. Would she like him at all? Would he like her?

They got out in front of a garage and Jane smelled the strong, salty air and felt the sand sift into her sandals and between her toes.

"Dad's car's here but I don't see him around. Must be—" But his words were cut off when Jane heard a growling sound. She turned to Graham questioningly but her attention was diverted by two lean Doberman pinschers bounding toward Graham from around the corner of the garage.

Instantly, her training making her reaction automatic, Jane threw herself between Graham and the vicious dogs who were still racing toward them, barking wildly, pink tongues flapping, sharp white eyeteeth gleaming. She crouched, putting one arm up to fend off the attack, while she searched the area desperately for a club or a rock or anything to use as a weapon.

"No! Jane, don't!" came Graham's voice from behind her and she froze, uncertain, poised between aiming a blow at a dog's head and obeying Graham's command, but then it was too late to do anything because suddenly the animals were leaping through the air, knocking Graham clean off his feet and... Amazingly, their short tails were wagging and Graham was gasping and laughing and pushing the beasts off him.

"It's only Heckle and Jeckle," he was telling her as he tried to avoid their sloppy tongues, "Dad's watchdogs."

Jane straightened, put her hands on her hips and cocked a brow. "Why didn't you warn me?" she asked, hovering between irritation and amusement while she watched Graham struggle to get up.

"I forgot. Now give me a hand, will you? These stupid mutts..."

She slapped her thigh and called forcefully. "Here, Heckle, here, Jeckle. That's enough, you two bad dogs!"

They obeyed, turning toward her, their ears alert and upright, their noses testing; then, tongues flopping happily, they trotted toward her, ready to renew the game.

"My God, these are the worst trained animals I've ever seen," she said to Graham. "Get down!" she snapped at the dogs but they were bent on leaping up at her now, their sandy, salty paws leaving smudges all over her white shorts. "You two wouldn't last a day on the ranch. My dad would shoot you and hang you out to cure!"

"He wouldn't," said Graham with assurance.

"He just might," Jane replied under her breath.

With the dogs at her heels, she followed Graham inside. "Are they allowed in?" she asked, trying to close the door in their faces.

"They have the run of the house." Graham shrugged, then laughed at Jane's expression of disgust.

"The least you could do then," she said, "is teach them some manners."

He tried to check his laughter. "We did. But they were smarter."

"Very funny."

Jane followed Graham into the living room while one dog playfully chewed at her ankle.

"Anyone home?" Graham called. "Dad?"

"Out here, on the sun deck!" came a slightly accented voice.

For a moment Jane stood in the center of the room and looked around, bemused. The place was as close to the interior of a ship as an architect could make it. Triangular in shape, two walls were wood-paneled, while the other, which faced the ocean, was entirely glass. On one of the wood walls was a large fireplace and on the other hung paintings of seascapes, adding color to the room. Beneath her feet was a blue rug, recently vacuumed, Jane noted. The furnishings were serviceable and looked comfortable: a big couch with lots of pillows facing the fireplace, several floor lamps, a glass coffee table with sea shells scattered on its top. In front of the glass wall sat an antique dining table, its rough wood faded and bleached, an old whaler's lamp sitting in the center. There were benches on either side of the table. No chairs.

"What a great room," Jane declared.

"Dad thought it up. I like it a lot, too." One of the dogs hopped up onto the couch. "Get down, Heckle," Graham said, glancing at Jane sheepishly.

"Oh, brother," she mumbled, giving in and, against her better judgment, petting Heckle's head.

"Maybe I'll give them to you for Christmas," Graham said, leading the way out onto a spacious deck that faced the ocean.

Jane's first sight of Graham's father was startling. It was hard not to stare.

Smedley Smith, all six feet two inches of him, was maneuvering on some strange contraption made of what appeared to be old beach junk: gray rotted wood planks; rusty bolts and nails; a rubber tire; faded, stretched cords; a vintage bicycle speedometer.

If forced to put words to the homemade *thing*, Jane would have said it was a rowing machine but that would have been stretching the imagination.

"Dad," Graham was saying, "this is Jane, Jane Manning."

"Hello!" he called cheerfully, pumping his sun-scorched arms and legs madly, gasping while the contraption creaked and protested.

Her first impression of Smedley was one of beautiful clear-blue eyes and a strong, masculine face. His hair, which was silvering strawberry-blond and on the long side, was being whipped around from the strong ocean breeze. He was still well-built, but his clothes—Jane tried not to gape—were not at all what she had expected from a well-educated, purportedly sophisticated gentleman. Whereas Graham dressed impeccably, his English-American father was wearing old worn madras shorts, sixties' vintage; a torn, faded T-shirt that read Wink's Groceries; and Topsiders without socks, with a big toe showing through one of them.

"From…Colorado," he breathed, "Graham tells…me. Great state, that."

"Yes," Jane replied awkwardly, "I was born and raised there."

"You can…tell me all…about it at…dinner, Jane. For now—" gasp, pump, pant "—why don't you…two go for a…swim." Jeckle stuck out his drooping tongue and licked Smedley's ear with a slurp. "Go…away!"

"Hey," said Graham, "a swim sounds great. Are you game, Jane?"

"Sure, why not?" Anything to collect herself for a few minutes. This place was . . . unusual.

Before fetching their suitcases, Graham showed her to a guest room down the hall from his own. It was a small tidy room, sparsely furnished. On two sides were windows, one facing north toward the sand dunes, the other facing the ocean. Both windows were open and Jane went to one to close it as she was unused to the constant, roaring drone of the sea. As she tugged it down, she noticed a wire hanging out of the window, leading down into a small puddle. She wondered what it was there for, then shrugged, dismissing it.

There was a double bed, a low dresser and shaving mirror, a rocker and a plant stand. In spite of all the sunlight, the plant was as dead as a doornail.

"Here's your suitcase," Graham said, placing it on the floor. Coming over to her, he pushed her playfully down onto the bed, then bent over and covered her lips with his. "Umm," he groaned against her mouth, "you taste good."

But Jane was embarrassed. What if his father . . . "Stop it," she protested, albeit unconvincingly. "Your dad."

"He's still exercising." He slipped his hands up under her shirt and unsnapped her bra.

"Graham!"

Then his fingers were on her breasts, lightly tracing teasing circles around her nipples, and Jane knew that if he didn't stop in a minute she'd be lost. She pushed him away. "Not in your father's house. Promise me."

"Ah, come on, Jane."

"No." She stood and straightened her shirt. "Promise me."

"Oh, all right," he relented, his eyes twinkling. "But I'll bet you've never done it in the ocean."

"Graham." She tried not to smile.

"Okay. I guess I better let you change, huh?"

"Uh, Graham, what's that wire doing hanging out the window?" She had to ask.

"You'll never believe it if I tell you."

"Yes, I will. Please tell me."

"Well, during thunderstorms Dad runs the wire into the large puddle that forms outside the window. Then he hooks the inside end up to a battery charger." He hesitated. "It's really strange, Jane. Sure you want to hear?"

"Go on."

"Well, then he hooks himself up to the charger and—"

"Hooks himself up?"

"He uses pads covered with aluminum foil and tapes them to his chest. Then he regulates the current, you know, he gives himself electrical shocks."

"My God, you mean like...*Frankenstein*?

Graham tried to look casual. "Sort of, I suppose. Dad claims the electricity is good for his heart. Keeps it in balance, he says."

Jane was utterly speechless.

"I warned you," he said, making a hasty exit.

She put on the new lavender swimsuit she'd bought especially for this trip. It was cut high on the thigh and plunged rather daringly in front and back, but she was pleased with the effect. Pulling on an oversized shirt and slipping into her sandals, she went to join Graham and his father on the sun deck.

"Hello again, Mr. Smith," she began uncertainly, unable to forget the wires and the battery charger.

"Call me Smedley, please." Without asking he handed her a glass of thick, reddish liquid. "V-8 juice. Good for what ails you."

"Thank you," said Jane dubiously. She'd have preferred an iced tea or a lemonade in this heat. She drank it anyway and was surprised. "It tastes good."

"Perfect on a hot day. It gets the juices flowing."

"I certainly hope so," replied Jane, "because I'm so hot I feel like I can't move."

"A swim will do you good. And then we'll all fish for our dinner."

She cocked her head. "You mean, you can swim right alongside your dinner out there?"

Smedley and Graham laughed, their deep male tones drifting on the offshore breeze. "I suggest you take your ring off, though," said Graham, sobering. "The bluefish have been known to take a shiny finger as bait."

The dogs were running in and out of the surf, barking wildly, as Jane and Graham swam. But this was no lake, she was discovering. There was a strong undertow just beneath the surface of the water.

"Don't go out any farther!" Graham called and Jane moved into shore a few feet, noticing that there were no lifeguards nor was there another living soul anywhere up or down the beach. They could have been marooned on a deserted island. Cooled off, they got out the fishing poles and Graham taught Jane how to cast out over the breakers.

"What if I get a shark?"

"We'll eat it and call it scallops. Plenty of people do."

"Say, where's your boat?" asked Jane.

"It's down the coast at a marina."

"Can we go see it?"

"Sure, we'll check out the old girl tomorrow."

Neither Jane nor Graham had put their shirts back on. She glanced sidelong at him often, too often, enjoying the sight of his strong legs flexing, his feet embedded in the soft sand, the muscles of his thighs and back moving fluidly as he cast his line. And she knew he was looking at her as well, in her lavender suit that hid absolutely nothing. Her legs were sandy, her skin salty, her hair stiff and brushed back off her forehead and she felt totally natural and uninhibited, as wild as these Outer Banks of Graham's, untamed and ready for anything.

They fished in their wet swimsuits while the hot afternoon sun gilded their skin. Her senses were keen and aroused, the world narrowed down to a universe of simple, totally physical sensations. She could feel the cool water sucking the smooth sand out from under her toes, the reflected heat of the beach on her back, the pull of the rod against her arm muscles. And there was Graham standing next to her, tall and carefree. Sinews stood out on his arms as he threw the line out, his thighs tensed, his hair tossed in the breeze. There was something about Graham, something special and innocent and vital. She wanted him right then, fiercely.

Evening fell over the Outer Banks with a red sun setting behind the dunes and lighting the waving sea oats to a golden color. They fried Graham's fish outside on a grill and Smedley, an expert chef, watched over the charcoals. "Tomorrow you'll catch a fish," he told Jane. "Graham's had lots of experience. You have to know when the blues are just sniffing around and nudging your line or when they've actually bitten. You'll master it." He took the spatula from Graham. "Here, you're not doing it right."

"Geez, Dad," said Graham, "do you ever think I'll be old enough to fry fish?"

Jane laughed and sipped on a beer. "My dad is the same way. It was only last summer that he let me take the trash out because he said I didn't know how to put the lids back on the cans right!"

"Really, Jane," said Smedley, turning the fish, "I'm not that bad," and Graham winked at her from behind his father's back.

They ate the meaty bluefish out on the deck and Jane had an extra helping of corn on the cob. The butter dripped from her fingers and chin. They cleaned up in the kitchen, then went back out onto the deck to sit and enjoy the evening. Smedley entertained Jane with his knowledge of local folklore while Graham rested easily in his chair, his feet propped up on the rail surrounding the deck.

"Ten miles down the beach," Smedley was telling her, "is what's called Nags Head."

"Nag? Like in a horse?" asked Jane.

"Exactly. Three hundred and some years ago pirates used to inhabit the coastline here. They'd wait for a storm to brew, then tie lanterns to the necks of donkeys and let the animals loose to walk up and down the beach. The treasure ships that passed here on their way to England would get blown off course in the storms. The lookouts would see the lanterns and think they had spotted a safe port but instead, the ships would get wrecked on the terrible shoals out there. The next day," Smedley told her, "the pirates would hop into their small boats and collect the booty."

"Is that true?" asked Jane dubiously.

"Absolutely. In fact, they've charted over a thousand old wrecks out there. The coastline here is called the Graveyard of the Atlantic."

"That's a wonderful story," she said.

"And their children's children's *children*," concluded Smedley, "still live here. But today they rob the tourists instead!"

"Tell her about Virginia Dare," Graham suggested lazily, his hand reaching over to Jane's arm and trailing a feather-light touch across her flesh.

"Virginia Dare," Smedley explained, "was the first white baby born on the continental U.S. Long before the pilgrims dreamed of sailing for Plymouth Rock." He snorted at his inside knowledge. "Yes, indeed, she was born on Roanoke Island just south of here. The colony disappeared into the mists of time, my dear, but today the state of Virginia still celebrates her name and the county here is called Dare County."

"But I didn't know half of that," said Jane wonderingly.

"You wouldn't," Smedley was quick to tell her, "since they wrote the first history books up north."

"Don't get Dad going on politics," warned Graham.

The sky grew dark and a haze formed over the ocean. On the horizon, ships passed northward silently, heading toward Chesapeake Bay, their lights twinkling in the darkness. The moist night air embraced Jane and her fingers glided over her arms to fend off the chill damp from the ocean. Even her own touch was somehow arousing.

Smedley slipped inside and reappeared with a silver tray, three snifters and a bottle of cognac. Over his arm was a jacket for Jane.

"Thank you," she said, smiling up at him.

They sipped their cognac in companionable silence. The setting was so terribly evocative that Jane could have sat there forever, feeling the ocean air moisten her skin, hearing the distant call of a foghorn from a lighthouse, listening to the never-ending roll of the tide. Perhaps she would reopen the window in her bedroom.

Eventually Smedley disappeared inside.

"Is your dad going to bed this early?" asked Jane.

"Probably not. More than likely he's out in the garage fiddling. If you can believe this—" Graham chuckled "—he has an old screen door set up in there and he uses it to filter sand from the beach."

"What on earth for?"

"Gold, diamonds, who knows?" He shrugged. "He thinks that the ocean, from beating against the coast when it was rocky, say, a million years ago, crushed the rocks into sand and that there are plenty of precious stones just waiting to be filtered out of the sand."

"Well, it makes sense in a way, doesn't it?"

"I suppose. And he does have a few old pill bottles full of what he *tells* everyone is gold dust."

"You sound skeptical," said Jane. "Maybe it is gold."

"And maybe not."

"Don't be so hard on him."

"Oh, I'm not really. I like to rib him, though. He *does* take some getting used to."

"Well, I like him."

"And," said Graham, leaning close, "I can see you like Heckle and Jeckle, too." He glanced down at her hand. She was toying idly with Jeckle's ears while the dog practically purred. "I wish you'd play with my ears like that."

Jane sighed. "Back in New York, Graham. Not here. You promised."

"I did, didn't I? But I've got a plan. You did say, 'not in your father's house?'"

"Yes..."

"Ah, my sweet Janey, now you're curious! You know I've been scheming away but I'm going to torture you and not tell. You'll have to wait till tomorrow."

"Graham," she said, mock-angrily.

Later he saw her to the guest room door. "Just a good-night kiss?" he asked softly.

"Well, the light *is* still on in the garage. Maybe just one," she conceded.

His arms came around her waist and he pulled Jane close. "This is becoming a pleasant habit," he murmured, his lips covering hers finally in a slow, tender kiss.

A few minutes later Jane turned out her light and lay on the bed in the darkness listening to the drone of the ocean. She thought about the long day, about all the new sights and sounds. About pirates and their donkeys and a baby named Virginia who had passed ages and ages ago into the dark unknown. And of Graham who was a part of all this as much as he was a part of the throb of the city. A man with many faces. And *that*, Jane decided as sleep crept up on her, was what was so exciting about him.

Not surprisingly—at least not anymore—Jane found Smedley on the beach at 6:00 a.m. He was on his hands and knees, with a magnifying glass, searching for stones in the early light.

She brought him a cup of coffee. "Find anything?" she asked against the roar of the tide.

He pulled an interesting turquoise stone out of his frayed pants pocket. "This is a beauty. I'll have to drop it in some acid and see what I've got here." He exchanged the cup of coffee in her hand for the stone and they took a walk together.

"That son of mine," said Smedley about half a mile down the shore. "If he'd get his lazy bones up out of bed, he'd find there's a beach full of treasures out here. But if you wait too long to go beachcombing, a tourist is apt to get there ahead of you. You always wake up early?''

"Yes," said Jane. "On the ranch we had to. And now I jog sometimes in the city before all the cars are out."

"City's no good for you. Bad for the lungs and heart."

"I'm sure you're right," she commented, thinking once again about the wires hanging out of her window.

"This is the place, Jane. Out here in the wilds. Why, most of the ninety miles of beach here are still National Seashore. Protected. The government says it's to preserve the bird life, but I say it's really to preserve the people!" As if to underscore his words, a group of gulls swooped down ahead of them and began scavenging a dead horseshoe crab. "Birds do just fine," said Smedley, his strawberry-blond hair aflame in the first rays of the sun. "Yes, the animal life is going to take over the earth as it is. Especially the bloody insects! By God, North Carolina is already mosquito capital of the world!"

"What about baby harp seals?" asked Jane mischievously.

"*They're* in Alaska," she got as an answer.

Graham was on the deck when they returned, a coffee mug in hand, an early morning sleepy look to him. "In the city," he said, "this is positively an indecent hour."

"Lazy," said his father, grumbling. "Now Jane here, I like this young lady. She knows what's good for her."

There was a sudden commotion at the screen door. The dogs were whining and scratching to get out, pressing against the screen, enlarging an already respectable hole.

"Stop that!" hollered Smedley. "Confounded dogs! That does it, I'm going to drown them!" But as he opened the sliding screen door and let them out, his angry expression changed and soon he was tossing an old tennis ball down onto the beach for them to chase.

"It's really quite interesting around here," said Jane in an aside to Graham.

"Oh, I've seen worse," he commented. "But for the life of me, I can't remember just where."

All morning long Jane couldn't forget Graham's teasing promise of the previous evening—that he had a surprise for her today. It couldn't have been the visit they made to the Wright Brothers' National Memorial near Kitty Hawk. Nor did she think his surprise was their stop at the purported site of the Lost Colony where Virginia Dare had once walked the gently wooded land. And she seriously doubted that a stroll out onto a fishing pier to see what the locals were catching could have been his ultimate scheme. But when he pulled into the marina and parked in front of the lovely old mahogany sailboat, the *Renée*, Jane was beginning to get a glimmer of his plot.

It was a scorching morning on the Outer Banks, the radio in the Porsche calling for a heat wave throughout the South and possible afternoon thundershowers. Jane felt the perspiration soaking her head and the back of her tank top was plastered to her skin.

"Ever been sailing?" asked Graham as he maneuvered the twenty-two footer out of the bay and through the narrow, shallow inlet into the ocean.

"Never," replied Jane while she fumbled with ropes and tried to follow his instructions. Lord, this was complicated stuff, much worse than hitching up a team of six horses to a wagon.

The bay was calm, the inlet a bit tricky with waves going both east and west, meeting, crashing, sending plumes of sparkling white spray high into the air. Once they were actually out on the ocean, the water calmed again and the *Renée* glided smoothly over the rolling sea, her white sail billowing out and snapping before the northerly breeze.

The freedom of sailing struck Jane; the boat depended on nothing but the wind. And, oh boy, was the wind a powerful force out there on the ocean! It filled the sail and tilted the whole boat over with its force, skimming it along on the surface of the water. Once Graham let Jane hold the wheel for a while and she could feel the living energy of the wind quivering in her hands as the keel dug into the water to keep the boat upright and the sail fought it, urging the *Renée* onward.

"This is fabulous!" Jane called later through cupped hands, bracing herself against the cabin on the slanting deck, watching as Graham tacked backward and forward to make progress against the wind. The word "tack" suddenly took on new meaning. It was a different world, a wonderful new experience that thrilled and excited Jane. Another gift given to her by Graham. "I love it!" she yelled to him over the hiss of the hull on water and the crack of canvas.

"It's okay now but we have to watch out for a change in wind this afternoon. And storms as well. You can climb the mast and be my lookout!"

Graham was near the prow of the boat, leaning over the side, fiddling with a rope. He was wearing cutoff jeans, a faded blue shirt and Topsiders to keep his footing. His hair blew in the cool breeze, catching the sun and gleaming like gold. His arms and legs looked tan and strong and capable as he worked. His expression, Jane saw, was alive and happy.

"You'd have made a perfect pirate," she said.

"And that's exactly what I would have been doing...three hundred years ago."

"No qualms about stealing from the poor, innocent ships?"

"None." He laughed and a devil-may-care gleam appeared in his eyes. "The old ships were stealing the natives blind in the name of their kings. At least I'd have been keeping the booty in North America."

About three miles offshore Graham swung the sail out of the wind and the *Renée* lurched, rolling and drifting.

He turned to Jane. "I hope you don't get seasick."

"I feel okay. Why are we stopping? Are we going to fish?" But even as she asked, Jane knew the answer; it was written all over his face. It was in that rakish grin and the gleam in his eyes.

"Fish?" he said casually. "Maybe later." He pulled off his shirt and tossed it on the deck. Then he caught her arms and pulled her against him almost fiercely, his lips covering hers in a passionate kiss, bending her head back, crushing her breasts against his bare chest.

Graham had never been rough with her. And certainly this was not rough, exactly, but his urgency, the demand in his eager hands, the force of his manhood pressing against her was a new experience for Jane and her response was immediate and strong. He was playing her pirate and she loved it. Her arms went around his back, her hands kneaded the rippling, corded muscles of his shoulders.

They discarded their clothes on the deck then stumbled, laughing and excited, below to the single, narrow, pull-down cot. It was even hotter down in the cabin and the air was dead and salty, close. Both of them broke out in a sweat and when Graham poised on top of Jane, their legs and bellies glided smoothly together.

He spent very little time on preliminaries. His hands stroked her breasts, pushing the flesh beneath upward to meet his lips, flicking her taut nipples with his tongue until she could no longer stifle a cry. He kissed her neck, forcing her head back, kissed her shoulders, her nipples again and a hot ache coiled deep in her belly and her hips rotated against his, longing, craving, desperate to be filled by him.

Graham slid his hands beneath her buttocks and pulled her upward until her back arched and her legs parted, quivering, tense, expectant. Then he drove into her, filling her completely for a long, exquisite moment until he pulled out. He plunged again and again. She felt her body tightening, the blood pounding in her ears. Then she was gripping his shoulders and her hips lifted, straining, pressing, rolling against his until it was there, so near, so near...

Jane cried out and shook, her limbs straining, her body rocking, and then slowly the sweet ache abated and she felt his climax come, a pulsing throb deep inside her as he gasped and clutched her to him.

When it was over they lay together sweat-slicked and sated. "I hope I didn't hurt you," he breathed in her ear.

Jane laughed softly and nuzzled her face against his damp neck. "I hope I didn't hurt *you*."

They swam alongside the boat, holding onto a rope, cooling down. Then, dried off and dressed, Graham turned to her. "Okay, first mate, it's time to earn your keep. Out with the fishing poles."

"Aye, aye," she said, determined that today *she* was going to catch dinner.

By three o'clock Jane had caught two sea trout and one small yellowfin tuna. Graham, she was delighted to point out, had not caught a thing.

"Want me to show you how I did it?" she couldn't help saying but Graham suddenly had a sober expression on his face and was paying no attention whatsoever to her. Instead, he was looking over her shoulder out to sea.

Jane turned around curiously. Moving in from the north was a black bank of clouds, with lightning streaking the huge mass. "Oh, no," she said, alarmed. "What do we do?"

"We set sail and beat a path to the inlet. Pronto."

It was only a minute or two after Graham raised the sail that the wind rattled and shook the *Renée*. It was a cold, ominous wind that brought goose bumps to Jane's flesh. The *Renée* responded to the gust and leaped forward into a swell, rolling to one side. Jane stumbled, frightened suddenly, recalling Smedley's stories about the Graveyard of the Atlantic.

"Are we going to make it?" she called to Graham who was working with the rigging, straightening out a rope.

"We'll make it, all right," he assured her, "and in record time. But I want you to hold on tight, Jane. I mean it."

The wind was growing stronger, the black mass advancing on them and yet, strangely, the sun was still out bright and hot on her shoulders. She could see whitecaps ahead of them and behind them as the sea responded to the oncoming storm and kicked up spray and foam into the sun-drenched air. The *Renée* flew across the waves, pitching, heaving, the sail full and cracking like a shot and Jane was abruptly afraid it would tear into tatters and they would be stranded.

"I thought it was supposed to be hot and calm today," she shouted to Graham from where she hung on, helplessly watching him scramble around the deck.

"They've never been able to forecast these quick storms," he called back. "I should have been paying more attention to the horizon."

Jane put up a hand to shade her eyes and strained to see the shore. The inlet was there, all right, but it looked so far away. "We'll make it in, won't we?"

"Sure, sure we will." He flashed her a reassuring smile. "Come on, don't look so forlorn! This is fun!" And she could see that Graham was truly enjoying himself. She wished some of his confidence would rub off onto her. He'd said he loved the fact that she wasn't afraid of anything. But that was on *land*!

The inlet to the bay was treacherous. Behind the *Renée* were huge swells, pushing the boat, threatening to swamp it, and ahead were the smaller waves from the bay, rushing out to meet the sea. Graham was working the sail feverishly by then, trying to avoid the collision of waves that could capsize them with no trouble whatsoever. Then, finally, mercifully, the *Renée* dipped into a trench, came out of it with her bow nosed into the sun and *plop*, the water smoothed out and she glided sure and sound into the sparkling blue bay.

"Wow," breathed Jane, "for a few minutes there..."

He tipped his head back and laughed heartily. "Had you worried, did it?"

"Oh no, not at all." She laughed along with him, relieved, happy, feeling very much alive and glad that she'd shared the adventure with him.

WHILE THE STORM WHIPPED AROUND the sides of the house and spattered the windows with salt and rain, Jane helped Smedley cook the fish.

"Someday that boy of mine is going to push it too far," Smedley was telling her.

"Didn't you ever get caught out on the sea in a storm?" asked Jane. He had, after all, owned the boat for thirty-five years.

"Sure I did. But I never had my wife along with me."

"Do you think she'd have been any happier waiting at home?"

"Well, I don't really know. The point is, young lady, I had the good sense to make her stay onshore."

He was a hard man to reason with, Jane decided. He had strong opinions; he was unbendable and not a little eccentric. Nevertheless, she was growing fond of him, enjoying his stubborn banter. He reminded her of her father in some ways. Strong, old-fashioned men, they both did and said exactly what they wanted and damn the rest of the world if it didn't like it.

Graham built a fire and they ate at the old wooden table, sitting on the benches with the whaler's lamp lit. Graham's knee was pressed up against hers familiarly. Her fish was excellent, broiled to tender perfection, swimming in butter and lemon and parsley. Outside the wind howled and behind their backs the fire blazed. The dogs lay near the hearth. One of them—Jeckle, Jane thought—was snoring, his mouth sagging, twitching as he dreamed.

She went to bed that night with a book from Smedley's collection of mysteries. Her room was cozy and secure and she allowed Jeckle to rest at her feet until he took up too much of the bed and was banished, groaning, to the floor with Heckle. Finally she put the book on the nightstand and snapped off the light and lay there with her arms behind her head, thinking.

There was an otherworldly, untamed quality to this long barrier island of Graham's. It was in the air, in Smedley's lore of long-ago times, of pirates and graveyard shoals. It was in the way the sea wind tore through Graham's hair and lit his eyes to the color of aquamarine, in the way his gleaming teeth were bared as he worked, grinning, daring nature to test his mettle.

Graham Smith, she was beginning to realize, was everything she'd ever wanted in a man. She wouldn't change a thing about him. But as the weathered gray boards of the house creaked in the wind, Jane had to wonder if *she* was everything he'd always wanted in a woman.

CHAPTER NINE

JANE WAS IN HER ROOM, just pulling a tank top over her head on Sunday morning when she heard both dogs start barking hysterically. The frantic scratching of canine claws on the screen door filled the brief moments when Heckle and Jeckle paused for breath.

Running barefoot out into the living room to see what the commotion was all about, Jane got there in time to catch the dogs' glossy black backs disappearing through the front door, which had been opened by someone, someone who was scolding the dogs by name in a loud, imperious, feminine voice.

A neighbor?

The dogs' barking subsided and the door opened again to admit the caller. Jane's first impression was of a tall woman in, perhaps, her late fifties, marvelously well-preserved, with artfully streaked silver hair and classic features. She wore a simple peach-colored linen dress with such perfect lines to it that Jane immediately sized it up as a Halston original, like the one she'd seen in the window of Saks Fifth Avenue that cost a mere three hundred dollars. White pumps and coral beads—two long strands—a straw bag and a large diamond winking on her ring finger completed her ensemble. Her stance was elegant as she halted in surprise upon the threshold and her eyes were a frigid blue that pierced Jane with an arrow of appraisal. "And just *who*," demanded the woman, "are you?"

Jane drew herself up, trying to ignore her hastily combed hair, bare feet and casual attire. After all, Jane had been invited to Smedley's house while this woman certainly had not. She was about to ask the lady just who she thought *she* was when Jane was aware of Graham coming up behind her. She turned to him for help when she saw his face light up.

"Mother!" he exclaimed. "What a surprise!"

"Graham," said the woman breathlessly, "I had no idea *you'd* be here! How wonderful to see you! Oh, you've gotten too much sun again and . . . have you lost weight?"

Jane remained where she was feeling decidedly out of place. And to think that she'd been about to accost Graham's mother as an intruder. Thank heavens Graham had come when he did!

But he was pulling his mother toward Jane and saying, "Mom, I want you to meet a very special friend of mine. Jane Manning, Renée Smith."

Renée's dark blue eyes had softened. She held her manicured hand out to Jane. "You'll have to excuse me—I was very surprised, you understand."

Jane clasped her hand. "It's so nice to meet you, Mrs. Smith. Graham's told me a lot about you."

Renée's curved eyebrows rose. "So my son talks of me, his mother, when you two are together?" There was a slight lilt in Renée's voice, a shadow of inflection that made her speech musical and graceful.

Graham laughed, "You know me too well, Mom. Do you have some luggage in your car? Did you drive down this morning?"

"Yes, I flew into Norfolk last evening and got up very early this morning. Graham, *mon chéri*, there are a couple of things in the car, if you don't mind . . ."

"Two steamer trunks, I bet," Graham said, rolling his eyes.

"But of course not, two very small—"

"*Renée*." The voice came from behind Jane. She turned to see Smedley in the hallway, one hand out, touching the wall as if groping for support.

Renée nodded, expressionless. "Hello, Smedley. You're looking well."

"Renée," Smedley repeated, making his way into the living room. He seemed stunned.

"*Oui, c'est moi*, it is I," she said.

"But you . . . you should have called," said Smedley. "I mean . . ."

"I did not, I just came. If I'd phoned you, you would have given me an excuse and told me you were busy or something."

"Renée—"

"Do you have some coffee made?" the woman asked, interrupting him. "I started very early this morning."

"Coffee? Coffee. Oh, not yet. We all just got up."

The dogs were whining and pressing against the door from outside now. Renée let them in and they tried to jump on her, stubby tails wagging, tongues lolling.

"No!" she cried, shaking her finger at them, then she pointed to a corner. "Go sit! Naughty boys!"

Meekly, Heckle and Jeckle slunk to the corner, turned a couple of times each and thumped down, panting. Jane was impressed.

"Those dogs," Renée said in disgust. "So, shall I make coffee and, perhaps, some crepes for breakfast? I can see that no one has begun anything. You have flour and butter and eggs, Smedley?"

"Yes." Smedley seemed to be recovering.

"*Mon Dieu*," Renée said, "this place is a mess. Don't you clean the stove, Smedley?"

"Mother," Graham said gently.

"Oh, sorry. I must not say a word. You may live like a pig if you like. You have my permission."

Smedley ran a big knuckled hand through his mussed hair. "Renée, it's clean."

She shrugged and turned toward the kitchen. "Graham, my things? And perhaps, Jane, you might help me set the table."

Wow, Jane thought. She was beginning to see what Graham had been talking about. Renée was a controller. But Jane didn't want to make too hasty a judgment. The woman's officious manner *could* be a guise for nervousness. Arriving unannounced like that must not have been the easiest thing Graham's mother had ever done.

Graham came back with two large leather suitcases. "Where do I put them?" he asked, a little embarrassed.

Jane realized that both guest rooms were filled. There was only Smedley's room. Oh dear, how awkward.

Smedley had retreated to the deck. "Put them in my room," he called through the screen door. "I'll sleep on the couch," he mumbled.

"No, don't be ridiculous. *I'll* sleep on the couch," announced Renée.

"Renée, you're my guest. I'll take the couch," he yelled.

"Hey, I've got a great idea," said Graham brightly. "Jane and I will sleep on the boat and you two can have the whole house to yourselves!"

Renée gave him a look of disapproval. "Certainly not! That's indecent and I won't consider it!"

Impasse.

Graham diplomatically left the bags in the living room and they all sat down to breakfast. Renée had brewed coffee, thawed orange juice and was in the process of cooking wafer-thin crepes, which she deftly rolled around dabs of jam and then sprinkled with powdered sugar.

Renée was the grand hostess, Graham was witty and charming, Jane tried to keep up her end of the conversation and Smedley gradually relaxed and started to be his old self.

"So, Renée, how is Montreal?" he asked cautiously.

"Rainy. My sister had a soirée last week. The prime minister and his wife came. And do you remember Ian Pembroke from the London embassy? He was there with his *new* wife. She was not a day over thirty."

"Ian remarried?"

"Yes, and Catherine Baldwin asked after you."

"How nice."

Renée finally turned to Jane. "And how long have you known my son?"

"Let's see. About three weeks, isn't it, Graham?"

"You met in New York?"

"Well, no, Mom. We met in Colorado. Jane just moved to New York for her new job."

"Ah, your new job. What do you do, my dear?"

"I'm a bodyguard at Mercury Courier," Jane said proudly.

For a moment there was an acute silence.

"Did you know that Jane's family raises rodeo stock on their ranch?" Graham put in hastily.

"Rodeo stock," Renée repeated tonelessly. "And do you ride this stock?"

"Yes, I ride the horses. I raced a little. Nothing serious."

"I ride in Montreal," Renée said, obviously relieved to have found some common ground. "Do you jump?"

"Well, a few irrigation ditches from time to time."

"Oh."

"These are *Western* horses, Mom," Graham explained.

Renée looked at him blankly and Jane hid a smile behind her coffee cup.

"How is Lew?" Smedley asked expediently.

"He's fine," Graham replied. "Having a little trouble with the business."

"What kind of trouble?"

"Oh, I'll tell you later. It's boring stuff."

Boring? thought Jane. But he probably didn't want to get into it at the table.

"And is Fiona doing well?" Renée asked.

"That's Lew's wife," Graham told Jane. "She's fine. Still complaining about her weight."

"And so she should," Renée sniffed.

"Did you know I got an invitation to George Mondragon's retirement party?" Smedley said to Renée.

"You mean he is just now retiring?"

"Yes, at seventy. There's going to be a big bash at his house in Hamilton. Formal. You know Eleanor."

Graham explained to Jane: "George is an old friend of Dad's and the consul general for Bermuda. Eleanor is his wife."

"Oh," Jane said, her head whirling with all the names.

"And so, are you going?" asked Renée, studiously casual.

Wouldn't George have invited both Smedley and Renée? Jane wondered. After all, they were not divorced.

"I don't think so. Seems a lot of hoopla for the old geezer's retirement. Still, it might be fun."

"Have you kept the moths out of your dinner jacket?" Renée asked with asperity.

Smedley looked down at his plate and began cutting up a crepe into many tiny pieces. Jane could see that Renée was *dying* to go to this George's party and was angling for an invitation. How uncomfortable.

Jane and Graham did the dishes while his parents wandered out on the deck, arguing about who would sleep where.

"You see what I mean?" asked Graham.

"I sure do," replied Jane. "What a shame. Your mother is very beautiful."

"Yeah, I guess she was a real knockout when she met Dad. He always told me how gorgeous she was."

"Still is."

"Not as gorgeous as you," Graham said with a glint in his eye. He bent his head and nuzzled her neck while soap dripped from his hands onto the floor.

"Graham, your mother might come in."

"Bashful, aren't you?"

"I don't know your parents very well. I mean, would you like me to grab you and kiss you in front of *my* family?"

His eyes lit up with merciless merriment. "Only if their shotguns were unloaded."

"See what I mean?"

"I missed you last night," Graham said. He wiped his sudsy hands on his shorts and pulled Jane close to him, his hands on her waist, so that she leaned out from his embrace and looked up into his face.

"Me, too," she admitted, "but I did have Heckle and Jeckle to keep me warm."

"I'm jealous."

"Don't be. They both snored and twitched all night."

"Damn mutts."

"Let's get the dishes done. I want to get out onto that beach," Jane said. "It may be old hat to you but to me it's an adventure."

So there was another day of heat and sun and swimming in the rough water, a stroll on the beach, throwing driftwood for the dogs, laughing together at their antics, finding seashells in the sand.

Late in the afternoon she and Graham drove down to Nags Head to get some groceries that Renée wanted. The top of the Porsche was down and Jane's hair was windblown and sticky with salt but she didn't care. The island offered total freedom and a time apart from the real world.

"I think," announced Graham on the way home, "that Mom is tired of living alone. I *think* this unscheduled visit is an attempt at rapprochement."

"What about your dad?"

Graham thought for a minute. "Once the shock wore off I noted a hungry stare in his eyes. I *think*."

"Maybe they'll get back together," said Jane, sensing that Graham wanted to hear that.

"Maybe," he said. "I just wish Mom would lighten up sometimes."

"She was probably nervous. It was hard for her to just show up like that."

"Um, I guess so. She tends to get real bossy and real busy when she's upset."

"If your father would have welcomed her, I mean really seemed glad to see her, I'll bet she would have melted."

"It's true. Smedley has a problem with intimacy. It's that old stiff upper lip routine. He went to an English public school, you know."

"Well, *you* sure don't have an intimacy problem," Jane quipped.

"No, it's that hot Gallic side of me," he said lasciviously, putting a hand on her bare thigh and squeezing.

A few minutes later they pulled into the driveway. Renée met them at the door and took the groceries from them.

She'd changed to beautifully cut pale lavender slacks with a white silk shirt. Jane wondered how she was going to cook dinner without ruining the outfit.

"Where's Dad?" asked Graham.

"Looking for stones on the beach," Renée answered. "I think he's trying to avoid me." She said it lightly but Jane sensed the pain behind her words.

"Now, why would he do that?" asked Graham.

"Because, *mon cher*, your father is an abject coward."

"Mom..."

She bent and rattled pans in a low cupboard. "He is and always has been," Jane thought she heard Renée say amidst the clatter. A second later the woman straightened and, holding a pot by its handle, she shook it in Graham's direction. "At least I didn't raise you to be a coward like your father, *mon Dieu*!"

"Hey, Mom, give the guy a chance."

Renée stopped brandishing the pot. She stood tall and said, very clearly and deliberately, "But that is exactly what I am here for."

Before dinner, Jane and Graham strolled down the beach. His arm was around her, his head bent close as they walked along the receding tide line, bare feet splashing in the sliding water.

"What a wonderful place," Jane said with a sigh. "I could stay here forever."

"Lew wouldn't like that."

"No, he wouldn't."

"But we can come again. It's wonderful in the fall when all the tourists are gone."

"I'll never manage to get four days off again. I'm lucky Lew gave them to me this time."

"I guess you just know the right people." Graham grinned.

Jane disengaged herself from his arm and faced him, hands on hips. "Did you get me those days off? Graham, I will be so angry with you if you did!"

"I confess."

"That's not fair!"

"But there's method to my madness."

"What *method*?"

"I'll tell you tomorrow. I needed you."

"Graham, you're disgraceful!"

"Yes—and no. Reserve judgment until tomorrow morning."

"I *hate* mysteries!" cried Jane.

He put his arm around her again and started walking. "You're beautiful when you're angry. Did anyone ever tell you that before?"

"No." She started to finally laugh, unable to sustain her temper. "Mostly they just hightailed it and ran when they saw that look in my eyes."

Frantic barking came from beyond a dune. Two dogs.

"We've got company," Graham said wryly as the two black and tan beasts bounded over the hill, spraying sand, barking, flinging themselves at the receding water and biting at it.

Smedley trudged into view, hands behind his back, head bent, eyes fixed on the ground.

"Hi, Dad!" Graham called.

"Oh, it's you two. Did Renée send you?" he asked warily.

"No, she's busy whipping up something spectacular for dinner."

Smedley's eyes lit up. "Do you suppose she's making shrimp Newburg? She knows I love it."

"Well, shrimp was on the shopping list."

"Haven't had it in a year. And those little round rolls she makes?"

"I did buy some yeast," Graham admitted.

"Um," came from Smedley as he kicked sand with one bare foot. "Suppose I'll have to show up for dinner."

"It would be a good idea." Graham eyed his father speculatively.

"Although, *confound it*, she has no business just popping in here unannounced. And now she's taken over the kitchen. I'll never find my pots again." He bent to examine a pile of stones, fingering one with a reddish tint. "I'll tell you, it's been peaceful around here without her constantly nagging and organizing."

"I think I'll walk on ahead," Jane said meaningfully, catching Graham's glance.

"You can stay right here, young lady," Smedley was quick to say. "I haven't got any secrets. And you know something else," he went on without pause, "she emptied my jars of diamonds out onto the sand!"

"I'm sure she—" Graham began.

"She *knew* I'd been collecting them for years! I had to spend an hour picking up what I could out of the sand. Now I've got exactly one jar left!"

"I'm sure she—" Graham tried once more.

"And don't think I don't know she'd like to go to that party in Bermuda."

"It seems natural to me that she—"

"Sure, sure, Renée comes flying back into my life and takes over again. Well, if I go to Bermuda, it'll be alone!"

"*Dad*," Graham said, exasperated, "I think you're being unfair just because Mom dumped out a few jars of beach junk."

"Beach junk! That's how much *you* know!" And he stalked away, growling under his breath.

"God, he can push my buttons!" Graham said heatedly to his father's hunched, retreating form.

"He's confused, that's all. Can't you see how strained everything's been since your mom got here?" Jane noted Graham's frustrated expression and felt sorry for him; it was clear he would like nothing more than to see his parents reunited. "These things take time."

"Sure," he replied then smiled. "I know."

"Come on," Jane urged, "let's finish our walk. There's nothing we can do to help your mother and father. Come on, where's that old Graham who doesn't let anything bother him?"

"Beats me." He took his hands out of his pockets and cocked his head. "Wanna race back to the house?"

"I've never run in sand. You'll beat me."

"Exactly what I was thinking." Graham took off ahead of her. Jane smiled to herself and continued walking slowly, enjoying the feel of the foamy tide at her feet, watching his footprints disappearing swiftly along the edge of the water, looking up and shading her eyes while she watched a gull screech overhead and swoop down to pick at a ripple in the surf. She arrived on the sun deck ten minutes after Graham.

He was still breathing hard. "Cute trick."

"I never said *I* wanted to race."

Somewhere Renée had dug up a cut glass decanter and filled it with wildflowers. And she'd located matching glasses. There were even candles stuck in bright pottery holders and shrimp Newburg, rolls and a crisp Caesar salad. Smedley had changed into khaki pants and a clean white shirt and looked very handsome at the head of the table. It was obvious to Jane that they were all trying very hard to be a family.

"This is a wonderful meal, Mrs. Smith," Jane said. She noticed that Graham's mother did not request to be called Renée.

"Thank you. I wonder sometimes if Smedley sees to eating properly."

"I do just fine, Renée."

"You look well," she admitted grudgingly.

"Are you two going to take the boat out tomorrow?" Graham asked. "Jane and I have to leave and someone should use the poor old thing."

"Old thing?" objected Renée.

"Old for a boat. Come on, Mom, where's your sense of humor?"

After a couple of glasses of wine Renée did loosen up. She told Jane stories of Graham's childhood. "Oh, but he was an enfant terrible! The trouble he got in! He used to invade my parties in his Ninja costume, screaming in Japanese and throwing darts."

"Mom..."

"What a time that boy gave us," mused Smedley, catching his wife's eye.

"Must we tell *Graham* stories?" asked Graham, looking down at his plate.

Renée folded her hands, elbows on the table, and gazed at him lovingly. "But your father and I adore these memories, *mon cher*." She glanced at Smedley. "In high school he locked himself in the office and took over the school's public-address system. I can't tell you how humiliated I was!"

"Sounds like Graham. Did he tell you about his ride on Pard at our ranch in Colorado?"

"Pard?" asked Smedley.

So Jane had to repeat the story. Graham laughed louder than anyone at her description of his fall, as seen through the kitchen window.

"So you *did* see that," said Graham finally.

"I was waiting for it," Jane quipped. "You think I was brought up by the Manning men to be dumb?"

When the meal was over, they all helped to clear the table. Jane was carrying in the last of the clutter when she heard Renée say to Smedley in the kitchen, "I am so sorry about throwing away your gems today," and Smedley's reply, "Oh, er, no harm done. Here, let me scrub that pot. You'll ruin your nails."

"Good sign," Graham said when Jane told him, "I *think*." They were sitting on the deck, watching the sun's rays slant across the water. It was a peaceful time, the only sound the muted soughing of the ocean as it sucked at the shore. Jane half sat on the railing, her back against the house and Graham was in his usual chair with his feet propped up. A warm breeze laden with a salty ocean smell and moisture blew her bangs off her forehead. She was so terribly aware of Graham nearby, of his long lean body that was so relaxed, of his lazy smile as he watched the dogs fighting over a stick on the beach. She was acutely conscious of every sensation, every harsh call of a sea gull, every glint of the setting sun on a whitecap. She wanted to touch Graham, to feel him close; she craved his mouth on hers, his whispers in her ear. But his parents were there and they couldn't . . .

Graham reached out and took hold of her hand. "So now you've met my folks. And they've revealed to you the true me. What do you think?" Idly he played with her fingers and watched her from under sandy eyebrows.

His touch made her draw in her breath. What sweet torture it was to be so close to him. "I think I like your family very much," she said.

"And me?"

"You, too."

"You *like* me, that's all?"

"Well, I like you a lot."

"Janey, Janey," he said with mock-despair, "I guess that'll have to do for now."

She closed her eyes and leaned her head back against the rough silvered wood of the wall. What did he want from her—a declaration of love? It was too soon, wasn't it?

"Down-to-earth Janey," Graham mused as if reading her mind. "You're very good for me, you know."

"Am I?"

"And I'm very, very good for you," he murmured, and their eyes met and locked and spoke eloquently to each other.

Renée and Smedley joined them and the talk was quiet for a while, about the weather and the ocean and fishing. It was hard to imagine Graham's parents were separated and hurting each other. They seemed so well suited but Jane supposed that could merely be the habit of years. Maybe they could work things out, she thought hopefully.

Dusk fell and the drone of the ocean seemed to grow louder, to fill the air. That huge body of water was a powerful entity, Jane was beginning to realize, as powerful as the sun was back home, an entity affecting the climate and way of life and mood.

Graham stood up and announced, "I think I'd better check out the *Renée*."

"What? At night?" asked his mother.

"Yes, I'm not sure I secured her properly yesterday."
Then he grinned self-consciously. "I need company. Jane,
will you come?"

Jane was beginning to follow the direction of his plan.
"Sure," she said, trying to hide a smile.

"Good. Well, see you later," he said lightly to his parents.

"That was embarrassingly transparent," Jane commented, as they drove through the hot night.

"But you're here, aren't you? Look, this way we kill two
birds with one stone. We give them time to be alone together and we get the same thing. I thought I was brilliant."

He was right. Jane's heart was pounding. She couldn't
wait to be alone with Graham, to breathe in his sweet scent.
When she closed her eyes and felt the hot wind on her face
she could imagine it was the illusory touch of his fingers.

The *Renée* rocked gently in a strip of luminous, moonlit
water and the cabin was close and dark. He pulled her into
his arms. "God, I'm crazy about you," he breathed. "I
couldn't sit there another minute. I thought I was going to
leap on you and growl, like a tomcat."

She kissed him, melting against his chest and he crushed
her to him, hard. They found the bed in the darkness and
sank down onto it, still holding each other. His body was
familiar to her now but each time was a new experience, a
new adventure. He thrilled her and fulfilled her and she
couldn't get enough of his mouth and his hands and his
passionate murmurings.

The boat rocked lazily as they came together in wild ten-
derness, crying out, sweating in the stuffy cabin, lost in
each other until the moon stood overhead and washed the
Renée in bright liquid silver.

RENÉE AND SMEDLEY stood together on the steps to see Graham and Jane off on Monday morning.

"Drive carefully," Renée was saying. "That little car goes too fast."

"Don't worry, Mom," called Graham, throwing the bags in the trunk.

"Thank you again," Jane said, poised by the car door. "I had a wonderful weekend. I'm so glad I met you both."

"Come again anytime," said Smedley.

They drove away and Jane looked back one last time to wave to the attractive couple. Renée was gazing at her husband, and Jane could swear there was a wistful expression on her face. How sad, Jane thought, turning away, that Graham's parents, while growing older, had become dissatisfied with each other. They were looking for more but failing to see that there really wasn't *more* out there; they already had what they needed. She vowed to remember this lesson if she ever got restless after years of marriage.

"I wonder how they're going to get along," Graham mused. "I feel like I'm a rat deserting the sinking ship."

"Maybe not sinking," Jane replied. "You did notice your mother's suitcases were gone last night, didn't you? And they weren't in *my* room."

"Nor mine," Graham said lightly. "So that means they were—"

"In your dad's room."

"Well, what do you know," he said.

"Do you think your father will take your mother to that party in Bermuda?" asked Jane. "I just know she'd give anything to go."

"Oh, she'd love to arrive dripping in jewels with a new creation on and see all their old buddies," agreed Graham. "It all depends on my father's nerve. In some ways he is a coward."

The miles flew by; a white haze burned off the surface of the ocean and the sun blasted out of a heat-bleached sky. They got held up at a drawbridge on the Inland Waterway and Graham leaned over and kissed Jane. "Sorry I didn't sneak into your room last night?" he asked, his warm breath sending rippling shock waves down her hip. She leaned against him, feeling the whipcord strength of his body, loving the nearness of him but a little afraid, too. She was falling in love with this man, this Quicksilver, and it was all happening much too fast.

In Virginia, Graham turned west at the sign that read Washington, D.C. "Are we going a different way?" asked Jane.

"Sort of. This is the surprise I told you about."

"Oh, I'd forgotten about that."

"I'm going to pick up some Picasso sketches at the National Gallery and deliver them to the Met in New York."

Jane sat straight up. "You mean you're on a job?"

"And so are you. Lew assigned you to me as my bodyguard."

"Graham, why didn't you *tell* me?"

He shrugged and pulled out to pass a truck. "Lew told me not to tell anyone till I'd left New York."

"We left New York three days ago!"

"We did, you're right. But I didn't want you worrying. It was supposed to be a vacation."

"Oh, Graham! You should have told me!"

"Why? Would you have practiced karate on me all weekend if you'd known?"

"No, it's just that...oh, I don't know. You can be really...infuriating sometimes."

"And you love every minute of it."

Some time later they pulled up to the rear service entrance of the national Gallery. "I'm going to check out the area," said Jane, stepping out of the car.

"There won't be any theft attempt," Graham was quick to tell her. "Lew was very careful to make sure no one in the office knew about this job."

"Nevertheless," Jane retorted, "I'm going to treat this like any other job. And, besides, someone in Washington could have talked about it."

She found it to be a typically deserted parking lot with trash Dumpsters and cars and piles of empty boxes. There were a million places for someone to hide. Graham still sat in the car, smiling sardonically, but she ignored him. She wasn't going to take a chance on anything going wrong.

Finally she let him go inside while she waited at the door to keep an eye on things. He was accompanied to and from the storage room by a museum guard and the curator and returned shortly with a one-foot square box that had been sealed very carefully.

"That's it?" she asked.

"They're small sketches, I guess," he said. Then he thanked the two men and stepped toward the door.

"Hold on," said Jane. "I have to secure the area. You wait here."

He looked at the guard and they exchanged smiles that clearly said, "Oh, boy, look at the amateur, following all the rules in the book."

Nevertheless Jane checked the area thoroughly: behind Dumpsters again, around the corners of the building, in the bushes, everywhere people could conceal themselves. She was ready to call Graham out to the car when she heard a squeal of tires and a horn honking behind her. She jumped as if she'd been shot and whirled around.

There was Graham in his red Porsche, grinning like crazy. "Come on!" he yelled. "I'm hungry for lunch."

"That was stupid!" she blurted out angrily as she got into the car.

"But you were so busy securing the area I knew I'd be safe."

"Where are the sketches?"

"Locked in the trunk."

"Damn it, Graham, *you* may not take this job seriously but I do!"

His smile faded. "I'm sorry, Jane, I could see you had everything under control," he said contritely. "I'll never do it again, I promise. Forgive me, my beloved bodyguard. Gee—" he brightened "—Beloved Bodyguard, isn't that a great name for a book?"

Jane snorted in derision. He was impossible. He wasn't capable of sticking to rules. She was beginning to understand his nickname, Quicksilver. And yet, she wondered, as they peeled out of the parking lot and darted through Washington traffic toward the beltway, wasn't that a part of Graham that attracted her?

But the romantic interlude was over for Jane. She was on the job, acutely aware of every car on the road, every broken-down vehicle on the shoulder, every possible hiding place for a pursuing vehicle. Graham insisted on stopping for lunch although Jane would have gladly gone without to avoid the possibility of problems. She was well aware that they were safer on the road, moving.

"But I'm hungry," Graham complained.

She insisted he stay in the car while she went into a McDonald's. Walking out of the place, Jane was brought up short by a hard poke in the ribs and a voice whispering harshly, "Stick 'em up!"

Adrenaline flared in her veins and she dropped the bag of food, smashing her elbow into the hand at her back, knocking it aside, then spun around, ready to slam a knee into the assaulter's groin.

"Graham!" she gasped.

"Damn it, you were ready to emasculate me!"

"You're right! Oh, darn you! *Darn you!*"

He picked up the bag of hamburgers. "I think your drink spilled," he said mildly.

She insisted on driving.

"Okay." Graham gave in. "Okay, do whatever you want. I've been a bad boy."

Silently Jane took the keys from his outstretched hand, got in and started the car, waiting without saying a word.

"Okay, so you're mad at me. But you're forgetting that I used to work in security. Everything was safe, Janey. I wouldn't have jeopardized the Picassos just to tease you."

She shot him a hard look as she pulled back onto the interstate. "I'm not putting down your capabilities, Graham. I'm only trying to do my job. I simply can't take things as lightly as you do. And you can't just keep apologizing like a little child, then turn around and pull stunts like that." She caught his glance and decided that he wasn't taking her seriously. "From now on," she said, determined to drive home her point, "I'll just tell Lew that Norma has got to go on jobs with you."

"You wouldn't!"

She fell silent, satisfied.

The delivery at the Metropolitan Museum of Art at Central Park went smoothly. Graham got all his papers signed while Jane scouted the area and he *did* behave himself.

"Can I drive now?" he asked as they stood on the curb together.

"Of course."

"The keys?" He smiled, a mixture of devilry and sincerity tilting his handsome mouth.

She handed them over. "I'm sorry I got so mad back at that restaurant," Jane began as he pulled out into traffic. "You've just got to understand how seriously I take my work."

"Okay. Friends then?"

She nodded.

"Lovers, too?" He tipped his sunglasses up and winked at her.

Graham pulled up in front of the Barbizon Hotel, double-parked, swiveled in his seat and took her chin in his hand. "Jane, that was the best weekend I ever had. Can we do it again?"

"I'd love to."

"You did have fun? Even with the dogs and Mom and Dad and all that stuff?"

"It was wonderful."

"Gosh, I'm going to miss you. I have that Amsterdam job coming up shortly. The diamonds. Norma's going this time—Lew's orders. I wish it were you going along, Janey. What a wild time we could have." He kissed her gently and her stomach rolled, quivering with delight. "Norma's an old grouch."

"Norma's a great lady and I'll bet she's a terrific bodyguard."

"Not like you, Janey." He kissed her again. "Come over for dinner in a couple of days?"

"Um, I will. But I'll cook this time."

"Anything you want."

A car honked furiously behind them.

"Uh-oh, I gotta go," said Graham. "Bye, I'll call you."

She got out quickly, waved at the angry driver and blew Graham a kiss.

Riding up in the elevator, Jane started to daydream. What if Norma got sick—oh, nothing serious, maybe a sinus attack or something—and she had to go to Amsterdam with Graham in Norma's place? She closed her eyes and imagined the trip. Wow. The old-world charm of Europe, millions in sparkling diamonds and Quicksilver, all to herself.

CHAPTER TEN

WHEN NORMA SWEPT INTO Jane's tiny office it felt like the woman was sucking all the air and a few of the loose items from the rest of the building in with her. "I found you an apartment," was her pronouncement.

Jane's head snapped up. "You *did*?"

"You're still looking, I take it?" Norma asked briskly.

"You bet! But I haven't found anything I can afford."

"'Course not. You have to *know* someone. I know someone. An old friend of mine is the landlady of a building up on 84th and First Avenue, East side. Somebody moved out on her and she needs a tenant—quick."

Jane felt excitement stirring but tried to bank the embers against disappointment. She couldn't help the grimace on her face when she asked, "How much?"

"Two hundred and fifty. A steal. It's rent controlled."

"Holy cow, that's cheap!"

"It's a one-bedroom shotgun apartment. She'll let it for first and last, no damage deposit. It needs a little fixing up."

"If it's got walls and a door and indoor plumbing I'll take it."

"Call her. Give her that old 'I'm-a-great-tenant' routine. I'm sure she'll let you have it but there'll be the usual lecture on her waiting list." Norma thrust a scrap of paper at Jane, then turned to leave.

"Gosh, Norma, *thanks*, I mean it."

"No problem." Norma disappeared down the hall and Jane felt the urge to kick her heels in the air.

"Oh, boy," she whispered to herself. An apartment, a home, her first bachelor place all her very own. Graham would love it; he hated that old Barbizon that wouldn't let him go beyond the lobby. She could clean and fuss and cook for Graham. She could have friends over and if one of her brothers wanted to come and visit, there would be a place for him to stay. She'd be a New Yorker, not a hotel dweller but a real, live, bona fide New Yorker!

Wait a minute. She had to call and get the place. What if someone got there first and snatched it away from her? What if she didn't hit it off with the landlady? Fingers shaking, she dialed the number on the scrap of paper. A hoarse voice answered.

"Lily Sypnewski?" asked Jane, stumbling over the last name.

"Yeah."

"This is Jane Manning. Norma Stedman told me you have an apartment to rent."

"Who'd you say this was?"

"Jane Manning. I work with Norma Stedman."

"I *do* have a waiting list."

"Yes, I'm sure you do, but I'd be such a good tenant. I'd always pay my rent on time, I'm a good housekeeper. I have a steady job and—" Jane thought quickly "—and I never make any noise."

"Well..."

"Oh, please, Mrs. Sypnewski, I'm absolutely desperate." There was a long pause on the other end of the line and Jane did not breathe once.

"Norma's friend?" the woman asked rhetorically. "Well, I suppose for Norma's sake. Five hundred is what

I'll need up front. And a little elbow grease on your part. I suppose you'll want to see it first?''

"No, it'll be fine, I'm sure. I'll take it. Can I bring you over a check today?''

"Sooner the better,'' rasped Lily.

"I'll be there after work, by six,'' said Jane firmly.

Of course, she couldn't think of anything but the apartment all day. She and Lukas had to deliver some new perfume samples that afternoon to a plant way out in Hoboken somewhere. They got lost and hit the Lincoln Tunnel on the return trip during rush hour. She sat behind the wheel fretting and impatient as they crawled along, in the traffic.

"I'll never make it,'' she muttered, checking her watch again.

"Make what?'' asked Lukas.

"Look, do you mind if we take a quick detour? I have to drop off a check for an apartment I'm going to rent. I'm afraid I'll be late if we go all the way to the office first.''

Lukas shrugged his heavy shoulders. "I am a gentleman. Besides, this way I know where you live.'' He leered at her.

She shot him a disgusted glance. "I thought we had all that straightened out, Luke.''

"We do, sure we do. You got a boyfriend. A little skinny, maybe, but he's a nice guy. So, I make a little joke.''

Shaking her head, Jane headed crosstown. The address. She rummaged around in her purse with one hand until she found the piece of paper—84th off First Avenue. Damn, every street she passed seemed to go one way, the wrong way. New York was laid out simply but it worked only in theory.

The building was small and old, in the center of the block. Someone had tried to grow geraniums in a window box but they had wilted in the heat. It was a nice residential neighborhood in Germantown, quiet, with a deli on the corner. Jane left Lukas in the car, ran up the front steps and pushed the button marked Super. Her heart pounded so hard she put a sweaty hand on her chest as if to still it. It was 6:05 p.m.

The door buzzed open and Jane stepped into the hallway. A voice came out of the dimness to croak, "You're late."

Jane blinked and strained her eyes in the weak light. "I'm sorry, the traffic..."

"Sure, I know. You're Jane, huh?"

"Yes. Mrs. Sypnewski?"

Lily was under five feet tall. She was dressed in a conglomeration of gauzy, silky clothes, layers of skirts and blouses and scarves in bright colors, giving her a gypsylike aura. Her hair was dyed jet-black and pulled back into a bun and her face was soft and velvety with tiny wrinkles. Her minuscule feet were shod in black patent leather Mary Janes and in her hand—perpetually, Jane was to learn—was a king-sized cigarette.

"Come on," Lily said, jangling a ring of keys, "I'll show it to you."

The door opened directly into the living room that opened directly into the kitchen that led to the bedroom that... "Shotgun apartment," murmured Jane to herself.

"Yeah, if you shot a gun at the front door it'd go straight through to the back," put in Lily.

There were a few basic pieces of furniture, the kitchen was old-fashioned, the stove desperately needed cleaning, the mattress had seen better days, the bathroom was...ugh. Jane saw what Norma had meant: it needed "a little fixing up."

"It's a rat's nest, isn't it?" Lily was commenting. "Poor old Mrs. Singer, her son finally had her carted off to an old folks' home up in Yonkers."

Mrs. Singer hadn't been too spick-and-span, Jane noted. "I'll take it," she repeated firmly, pulling out her checkbook and scribbling out a check quickly, as if afraid she might change her own mind.

Lily handed her three keys. "It's all yours, honey. No pets, no dope, men are okay as long as they don't make noise. I get up late so don't bug me until I've had my cigarette and my coffee, okay?"

"Okay, Lily." But the tiny figure had scurried out and all that remained was the scent of cigarette smoke mixed with baby powder.

"My Lord," breathed Jane. Lukas was waiting in the car. She closed her eyes, hugged herself and spun around in the center of her new living room then rushed out, struggling with the three different locks on the door, wishing she could stay and start cleaning and planning....

"GRAHAM!" SHE SAID BREATHLESSLY into the phone that night when he called. "I've got an apartment!" Then she had to tell him the whole story, about Norma and Lily and the heavy traffic.

"Janey, that's wonderful! When are you moving in?"

"Well, it needs some work. It's a mess. Probably this weekend."

"Want some help?"

"Oh, yes, would you mind?"

"No, sweets, I wouldn't mind a bit. I even know this great Goodwill store where you can get everything you need. Make a list."

"I'm so excited I don't know what to do!"

"I'm jealous," he said mock-seriously.

"Now you can come over to dinner at *my* place," she replied proudly.

"And you'll let me in past the lobby?"

"I certainly will," she said, laughing. "As long as you don't make too much noise!"

"Noise?"

"Lily's rule. Men are okay if they're quiet."

"Sensible woman," he agreed. "Janey, I miss you, babe. And I can't wait to see your apartment but I'll be out of town until Friday. Okay? Saturday morning we'll go to work on that place, I promise."

"You're too good to me," Jane said softly, "and I miss you, too."

"Damn, Janey, I wish you were here!"

"Me, too."

"See you Saturday."

"Bye, Graham."

It was so hot and humid on Saturday morning a person could cut the soggy air with a knife. The apartment smelled moldy and looked dingy when she ushered him in.

Jane had taken care of the utilities and phone during the week; she'd done some scrubbing in the evenings and hung some clothes in the closet. Lily had lent her a vacuum cleaner. But still it had been discouraging.

Graham changed all that. He rubbed his hands together, grabbed Jane and kissed her soundly. "It needs a little work is all," he said cheerfully. "I've seen lots worse."

He whisked her off to the Goodwill store. "My mother showed me this place years ago. One half of New York donates stuff to this store; the other half buys the stuff from it."

The store was housed in the basement of an old warehouse near the East Side docks in lower Manhattan. Jane had never seen so many things crammed into an area she estimated to be the size of a football field. It was dark and dusty and smelly in the brick building and there was no air-conditioning. She held on to Graham's arm, feeling uncharacteristically insecure, expecting wharf rats to leap out at her from the shadowy corners.

"Ugh," Jane said once as they meandered in and out of aisles that had stacks and stacks of used clothing, enough clothing to outfit an army. "I don't know about this."

"Nothing like it in Rifle?"

"That's for sure. Listen," she suggested, "maybe I could go to a department store, use my new credit card or something. I only need a few things, really."

"Nothing doing. You're getting too used to Bloomies and Saks. A bad habit. This place is for the real folks, Jane, the needy and the ones just starting out—like you."

"I'll bet *some* start out in Bloomies," muttered Jane as she twitched her nose over a pile of very worn sheets.

"Snob," said Graham good-naturedly.

It did take a full hour of shuffling through the piles of sheets and towels but eventually Jane was handing Graham a stack of linens. "These are in good condition. I'm amazed."

"I take it I get to do all the carrying."

"It was your idea to come here."

There were piles of chipped dishes and china—real china—and aisles and aisles of pots and pans and toaster ovens and vintage blenders. Everything. There were rows of furniture, piles of the old stuff stacked to the ceiling. There were chairs and tables and bed frames, even a brass one.

"I should get it," Jane exclaimed. "A real brass bed."

"There's a perfectly serviceable bed in the apartment."

"I know, but brass..."

"Come on," he said, shouldering her past the aisle, as his arms were filled, "I'd never be able to look myself in the mirror again if I let you overspend at the Goodwill."

"It was your idea."

"So you keep reminding me."

It was a silly old thing—an early sixties' clock radio, in dirty white plastic with a round clock face and a metal alarm tab that was missing its plastic knob. Jane fingered it thoughtfully and cocked her head. "You know, I had this same one, I swear, when I was a kid. The *same* one. Oh, Graham, it's even missing that clear knob for the alarm. Mine was, too."

"Must be yours then." He smiled and studied her face.

"It couldn't be. You're teasing."

"Maybe I am and maybe I'm not."

"Should I...? I mean, do you suppose it works?"

So they plugged it into an outlet behind the counter and lo and behold, WOR, New York, blared away. "I can't believe it!" breathed Jane. "It *is* my radio."

The price tag, no doubt placed on it fifteen years before, said a dollar fifty. The mountain in Graham's arms grew.

By eleven-thirty, they were both tired and grimy and sweaty as the temperature in the basement edged toward ninety degrees. "Can we go?" asked Graham hopefully.

"In a minute."

"I thought you hated this place."

"I never said that." And she stopped to dig through the stacks of moth-eaten blankets, adding, "There *must* be a winter here sometime."

By noon, the back of his Porsche was piled with pots and dishes, silverware, the sheets and towels, a few small tables, lamps and the old radio. They stopped at a hardware store and bought paint—white for the living room, pale green for the bedroom and bright yellow for the bathroom.

Lunch was thick ham sandwiches on pumpernickel and vinegary potato salad from the corner deli and they ate on Jane's new mismatched plates on her new table. She'd never tasted anything so delicious.

Jane put on an old T-shirt of Graham's that he'd thoughtfully brought along and they painted all afternoon as the old radio played. Graham sang along with the music, did an impromptu dance step once in a while, paintbrush in hand, and managed to get paint in his hair, on his jeans and on the floor.

Jane was happy. She loved being busy, having something physical to do. She loved having Graham there as if they were decorating their own place together, as so many married couples did. *Married couples.* What was she thinking? She and Graham...well, it was too soon. They'd only known each other a few weeks really. But still...

By late afternoon the windows were wide open in an attempt to let the paint dry. Jane put dishes in the cupboards and made up the bed with her "new" sheets and blankets. The watery sun threw lines of light across the freshly painted walls.

"I love it," Jane said. "My own apartment. Oh, Graham."

"I'd grab you and throw you on that bed but I've got paint all over me," he said.

"You could take a shower in my bathroom," she pointed out.

"So could you," he said, his eyes lighting up. "Sort of christen the shower."

"What would Lily say?"

"From what you've told me of her, nothing." He took her hand and led her through the bedroom to the small sunny bathroom. Pulling her T-shirt over her head, he bent to kiss one soft shoulder. "Lovely."

"There's paint in your hair," Jane murmured, running her hand through his thick, fair waves.

"I know."

The shower felt cool and soothing to her skin. She soaped Graham's body, scrubbing with a washcloth at the splotches of paint. She washed it out of his hair while he stood with his eyes squeezed shut and the warm water running down the flawless, tanned satin of his skin.

Then it was his turn. Gently he shampooed her hair and ran a soapy washcloth over her body until she shivered with pleasure. They both stood under the spray, locked together, hands slippery on wet skin, lips searching, pressing, as the warm water sluiced over them and the old pipes clanked and knocked on the walls.

Soaking wet footprints led to the bedroom, dripping bodies dampened the freshly made bed. "So what," whispered Graham. "I'll get you more sheets."

His kisses excited her, his hands intoxicated her. The newly painted green walls spun before Jane's eyes as Graham took her on an incredible journey with him, an odyssey of sensation and emotion.

"This bed is well and truly christened," Graham murmured some time later.

"Mmm," Jane said, running the sole of her foot up and down his calf.

"Isn't this better than the Barbizon Hotel?"

"Mmm," she repeated.

Graham rolled over on his back and put his hands behind his head. "We owe Norma one for this."

"I know." Jane stretched lazily, catlike. "I've been trying to think of what to do." She sat up suddenly, the sheet falling away to her waist. "I know! I'll have a party!

A real party. I'll invite Norma and her husband and Donna.''

"Don't forget Frank," said Graham.

"Frank. Of course," agreed Jane. "Saturday night."

"Am I invited?" Graham asked softly, stroking her side, his hand moving over her ribs to her hip and then lower...

"What will I make? I mean, I've never had a party like this before."

"Have it catered," he suggested wryly.

"*Graham*."

"Am I invited?"

"Yes, silly. I couldn't have it without you."

Saturday night came too soon. Jane had cleaned all day, arranged flowers in a vase she bought at Woolworth's, cooked her chicken and chili casserole, bought ice cream, paper plates, plastic cups and beer and wine. She wore her green and white dress and prayed for an evening breeze to stir the stagnant air in her apartment.

Norma and Martin arrived first, buzzing the door at seven sharp. Jane gasped in dismay, remembering Martin's wheelchair and the front steps but Norma muscled the chair up the steps as if she were a longshoreman. Martin held a wrapped package carefully on his lap.

"Oh, you shouldn't have!" admonished Jane. "This is a party to thank *you*."

The box contained a set of long-stemmed glasses. "I figured you wouldn't have any," stated Norma.

Donna and Frank arrived next. Donna wore red parachute pants, white high heels and a purple, orange and red filmy blouse that came to her knees. She looked, Jane thought, like a particularly bright, exotic flower. Frank appeared sulky and wore jeans, a Western-style shirt, a belt with a rather large silver buckle and his name etched on the back of the leather: "Frank." Jane had a sneaking feeling Donna had made him come to the party.

Donna brought a big box of Godiva chocolates that was immediately opened and sampled.

"It doesn't look half bad," Norma admitted, glancing around critically. "You've done a good job."

"Graham helped a lot."

"It's terrific!" said Donna, snapping her gum enthusiastically. "You lucky thing!"

Lily arrived next. Jane had invited her because her landlady knew Norma. She brought a bottle of Jack Daniel's. "I knew you wouldn't have any," she rasped, blowing out a stream of smoke. "Mind you, this is my bottle. I'm only lending it for the evening."

The buzzer sounded. It had to be Graham, but when he didn't appear at her door, Jane peeked out into the hall. The outside door was filled with a large, untidy lump.

"You weren't supposed to look," she heard Graham saying. "Dammit all, I'm stuck!"

He was trying to drag something inside. It was huge—taller than him and bulging against the door frame. Frank came to help and, with a few minutes of wrestling, it popped into the hallway.

"A horse!" exclaimed Jane. It was a horse, a stuffed horse, a *huge* fur animal with a pale, fuzzy coat, a bristly mane and tail and patent leather hooves.

Graham stood, hands on hips, puffing a little. "It's been hell getting it here."

They pushed and tugged some more and finally got it into Jane's apartment so that everyone could see.

"Helluva waste of money," grumbled Norma. "Impractical."

"I didn't want you to be homesick," explained Graham. "I thought he looked a little like Pard."

Jane stroked the soft neck. "I love him. Oh, thank you."
She felt her eyes fill with tears at thoughts of home, the
fragrant barn, her brothers and the big old, comfortable
house. And her new friends, too, her new life...and Graham.

Donna patted her on the back, Frank downed a plastic
cup of Lily's bourbon, Lily blew smoke rings in the air and
Martin chided Norma for grumbling.

"He'll keep you company," Graham was saying and she
gave him a brilliant, grateful smile through her tears.

Dinner was a success. Lily trailed the corner of one of her
scarves into the salsa, dropped ashes in the salad and told
hilarious jokes.

"How many Californians does it take to change a light
bulb?" she asked.

"I don't know," said Jane dutifully. "How many?"

"Five. One to screw in the bulb and four to experience
it." Then she laughed and laughed so hard that she went
into a coughing spasm.

Everyone ate on paper plates on their laps and talked
across one another. Even Frank loosened up—maybe it was
the booze—and smiled at one of Lily's off-color jokes
about bikers, but he seemed to be ill at ease and kept a hand
on Donna's arm or waist or knee, as if for security. By the
end of the evening Jane still couldn't figure out what
Donna saw in him. Oh well, to each his own, she told herself.

Graham was charming, even engaging Frank in conversation—about cars, Jane decided, as she overheard "carburetor" and "turbo" and "horsepower" from that corner
of the room.

So what if her ice cream was melted because the old,
chugging refrigerator didn't work too well or if the pipes

banged and grunted for ten minutes after someone used the bathroom? No one seemed to mind.

Martin told hair-raising stories of his former work on the high rises in the city. It was fascinating, Jane thought, to hear him talk about walking a six-inch steel beam a thousand feet above the ground.

"How could you do it?" asked Donna, wide-eyed.

"I'm half Mohawk Indian," Martin said. "All of us Mohawks are great high-rise workers."

His accident had not been due to a fall, he told them, but to a truck backing up into some equipment that had collapsed on him. "I paint pictures now," he said, without self-pity.

Norma patted her husband on the shoulder with her big hand. "He does paintings of the buildings he's worked on. He's getting real good, too. Sells 'em to the buildings to hang in the lobbies."

Everybody was gone by eleven-thirty and Jane settled back on the couch with a sigh. She felt tired but good, a successful housewarming, a pleasant evening with friends behind her. Inside the air was finally cooling off a degree or two; outside the summer city throbbed, sirens wailed in the distance, horns honked occasionally, New York beat like a heart full of anticipation. This was what she'd always wanted and daydreamed about when she'd been riding the desolate range with her brothers or tapping a pen against her teeth in class at Fort Collins. She'd made her choice—her *own* choice—and it had turned out perfectly. No, better than perfect because in her wildest imaginings she could never have conjured up someone as wonderful as Graham.

"It was a real nice party," Graham said, breaking into her thoughts as he dumped paper plates into a trash bag.

"Was it? Do you think everyone had a good time?"

"Absolutely."

Jane sighed again and rubbed at some ashes Lily had spilled on the coffee table. "My first party."

"But not your last, Janey."

She smiled at him. "I love Pard, Graham."

He sat next to her and pushed her damp bangs off her forehead. "I thought for a minute there, you were awful homesick and I thought maybe I'd just made things worse."

She ran a finger down his shirt front. "No, Pard is sweet and so are you and I'm very, very glad I'm here with you."

Graham stretched out his legs in front of him and yawned. "I'm getting old, I guess. Not even midnight and I've had it."

"Ancient," Jane agreed. "Will you stay?"

"I'm too tired to go anywhere," Graham said lazily, resting a hand on her knee.

"That says lots for my charms," Jane answered dryly.

"I can't say enough about your charms, Janey, my love," Graham murmured, walking his fingers along her thigh.

"Should I do the dishes?" asked Jane, looking around at the party litter.

"Later, Janey, later," said Graham, turning to her and pulling her into his arms while outside the city pulsed steadily on into the night.

CHAPTER ELEVEN

ON MONDAY JANE SLEPT right through her alarm and leapt out of bed when she realized the time: 7:35!

No time to jog or even shower.

What had gotten into her? Had it been that last-minute trip to Cleveland with Lukas the day before? They *had* gotten into La Guardia late. Then an impish smile curved her lips; perhaps it had been Graham's after-midnight phone call.

She was ready to leave, snatching up her purse, feeling guilty and harassed, when the telephone rang.

It was her father. "Jane, glad I caught you."

"Daddy, I've got to run. Can I call you later? I'm sorry."

"I was only checking to see how you're coming along. Haven't heard from you for a week. I was getting worried. Is that new apartment of yours safe?"

"Yes, there are three locks and I'm perfectly safe."

"Nice neighborhood?"

"Very nice."

"Well, Jane, honey, are you enjoying your new place?"

"I love it, Daddy..."

"Well, I was just wondering."

"Oh, Daddy, I'm sorry. Really I am. I've been so busy."

"You're all right then?"

"Fine. Honestly."

"Well, try to call more often, Jane. Reverse the charges if you like."

"Daddy," she begged off, "I have to go. I'll call you later. I promise."

She left her apartment thinking there was some truth to the words that you could never go home again. But whereas a month ago Jane would have felt a twinge of homesickness, now there was only a peaceful kind of acceptance.

It was pleasantly warm outside, certainly not like September in the Rockies with that cool, crisp, high country air, the light morning frost on the range, the breath pluming from the horses' nostrils. But New York would do just fine.

At 8:45, fifteen minutes late, Jane hurried up the steps to Mercury's offices, planning in her mind the excuse she would give Lew.

But nobody noticed her tardiness.

When Jane walked into the office it was in a turmoil. Donna grabbed her and cried, "It's Norma, they shot Norma!"

"What?" Jane gasped, bludgeoned by shock.

"Oh God, Norma's been shot! She was on a job with Peter. He just called from the hospital."

"How bad is it?" Jane asked, abruptly feeling ice-cold, her mind flying in a dozen directions.

"I . . . I don't know!" wailed Donna.

Lew strode up, his round face drawn in grim lines. He kept slicking his scanty hair back in a nervous gesture. "Where did they take her, Donna?" he asked. "Calm down. What hospital?"

Donna cried harder and searched blindly through papers on her desk. "I wrote it, I wrote it down. . . ."

No one seemed to know what to do. It was as if someone had cried "fire" but not a soul remembered the drill.

"What did Peter say?" Jane kept pressing Donna for a straight answer. "Is Norma alive? Donna, you've got to tell us. Which hospital?"

"Oh, God! Here it is!" Donna held up a scrap of paper. Jane grabbed it. She had no idea where Bellevue Hospital was. "I'm going," she said. "I don't have a job this morning. Anyone else?"

"Peter said she was going into surgery, emergency surgery," sobbed Donna.

"So she's still alive," said Rick. "Maybe it's not so bad. I'll go with you, Jane."

They caught a cab to the hospital while the others stayed behind to keep some semblance of order in the office. "Call us," Lew had ordered. "Keep me informed."

"God damn it," Rick swore as their taxi weaved in and out of traffic. "It shouldn't have come to this. Poor Norma."

But no one was more upset about Norma than Jane. A cold lump of guilt was sitting in her stomach like lead. She couldn't forget what had crossed her mind when Graham told her about the Amsterdam job: if something happened to Norma then Jane could go to Amsterdam with Graham.

They entered Bellevue through the emergency room where even at this early hour there were patients being wheeled to and fro on carts and children crying in their mothers' arms and white-jacketed doctors and nurses scurrying about.

Rick tried to find out Norma's status from the desk nurse but got very little out of her. "You'll just have to wait, sir, until Mrs. Stedman's doctor is through operating."

"What kind of injury is it?" asked Jane.

"I don't know," said the nurse. "Really I don't."

Tears burning in her eyes, Jane tried again. "Can you tell us anything? Please..."

And amazingly the sympathetic woman said, "All right, I'll see what I can do. Just please wait in the room over there. Go on now. I'll do what I can."

It was at least fifteen minutes before the nurse poked her head in the door. "It's a chest wound. Right lung." She started to leave.

"Wait!" cried Jane, leaping to her feet. "Is she going to be all right? What did they say?"

The nurse shook her head. "I don't know what's going on in the operating room, miss. Now, please, I've got work to do. You'll simply have to wait."

Jane turned to Rick and swallowed a sob. "Poor Norma. Oh, God, this is so awful."

It turned out that Peter had been at the hospital but the police had driven him over to the station house to make his report. "I wish to hell he'd get back here," Rick said. "I'd sure like to know exactly what happened."

Rick left shortly thereafter to get them some coffee and call Mercury. When he disappeared down the hall and into an elevator, Jane felt suddenly, horribly alone. She tried leafing through last month's *Smithsonian Magazine*, in between pacing, then peeking down the hall as if somehow, miraculously, Norma would be standing there, sound and fit as always. She kept telling herself that Norma was in excellent physical condition. The woman didn't smoke, drink or have an ounce of fat on her body. That counted for something, didn't it?

But still, a chest wound, a lung...

Nervous adrenaline pumped through Jane's body, making her eye twitch and her knees rubbery. Her heart was pounding and her mouth felt as dry as cotton. Where was Rick? Had anyone notified Martin, Norma's husband?

Would Martin be able to make it to the hospital on his own? Maybe she should find a phone and call Mercury to make sure someone had thought to call Norma's husband.

No, no, she decided. She'd better wait right there in case the surgeon came in.

The minutes ticked by slowly. Through the glass-paneled window in the waiting lounge Jane could see one of those round, white-faced generic clocks like the ones in her old high school. The sweeping second hand seemed to be moving in slow motion.

Where was Rick?

God, what she wouldn't do to get to a phone, call Mercury and then Graham. Graham should know, too. And, besides, Jane wanted him there, *needed* him to be with her. This waiting, the not-knowing, was ghastly.

Rick swung open the door at 10:20. Coffee sloshed unnoticed from two plastic cups onto his hands and trouser leg.

"Did you tell someone to get in touch with Martin Stedman?" she rushed to ask.

He nodded and handed her a cup. "Lew went to pick him up. They should be here shortly. Any word yet?"

"None. I wonder how long this sort of surgery takes?"

"I haven't the slightest idea. I imagine a while, though, what with having to go into a chest." Rick shrugged helplessly.

"And her lung... Oh, God." Jane fell silent, trying to remember details from her year at vet school but unable to think, blocked by her stress.

"Rick," she said, getting to her feet shakily, "I need to call someone. I'll be right back."

But Graham was not home. "Darn," she said, waiting and waiting for the phone to be picked up. After fifteen rings, Jane finally hung up slowly and sagged against the wall.

Why had she had those thoughts about Norma? How could she have been so mean and selfish? And where the devil was Graham?

Martin Stedman arrived, his wheelchair pushed by Lew, at 11:30. His frail, seamed face was the color of ashes.

"Have you heard anything?" asked Lew.

"Not a word," replied Rick.

Jane crouched by Martin's chair and took his hand gently in hers. "I'm sure Norma's going to be okay."

Noon came and went. Still no word. Martin kept asking: "Is it a good sign when it takes a long time?"

And Lew would reply: "I'm sure it is."

At 12:15 the door swung open and Graham stood there, tall and strong, self-possessed, his face creased by uncharacteristic concern. Jane's heart gave a great glad leap and she left Martin's side to run to Graham.

"I tried to call," she said in a whisper. "Oh, Graham, this is so terrible. Poor Norma . . ." And her broken voice trailed away.

Graham took both her hands in his. "I stopped by the office to see if you wanted to go to lunch. Donna told me." He gazed at her soberly. "How long has Norma been in surgery?"

"Since . . . 9:00, 9:30. I'm not exactly sure." Jane wanted desperately to tell Graham, to unburden herself of her awful guilt—wishing Norma would get sick—but she couldn't. Not there, not with Lew and Rick and especially Martin all looking at them.

"Do you want to walk down the hall or something? Get some air?"

"Well . . ."

"Come on. I'm sure nothing is going to happen for five minutes." His hand squeezed hers reassuringly. "Come on." He pushed open the door with his shoulder and gently led her along.

They got coffee; Jane had decaf because she already felt too shaky. Sitting at the cafeteria table, she lowered her eyes. "I feel like this is my fault," she confessed in a whisper. "I know it's crazy, Graham, but I wished Norma would get sick."

"But why? I don't understand."

Her face grew hot. "Because I thought if Norma were sick, I'd be asked to go to Amsterdam with you." There, it was said. But she felt no better.

"Janey." His voice was soft and caring, caressing. "Are you really blaming yourself? Come on, that's absurd."

"No, it's not. Well, of course it is *logically*, but in my gut I've always thought that if I wished for something hard enough, it would come true."

"What you're saying is that you've been able to set high standards for yourself and you've lived up to them. But this is different."

"It is and it isn't. But I can't help it if I feel miserable and guilty, Graham." She finally looked up at him.

"It's okay to *feel*, Jane. And if you feel guilty then go ahead. It'll pass. You're just upset right now and Lord knows you have a right to be. Norma has been very kind to you these past weeks."

"Almost like a mother."

"I know. And believe me, when she wakes up from surgery and you tell her all about how you wished this on her—" he smiled and leaned close "—Norma will have a good laugh along with you."

"Is she going to wake up, Graham? Is she?"

Of course, he had no answer. They left the cafeteria and headed back up to the third floor. There was still no news, nothing save a quick word from the desk nurse after her lunch hour.

"It's been over three hours," Martin said with a sigh as he wheeled his chair around the confined space of the lounge. "Why don't they let us know something!" He stopped moving and put his face in his hands.

The waiting was terrible, as if they were all being tested for some kind of masochistic endurance. But it didn't stop; there was no letup of emotion or the pain of their nerves being scraped raw.

Donna showed up at 1:30 p.m. Frank, amazingly, was with her, clean shaven, in a decent sport shirt, looking as solemn as the rest of them. "Peter just got out of the police station," Donna told everyone, "and he offered to man the front desk for me. He looked awful," she said, chewing her gum madly, as nervous as they all were. "And he's worried sick about Norma."

"Was Peter able to tell the police anything?" Lew wanted to know.

"Not much," she replied. "There were two of them. Big men. Oh, yeah, they were wearing those ski-type masks. Black and red, I think Peter said." She shrugged, tucking her arm into Frank's. "They got away with the jewelry, though," breathed Donna. "He said Norma should have just let them go."

"It was her *job*!" Martin Stedman came half out of his chair until Jane managed to calm him down.

"Peter was only worried, I'm sure," Jane said. "He didn't mean anything by it. Really."

"She's a hero," Lew was quick to add.

"A *heroine*," said Jane, patting Martin's arm.

The schoolroom clock crawled along at a snail's pace. 2:10. 2:15. At 2:19 the door swung open and a tall man in blood-splattered greens with his mask hanging around his neck stood on the threshold.

They all froze.

He pulled off his cap showing thick sandy hair and his lips split into a smile.

THAT HAD BEEN ON MONDAY. By Thursday Norma was moved from the Intensive Care Unit into a private room. Several of Mercury's employees were waiting down the hall for the nurse's okay to visit her. Jane was one of them. So was Graham, who had barely left Jane's side since the morning of the shooting. Even Lily Sypnewski was there, having been informed by Jane as to Norma's condition. Her diminutive figure was dressed in a mauve flowered caftan that dragged on the floor in the back. She kept muttering that she hated hospitals and reaching for her cigarettes, then remembering the No Smoking sign, she muttered some more.

"Damn fool job for anyone," she said to Jane, her fingers twitching toward the sagging pocket where she kept the cigarette pack.

"Now, you can't stay too long," the nurse admonished the eager entourage.

The first thing that met Jane's eyes was the oxygen tube, then a wire or two hooked to a blood-pressure apparatus and a heart monitor. Jane was intensely relieved to see Norma propped up and smiling, even though there was no color in her cheeks.

"Well, hello," she said, faintly embarrassed by all the to-do. "My, my. Everyone is here."

There were flowers all around and everyone chatted with Norma, making careful, cheerful small talk.

Graham said, "It's great to see you out of Intensive Care."

Lew asked, "Hey, when are you going to quit faking it and get back on the job!"

Peter chimed in with, "You know, you took a shot aimed at me."

"Nonsense," Norma responded. "I was stupid enough to chase those thugs down that alley." And then Peter and Norma had to rehash the whole incident while the others listened raptly. It seemed that while the two of them were making a crosstown jewelry delivery for a store that was moving, the robbers appeared as if from thin air, wearing ski masks, shoving Peter and Norma back in their car while wresting the briefcase from Peter.

"One of them had a gun," said Norma. "I should have let him go but all those years with the police... I just couldn't."

"Norma chased them down an alley," put in Peter. "But what gets me is why the thieves made a hit on us when there was a bodyguard along. They've never done that before."

"Norma was assigned to go along at the last minute," Lew said slowly, as if coming to a profound realization. "Maybe the crooks expected you to be alone."

All the talk about the robbery and Norma chasing the men down the alley and getting caught by a stray bullet barely scratched Jane's consciousness. She was thinking, instead, that it could have been *her* accompanying Peter that morning except that she'd been late getting to the office.

Had Norma gone in Jane's place because she'd been late to work? Oh, no...

"I really blew it, Lew," Norma was saying. "You could tell those two jerks were amateurs by the way they moved and handled the gun. I should never have underestimated them. I'm very sorry."

"Norma," Lew said, "it could have happened to anyone. It's not your fault. Hell, and don't get me wrong because I have the utmost respect for New York's finest, but Detective Sorello should have come up with a lead by now."

Norma nodded.

"But don't you worry, we'll get them. They'll pay for what they did to you."

"I worry about your insurance, Lew," Norma said. "It was bad enough and now this . . ."

"It's all going to work out in the end," answered Lew, "and I'll get my policy renewed. Now, you just rest and get better. Hear me?"

Norma smiled and nodded and the nurse came in, wagging her finger. "You'll have to leave now and let Mrs. Stedman be."

"Nurse," said Norma, "can I have a minute, please." Then she looked at Jane. "You stay, Jane. Just for a minute, please."

The nurse looked disapproving but did leave the room with the others, calling over her starched white shoulder, "I'll be keeping track of the time."

"Are you sure you shouldn't be resting?" Jane cautioned.

Norma beckoned Jane closer. "Later. I can sleep later. I had to talk to you alone." Then, when Jane was about to say something, Norma raised her hand. "I want you to hear me out. And remember, I've got a lot of years of experience and I'm not going to tell you this lightly, Jane. You just be brave for me, won't you?" Norma sounded a little breathless.

"Of course."

"Someone at Mercury is tipping off the robbers, Jane. I'm positive now. You see, I was asked to go with Peter only that morning—a last-minute decision on Lew's part because this other job I was supposed to go on was delayed."

"Did you go with Peter in my place?" Jane blurted out, unable to let the question rest another moment.

Norma raised a brow and looked at Jane for a second. Then she frowned. "Good Lord, girl, has *that* been on your mind all along? Listen to me now. My stupid mistake was none of your doing. Just get that bee out of your bonnet, you got that?"

Jane felt a surge of welcome relief. She squeezed Norma's hand and felt a reassuring, surprisingly strong clasp in return and smiled widely at her. "Boy, does that make me feel better! Now, you get some rest, Norma. The nurse said—"

"Wait a minute, Jane. Damn! These painkillers they dose me with make me so fuzzy. I hate them!"

"Norma—"

"Listen to me. We've got a problem to take care of. Jane, those thieves hit Peter because they'd been told he would be alone. And they were waiting for him. It was real obvious to me that they were hesitant the minute they saw me along. Surprised was the impression I got."

"So you think one of the masked men is a Mercury employee or getting information from a Mercury employee."

"Exactly. And, believe me, this is no news at Mercury, either. Detective Sorello questioned all of us, even asked if we would take lie detector tests. I wasn't sure if you were aware..." She grimaced in pain.

"Oh, I heard the scuttlebutt. Donna, you know. Now, Norma, maybe you better take it easy."

"Never mind my aches and pains. Anyway, we can eliminate you as a suspect because you weren't around for the earlier robberies," said Norma with assurance. "And it isn't me. Now, Donna we know was on the switchboard and Kelly, I'm told, was in Boston. Lukas, as well, was at Mercury all morning, and Rick showed up late for work but I doubt if he could have gotten across town and back that fast. You see, I've had plenty of time to think about this."

"Okay, maybe that's all true," Jane conceded, "but that sure doesn't mean one of them couldn't be in cahoots with the robbers."

"No, it doesn't. I'm merely eliminating possibilities. My old police brain working away." She cleared her throat roughly.

"Are you all right?"

"Fine. Now, let's see," said Norma, "there's Lew."

"But Lew *owns* Mercury!"

"So what? If he's in a financial bind he wouldn't be the first to rob his own place, collect the insurance and still have the goods to fence. It's done all the time, believe me."

Norma moved restlessly, as if searching for a more comfortable position. It made Jane terribly anxious and, besides, the nurse would be back any second. "Can I do something, Norma? Your pillows? A glass of water? I think you've talked enough."

"Listen to me," Norma said hoarsely. "You're the only one I can trust."

"I can't accept that it could be Lew."

"Hmm. Well, then, you won't like this, Jane, but there's always Graham Smith."

"Graham?"

"Yes. I know you two are—let's say, close—but, Jane, there's something funny about that guy. He's too slippery, too charming. Too sophisticated."

"No." Norma must be crazy, Jane thought in confusion. The drugs they were giving her . . .

"Think about it. The robbers were both big men. Graham's six one or two, isn't he? And he wasn't around that morning, was he?"

Jane's heart stopped, remembering the phone ringing and ringing at his place.

"I can see him as the Gentleman Thief. Oh, yes, he'd fit the bill exactly. And these old instincts of mine are rarely wrong."

Norma's voice was weaker. Jane should leave but she couldn't, not now. She had to convince Norma that she was wrong about Graham. She turned her back so Norma couldn't see the anguish on her face. "You're wrong, it's not him. He'd never hurt Lew. He wouldn't harm a fly, I know him too well."

But Norma wasn't through. "Jane, I realize this is the last thing you want to hear, but in my book, he's a prime suspect. And he may not even think he's hurting Lew. He might think the insurance company can afford losses."

"Not Graham." Jane came back around to face Norma. Her chest was aching. "You're my friend, Norma, and God knows I respect you. But on this one you're wrong."

"You're a sharp girl," Norma was saying, "and..."

But she couldn't finish because the nurse had pushed open the door and was ordering, "Out now, miss. I left you too long as it is!"

Jane turned to leave, her brain spinning.

"One more second," pleaded Norma. "Jane, you'll be going to Amsterdam now, you realize. You've got to be careful. It's all on your shoulders. Please, be careful. Watch Graham Smith!"

"You're wrong about him," reiterated Jane shakily. "I'll be perfectly fine. I've got to go. Take care, Norma." And Jane was out the door. For a long moment she leaned her back to the wall and breathed deeply. Poor, poor Norma! The shock, the wound, all the drugs they were pumping into her—no wonder she was suffering delusions.

Graham was standing down the corridor, talking to Lew while he waited for her. She studied him carefully from afar, saw the way he stood with his feet planted apart and his hands negligently in his jacket pockets. She took in the tilt of his head, the strong neck and shoulders, the thick strawberry-blond hair that she'd run her fingers through so lovingly, so often. He was a good man, a wonderful, loving man who simply liked to live life to its fullest.

Norma was sure reaching! Poor woman.

Jane collected herself, calmer now, and went to join the two men.

"Is Norma all right?" asked Lew, his graying brow furrowed.

"She's very tired, I think," said Jane, trying to sound casual. She felt Graham taking her hand. "She only wanted to tell me to be careful from now on." Jane smiled. "But you know me, I'm always careful."

"Yes, of course you are," Lew replied. "But Norma is right. You're going to really have to be on your toes now, Jane Manning." He made a grumbling sound in his throat then added, "I'm off to the police station. It's time I start pushing them for some answers. See you all later." And he disappeared into the elevator.

"Well," began Graham, "it's been a rough few days, hasn't it?" He reached up and pushed the bangs away from Jane's forehead in an affectionate, possessive gesture. "Can I buy you dinner, pretty lady?"

"Sure," said Jane staunchly, "a pizza. From Mario's."

"Mario's it is."

They walked onto the next elevator hand in hand and Jane allowed herself to mull over Norma's wild accusation. And, Jane decided firmly, that was exactly what it was: wild.

CHAPTER TWELVE

"I DON'T LIKE IT," said Lew. "Jane is very new to this profession. We're pushing her too fast and too hard."

Graham fiddled with a pencil sharpener on Lew's desk. "Yeah, I know the diamond job is risky." He glanced up at his friend and frowned. "And it's not that I don't trust Jane. Hell, she's good and her training is tops.... It's just that Norma has had twenty years' experience...." His voice faded and he and Lew exchanged expressions that said: and look what happened to Norma!

"I don't see where there's a choice, though," said Lew. "Everybody in the office knows about the job now and Jane is all we've got. I can't hire someone and have him, or whoever, ready before you leave. There's no time."

"Lew, I don't know. I'd really rather do this job by myself. You know Jane and I—"

"Yes, I know," said Lew humorously.

"Well, it's not such a great idea to be emotionally involved with your bodyguard, for heaven's sake."

"I've taken that into consideration. You're a professional, Graham. I trust you. And if it doesn't work, you always have the option of sending her back and finishing the job alone."

"Okay, okay. But I think you're wrong about one thing, Lew. Jane should be in on the whole plan."

Lew shook his head. "I can't allow you to tell her. Oh, as soon as you leave New York you can let her know that you're hoping to lure the crooks and nab them—it would be madness *not* to tell her that.''

"And unfair.''

"Very. But I won't have you telling her about the rest. I know it's your contingency plan and it's a damn solid one, clever. But in this office only the two of us are going to be in on it and that's final.''

"But who could Jane tell? Especially after we leave for Amsterdam?''

"How should I know? I just want it that way. I'm going by the book and the rules say the fewer who know the better. And besides,'' said Lew, "you and Jane are going to catch those crooks long before your contingency plan is even needed.''

"I never knew you to be such an optimist,'' said Graham teasingly.

"Well, you are going to get them, aren't you?''

"Sure, like I said, they're apt to be unarmed on this one because they won't be able to get a gun through airport security. Unless, and it's a possibility, they wait to snatch the stones until we get back to New York but I'm betting a hit will happen in Europe. The diamonds are worth too much to pass up and if they wait till we're back in the city to go for them, they'll have to figure they've got fewer options. In Europe,'' Graham mused, "they'll be able to bide their time and pick the most opportune moment.''

"And if they don't,'' Lew said, "you put into effect plan B.''

"Exactly. I'll make it so damn easy to steal the stones they won't be able to resist!''

"Hell,'' Lew said with a chuckle, "they'll probably think you're stealing them yourself.''

Graham's face dropped. "That's an ugly thought.''

"Just joking, son.''

"Real funny, Lew."

All the way home to his apartment Graham mulled over this new development: Jane was to accompany him to Amsterdam. The notion unsettled him and it must be because there was the possibility of danger to her. Certainly he was not feeling his usual carefree self as he strode along Seventh Avenue.

Of course, everything would go as smooth as silk. The crooks would try for the diamonds and he and Jane would thwart their attempt with ease. Heck, even Norma had said the creeps were amateurs! It was only Norma's mistake that had gotten her shot. Why, if the woman had known how to use her hands, she never would have had to chase the thieves down an alley! "Guns," he mumbled to himself, "useless hunks of metal."

Now, Jane was an expert with her hands. No problem there. Well, it wasn't going to do any good to stew over the situation. They'd do just fine in Amsterdam, he decided, feeling better.

Taking his apartment steps by two, Graham thought of Jane inside his place, cooking their dinner at that very moment. It was like coming home to a wife, being greeted by succulent aromas and a loving smile. How pleasant, how *right*.

"Hi, Jane!" he called, tossing his linen jacket carelessly onto the couch. "I'm home!"

"In the kitchen," came her reply.

"Mmm, what smells so good?" He gave her cheek a kiss, picking up the pot and pan lids. "Spaghetti?"

"Yes."

He opened the fridge and took out a Heineken and searched his junk drawer for the opener. "How did your trip with Kelly go?"

"All right." She wiped her hands on a dishtowel and began pressing garlic for the bread.

"What's the matter," he said lightly, "did Kelly make a pass? If he did..." Graham came up behind her and wrapped his arms around her waist, pulling Jane back against him.

"Stop it," she said, "I'm trying to clean up this garlic mess."

He nibbled her ear until she squirmed away. *"Graham."*

"Oh, all right." He let her go and backed off, leaning against a counter and sipping on his beer. Something was wrong. "What is it, Jane?"

"Nothing," she replied offhandedly. "I'm a little tired."

"Then we'll clean up here and go out to eat. You should have said something earlier."

"Everything's nearly done."

"So we'll eat here and I'll do all the cleanup."

"You're always so accommodating."

Of course, thought Graham, it was her time of the month. That must be it. He smiled, relieved, but then remembered: she'd had it last week. His mood flip-flopped. Frown lines deepened around his mouth. "Any trouble delivering those fashion designs?" he asked in a neutral tone.

She shook her head. "Everything went smoothly."

"Are you feeling all right?" He took a long swig of beer and watched her over the neck of the bottle.

"You're asking a lot of questions, aren't you?"

"Just making conversation. If you want, we don't have to talk." Maybe some music, some soft, easy listening music. Barry Manilow. Graham went into the living room and put on a cassette. There, that was nice and relaxing.

Having had an early lunch, Graham stuffed himself with the pasta and garlic bread. Jane, however, toyed with her spaghetti and barely looked at him. Then, when they were clearing the table, Jane dropped a dirty fork on the carpet and burst into tears.

Graham had had enough. He took the rest of the dishes from her, set them down roughly on the kitchen counter and pulled her into his arms. "Out with it," he said. "I know you too well and something's very wrong."

"It's just…Norma." She tried to free herself but he was having none of it.

"What about Norma?"

"Oh, Graham…she…" And he thought Jane was about to say something profound but instead she said, "I'm worried she won't recover."

"What?"

"You know. She could have a relapse."

"That's ridiculous, Jane. Now tell me the truth."

This time Jane managed to pull away from him; she was strong and to keep her imprisoned would have been a real struggle, one Graham wasn't so sure he'd win.

"Jane," he tried again, "I know you too well. I wish you'd be honest with me. Is it the trip to Amsterdam? Are you getting nervous?"

She stood several paces from him and put her hands on her hips. "I am *not* getting nervous. Now you're being ridiculous."

"Then what is it?"

"I'm—" she looked away "—not feeling well. Maybe a cold coming on or something."

"That's it?"

She nodded. But Graham didn't really buy her explanation. Jane was not the type to let a few sniffles get her down. He let it drop, however, deciding that she was feeling anxious about the upcoming trip and didn't want to admit it. Sure, that was all there was to it.

Jane seemed better as they did the dishes together, even slopping soap suds on his shirt once when he got in the way and laughing. It was good to hear her laugh. Then, after everything was tidied up they took brandies into the living room and sat close together on the couch.

"Listen," began Jane, relaxing back onto the cushions and curling her feet beneath her, "I'm sorry about earlier. That's not like me."

"All is forgiven."

"You're too good to me."

"Don't I know it!" He rose, put on another cassette, a mood setter, a slow, easy James Taylor recording, and turned down the lights. "Feeling sexy?" he teased, sitting back down and taking her brandy from her.

Jane wore a skirt, no stockings and a loose bittersweet-red shirt with buttons all the way down the front. He began with the first button, unfastening it, exposing the top of her bra, kissing the soft, satin-smooth flesh of her breasts. Moving on to the next button and the next, he kissed her each time languidly, his lips silk against her own smooth skin. Her belly. He felt her quiver.

"Janey," he whispered.

He reached around her back and unfastened her bra; it sagged below her breasts, which he cupped in both hands and caressed with his lips, one breast at a time, slowly, savoring her taste, flicking his tongue across her nipples until they hardened. This was going to be a long, delicious night, he decided, feeling himself pulse with expectation.

He kissed the softness of her belly above the waistline of her skirt and eased her shirt off her shoulders, his hands returning to cup her breasts, his mouth moving up again to taste her. As she moved and began to twist, her skirt hitched itself up and Graham brought a hand to her thigh and traced tiny, teasing patterns. A moment later, his hand slipped beneath the elastic of her panties, cupping her gently while his other hand kneaded a breast and his mouth drew a peak into its hungry warmth.

"Oh, Jane," he groaned against her, "I can never get enough of you."

Deciding that they couldn't wait until they got upstairs, he rose for a moment and began to undo his shirt. She looked so lovely lying there, half-dressed, her skin glowing peachy in the dim light, her mouth rosy and parted. And yet, somehow, as she watched him shed his shirt and unfasten his belt, there was a kind of sadness in those green eyes, a sadness and . . . indecision.

But why? What had happened between them? If only he could reach her tonight. He sat down beside her again and pushed her hair back behind one pale perfectly formed ear. "Are you okay, Janey?"

Her face was averted and he could only see the plane of her cheek, her little nose sprinkled with freckles, her eyelashes fanning out on her cheek. She straightened and pulled her blouse together then shook her head. "I guess I'm not feeling too great," she said in that throaty voice of hers. "Are you mad?"

"Of course I'm not. You should have told me, though. I want our lovemaking to be special for both of us."

"I know. Me, too." She reached up and pulled his head down and kissed him. "I'm just feeling off tonight. You know."

"Sure, I'm being a selfish lecher."

"Would you . . . mind taking me home?"

"Of course not," he replied, lying through his teeth. He minded very much but if Jane wasn't in the mood, well, he'd have to respect her wishes.

A half hour later they kissed good-night. It was a strained leave-taking, unlike any of the others they'd had.

"I'm sorry," Jane whispered. "I'll be better tomorrow."

"Sure, I'll call you, okay?"

She nodded and Graham watched her walk away from him to the door of her apartment building. Janey, tall and lovely. Was she really coming down with something? Maybe it was family trouble or an old boyfriend, that one she'd mentioned. Something at work? He wished she'd confide in him. Well, maybe it was just a matter of time. After all, she hadn't known him very long and he had no right to pry.

He waited until she was safely inside before glancing in his side mirror and pulling out into the traffic. A light rain began to fall and he turned on his wipers, idly watching them swish back and forth as he waited at a stoplight. How many women, he wondered, had he known in his thirty-three years? A few, anyway. And how many had stayed around? None. Was it because he'd scared them all off? Or because he really hadn't loved any of them? It was both, he decided, staring, hypnotized, at the bleary red stoplight.

Oh well, he was damn glad they'd all flown. If they hadn't, he'd never have found his Janey, his solid and steady lady who knew where she was going and realized her own worth and who was not in the least intimidated by his life-style.

Ah . . . Janey.

Another light. The drizzling rain continued, streaking his side windows, causing the city lights to diffuse colorfully in the glass.

Green light. He let the clutch out and moved with the flow of traffic. He knew—or at least hoped—he'd be involved with Jane for a very long time. Forever would suit him. Of course, there would be marriage, a couple of kids. He'd like one with clear green eyes just like Jane's. Naturally, he'd still travel as the courier business suited his need for action and diversity but he'd be able to pick and choose his jobs, stay home if he liked. That was okay; plenty of husbands had families and traveled. No problem...

Husbands!

Graham's mind exploded with the notion as the light turned yellow, then red. Husband! Quicksilver—in love and married? Holy cow.

He never braked for the light nor did he hear the scream of the siren behind him—not for two blocks, anyway.

JANE ROUNDED THE CORNER of 59th and Madison and made for Central Park. Already a half hour into her jog, the oxygen level in her brain had lowered, leaving her with a sort of euphoric well-being in which thoughts came at random, some crystal clear, others fog-bound and quickly lost. Every so often she remembered Graham. A spaghetti dinner, the smell of garlic and onions cooking, a beer in his hand. Her well-being fled.

She looked at her watch as she entered the park: 6:36 a.m. How *could* she have been so curt with him? Sure, anyone would have been upset by Norma's accusations and her warning but a sensible adult would have confided in Graham. A razor-sharp thought sliced through her head: *unless that sensible, reasoning adult no longer trusted him a hundred percent.*

"Damn," she said, breathing heavily. It had dawned cloudless and pleasantly cool in the city. It should have been a beautiful morning to Jane because she could add an extra few minutes to her run when the humidity level was lower. Instead she was beginning to feel sluggish.

6:39. At this rate she'd be dragging by the time she made her way back to the apartment. It was funny, Jane realized, but negative thinking affected every muscle, every bone and fiber of her body.

Why had she let Norma get to her? Graham had tried to make love to her. Yes, on the couch. Jane had a vivid mental picture flash in her brain of him standing above her and she recalled the feeling of reluctance that had swept her even as her insides seemed to be melting.

6:44. Another jogger passed her going the opposite way. He waved, breathed, "Morning," and his dog followed Jane for a few feet until the jogger called him away. At this hour the park was never truly empty. A bum or two slept on a bench, a bicycler sped by. There were always joggers and stray pets on the path. She circled the reservoir on her usual route. Sweat was now soaking her headband and the back of her T-shirt flapped against her skin wetly. She stayed close to the perimeter of the park, saw a mounted policeman, waved at him.

But if she trusted Graham, say, ninety percent, what exactly comprised the other ten percent? Doubt, of course. A small seed planted by Norma Stedman that had begun to swell by the evening before when Jane had cooked dinner.

Oh, boy! What if that seed grew and blossomed and became full-blown mistrust? She couldn't let that happen. My God, she was falling head over heels in love and she wasn't going to let a silly warning ruin a great relationship when she knew in her heart Norma was dead wrong.

6:56. Jane took a curve in the path and headed toward one of the park's many exits. She decided that by tomorrow morning—when they were to fly to Amsterdam—she'd have this unsettling doubt erased from her thoughts. It was all a matter of perspective, getting things straight. Very simple.

6:57. From behind her came the scratching sound of branch moving against branch, a twig breaking underfoot...

Jane spun around instinctively in time to ward off a blow with her forearm. She ducked, stepping backward to brace herself for another blow, then knocked the stranger's arm away, sidestepping agilely, cat-quick, panting evenly. The strike from the big man's fist had missed its mark entirely, causing him to stumble and Jane, arms thrust out for balance, kicked out and upward with a foot and caught the mugger squarely in the groin.

There was a deep, throaty groan of pain as he bent over and clasped at his crotch. He was backing off, staggering toward the bushes and Jane started after him. No way was this creep going to escape!

"Hold up there," came a command. Jane glanced quickly, afraid for a moment her mugger wasn't alone, but it was the park policeman, mounted still, trotting along a grassy embankment. "Hold it right there!" he called again but already, in the instant Jane had turned to look at the policeman, the mugger had ducked into the bushes and was out of sight.

"Damn!" she said, still panting.

"Stay where you are," called the policeman but Jane knew it was completely useless to pursue the thug—the horse couldn't make it through the undergrowth and Jane was winded. Her attacker had gotten away!

"Just swell," she grumbled, her hands on her hips, sucking in a lungful of air.

The police at the uptown station let her call Mercury. "Donna," she said, "I'm going to be running late. I'm with the police and have to make a report. No, everything's fine. I was jogging and almost got mugged.... Yes, I hurt him

pretty good.... No, he got away. Listen, I have to go....
Okay, see you in a couple of hours. Bye.''

Jane thought she was being helpful to the police but the
sergeant, a tall, thin, wiry man with kinky hair and horn-
rimmed glasses, obviously thought otherwise. Lazily, with
apparent unconcern, he took down the information given
him by Jane.

"Anything else?" he asked, sounding bored.

"A nylon stocking mask, long-sleeved checkered shirt...
I did tell you blue and white with shots of rust in it?"

"Sure, yeah, I got that down. Go on."

"Khaki trousers, Wilson tennis shoes."

"Yeah, Wilson, got that, too."

"I told you he was six feet and about two hundred
pounds."

"Sure."

"Oh, and his hair was very dark."

"You could tell that under the nylon?" asked the sergeant with deliberate sarcasm.

"Yes, I told you, I've been taught to observe."

"Isn't that nice."

Jane tried to keep her temper in check. "Are you really
interested in this, sergeant," she snapped, "or am I wasting my time?"

"Now, now, miss. I'm doing my best. You know how
many muggings there are in this city on an average day?"

"I read the papers. Now you tell me, how many victims
can remember so many details?"

He finally relented and grinned at her. "Very few, miss."

Jane sat back in her chair smugly. "So what now? Is
there any hope of apprehending this man?"

"To be honest, no. But if he ever gets caught, the information you've given me will come up out of the computer
and we can always call you in for an ID."

"I guess you never know."

"Never do, miss."

Jane rose to leave. "You know," she said pensively, "what I can't figure out is what he wanted from me. I mean, I wasn't wearing any jewelry, or carrying a wallet or purse."

"Rape, most likely, miss."

"Maybe," said Jane, without conviction.

It wasn't until she was back home, in the shower with shampoo dripping in her eyes, that it occurred to Jane the mugger might well have been after *her* specifically. First Norma—of course, that had been an accident—but was there a connection somehow? Norma was out of the way. Did someone want Jane laid up in a hospital as well? And if so, that would leave Graham very much alone and without protection in Amsterdam.

And then on the heels of that supposition came another, causing goose bumps to rise on her flesh despite the steaming hot water. Did Graham himself want to get his bodyguard out of the way?

CHAPTER THIRTEEN

THE 747 ALTERED COURSE SLIGHTLY and the sun, fiercely brilliant at forty thousand feet, speared into the windows on the right side of the plane and struck Graham dead in the face. He opened his eyes halfway and watched Jane from between his lashes. She was no longer reading but was sitting very still, staring out of the window, her face turned away from him. He could see the curving fan of her dark hair against her cheek, the sweep of her jawline, the corner of her mouth, that sweet, clinging mouth. Her hands were in her lap, small, strong hands with no-nonsense short fingernails. Those hands, Graham knew, could gentle a horse, break an assailant's wrist or drive him crazy with their touch.

He loved to watch her, sometimes at night waking to stare at her asleep or, if she wasn't there, to imagine how she looked in her own bed. He was getting awfully used to her, liking her more and more. He dared not say he *loved* her, not even to himself, but he couldn't imagine life without her. Graham knew himself well enough to know he wasn't about to turn down what fate had offered him and the idea of settling down didn't seem so dull anymore, at least not with Jane Manning.

She sighed and looked down at the book in her lap. Her brow was creased. He didn't blame her for being nervous; this was her first big job. Ten million in diamonds even made *him* nervous.

It was darn near impossible to think of Jane as his bodyguard. Although he'd die before admitting it to her, Graham felt very protective of Jane, as if the roles were reversed. Now, Norma, okay, he'd go along comfortably with her guarding him, but not with Jane. It must have been some old-fashioned previously buried instinct inside him but there it was—Jane was his lady and it should be him taking care of her.

Nevertheless he had a job to do for Lew. He supposed it was high time he let Jane in on the fact that they were to set themselves up as bait. She had to be forewarned and she had to cooperate. He had a feeling, however, that she wasn't going to like it one bit. And what on earth was he going to do if he ever had to fall back on his secret contingency plan? She'd like that even less.

He swallowed hard and broached the subject.

"You mean you told everyone in the office deliberately?" she asked in alarm when he had finished.

"We had to. Lew wants the thieves to follow us." If he blamed everything on Lew maybe she'd be easier to convince.

"That's *insane.*"

"But don't you see, the idea is to force them into making a try for the diamonds so we can catch them."

"The police are supposed to catch criminals," she said coldly.

"They've been trying for months and have come up with nothing. Lew doesn't have time to wait. By the time the cops find the thieves Mercury will be history."

She was stubbornly silent.

"So we're supposed to expose ourself a bit and keep a sharp eye out."

"I'd keep an eye out, anyway," she muttered.

"I know you would. But forewarned is forearmed, they say."

"Look, Graham, my job is to *prevent* attacks, not *allow* them. Rob taught us that if our charge was attacked, we'd already failed." Her voice rose a little.

"In this case we have to bend the rules a bit. You can see how important this is, Janey."

"Don't you Janey me! I don't like this. I don't like it at all. Lew should have told me himself if he wanted me to do it."

The man in the aisle seat had an ear cocked to the conversation, Graham was sure. He put a hand on Jane's arm to quiet her down. "Maybe Lew should have told you. That's my fault. I told him I'd take care of it," he lied.

"You figured I'd just go along without a question? Graham, you should know me better. My job is to protect you, not to set you up like bait."

A little boy's head popped up over the seat in front of them and the child stared curiously, thumb in mouth, until he was snatched down by his invisible mother.

"Jane, please, we'll discuss it later," Graham said quietly.

"Don't patronize me!"

Someone across the aisle leaned forward and stared over at Jane. Graham flinched inwardly.

"I'll send you back on the next plane," he said half-jokingly, trying to defuse her indignation.

"Try it!" Jane snapped, her small freckled nose thrust into his face.

This was awful. What had happened to his sweet, loving, passionate Janey? "Listen," he tried, "if you'd just think about the plan, you'd realize—"

"I know my job, Graham, and nothing is going to change my mind!"

In a minute, he knew, a full-fledged argument was going to erupt. Everyone on the plane would know their business and the thieves could even be on this flight!

"Shh," he said, smiling, putting a finger to his lips, "everyone's listening."

"So what? I can't believe you're worried about your image at a time like this!"

He'd seen it in an old Cary Grant movie; it had worked then, why not now? Graham leaped to his feet, unintentionally bumping his head on the luggage rack and said loudly, "All right, you win! I'll apologize to your mother, just put the blasted ring back on. We can't postpone the wedding again, Thelma!"

Up and down the aisle of the plane giggles broke out while Jane sat in her seat, frozen in mortification, her cheeks flaming scarlet. It was half an hour before she spoke. "I'll get you for this, buster," she warned. But she was trying not to smile.

They checked into a hotel near the diamond exchange, within the ring of concentric canals that encircled the city. It was a tall, narrow, gabled hotel called the Canal House, small and homey and charmingly Dutch.

"I really prefer this hotel to the big modern ones. I hope you like it, Jane," Graham said, watching her reactions as she stood in front of the place, looking up at the fanciful gables and staunch, rosy, seventeenth-century brick and baroque window motifs.

"It's beautiful, it's wonderful, Graham!" she exclaimed and he was inordinately pleased that she liked it.

The Canal House was even more picturesque inside. Narrow and cozy with ruffled lace curtains, dark beams and knickknacks, antique oil paintings on the walls—Dutch masters, naturally—and the gleam of a well-beloved old home.

"Do we need two rooms?" he asked, only half teasing.

"One will do," she said, straight-faced. She was getting nervous again. He wished he could get her to relax, to enjoy Amsterdam, at least for tonight. And he wished, too, that he could muster the courage to ask her if she'd decided to go along with his plan but he'd better give her more time to mull the whole thing over.

"Come on, now," he ventured when they were in their room. "Don't worry about a thing, at least until tomorrow. I want to show you this city, Jane. I want you to enjoy it." He pulled her close and kissed her forehead. "You've never been to Europe before. This is a special time and, just think, we can share it."

She tilted her face up to his, searched his eyes deeply and smiled wanly.

Graham put his hands on her shoulders, leaned close and kissed her freckled nose. "You know," he said, "I'm dying to hold you, Janey. I can't stand this tension between us."

"Neither can I." Her voice was so sincere, so soft and full of pain that his heart turned to putty.

"Well, what are we going to do about it?" he asked.

Her emerald-green eyes still held his with deep sadness then dropped. "I don't know. Maybe after the diamonds..."

He continued to hold her but it was as if he could feel her flesh shrinking away from him. He let his hands fall.

Jane gave a short, constrained laugh. "It's getting dark in here, Graham. It's getting late. If we're going to see the city..."

It was 7:00 p.m. and quite dark out, due to Amsterdam's northerly latitude; outside their narrow, lace-curtained window the night was damp and cool, the city's endless, self-indulgent nightlife illuminated brightly by streetlights that reflected on the canals.

Jane put a thin, rust-colored sweater and tweed wool blazer over her corduroy skirt, brushed her hair, redid her mascara and lipstick. Graham merely slipped on a navy-blue crewneck sweater under his gray herringbone sport coat. They'd both packed extremely lightly, using only a small carry-on bag each. There was nothing worse for a courier than to have to wait in a large, noisy, unruly crowd for luggage to be unloaded from a plane.

"Have I got a surprise for you!" he said as he locked the door behind them.

"Oh, no, not another one of your surprises!"

There, that was better. She was beginning to relax now.

"Ever hear of *rijsttafel*?"

"No, what is it?"

"Well, it's a kind of meal. It means, literally, 'rice table' in Dutch. But it's Indonesian. The Netherlands ruled the East Indies for hundreds of years and this is one of the few remaining customs."

"There are Indonesian restaurants in Amsterdam?"

"All over. We're going to a very special one. It's called the Bali."

There were slim, sloe-eyed waitresses in sarongs, fake palms and heavy wooden, Dutch-style tables in the restaurant. Jane took a menu and looked at it, then laughed. "You order. I'm lost."

He got the "deluxe combination." "Now watch out, some of this stuff is hot."

The waitress brought seemingly dozens of tiny, delicate porcelain bowls, each one filled with a spicy, delectable dish, each one with an odd Indonesian name: *saté babi*, bite-sized morsels of skewered pork cooked in a mouth-watering peanut sauce; *loempia*, a mixture of bean sprouts and vegetables wrapped in waferlike pastry and deep-fried, *kroepoek*, a large, crunchy prawn cracker. And rice, of course, to accompany every dish. Some of the flavors were vaguely reminiscent of Chinese food, some of East Indian. It was a mélange of delicacies.

"Where do I start?" Jane wondered aloud.

She exclaimed over each different flavor. "Chilis and peanuts?" she asked. "Fish with something . . ."

"Coconut milk and coriander," Graham supplied and she looked at him with respectful surprise.

He delighted in her pleasure. She was discovering something new and he loved her lack of sophisticated veneer. She showed her enjoyment. She was real, absolutely true to herself.

"This is almost better than Colorado beef!" she joked, tasting the suckling pig in a spicy sauce.

He watched her chew and swallow, watched the tip of her tongue flick a bit of sauce from her upper lip. Her face shone in the dim overhead lighting, her green eyes sparkled and her freckled nose wrinkled experimentally over each new dish. "Um, this is wonderful, some kind of shredded beef and ginger. And lots of garlic."

She held the fork out to him and he tasted it. What fun he and Jane could have together, years of fun, traveling, exploring, sailing the *Renée*, raising a family.

"Aren't you hungry?" she was asking.

"I've eaten plenty," he said with a smile.

"I was afraid I'd stuffed it all down. What a pig I am," she said without self-consciousness. "James always claimed I out-ate him two to one."

"You'd never know it to look at you," Graham answered.

"Let's walk around some," Jane suggested as they left the restaurant. "I want to see this city up close."

"Too bad we don't have longer. I'd love to take you to the Rijksmuseum—to see the Rembrandts—and Rembrandt's house. The van Gogh Museum, too. And then, outside of Amsterdam, are the windmills and tulip fields and dikes.''

"Next time," she said wistfully.

Graham took her hand as they walked along the Herengracht, "Gentlemen's Canal," the most important of the three canal rings built in the 1600s. Trees lined the banks. Tall, narrow, gabled houses, all four stories high, stood in sober ranks along the street, throwing wavering squares of light into the water. A motor launch chugged by and, in its rippled wake, the houses' long reflections in the water suddenly fractured into splinters of liquid luminescence. Jane drew in her breath in wonder and Graham squeezed her hand. "Nice, huh?" he murmured into her ear.

"It's so different," she replied, "so pretty. These houses, why, they've been lived in so long, so much longer than I can even imagine."

"Europe *is* old," he agreed.

The buildings lining the canals reflected the nature of the people: conservative, cautious about wasting precious space, but not above demonstrating their success. The upper stories of the houses had been used for storing tea, spices and furs, the riches of the Dutch colonies. Graham pointed out to Jane the heavy beams that jutted out from their topmost gables. "All that's missing are ropes and men to pull aloft." Then he smiled and added, "It's hard to believe that the red-light district is only a few blocks from here, next to the oldest church in the city."

Jane turned to him in disbelief. "You mean... prostitutes?"

"They're legal here. They even take traveler's checks."

Jane stopped short. "How do you know?"

"Oh, I've heard, you know, from, ah, friends."

"Friends," Jane repeated, "hmm."

"Right."

He turned up another street. "It's a nice city, isn't it?"

"Lovely. Oh, I wish I was just a tourist here."

He squeezed her hand and rounded another corner. "This is Prinsengracht. Anne Frank's house is on the next block."

"Anne Frank. Oh, that poor girl. I read the book when I was twelve, I think. I cried and cried." She started walking faster. "I want to see it, Graham."

They stood together in front of the narrow brick house that was indistinguishable from all the others. Jane was silent for a long time. "She must have stayed up there on the top floor," she finally said in a hushed voice. "Oh, Graham, I can't believe someone went through that, a little girl." And he felt her hand tighten on his.

Jane wanted to walk some more since it was her only chance to see Amsterdam. Tomorrow they'd go straight to the diamond bourse, pick up the stones and head to the airport. Not much time for sight-seeing. He led her toward the oldest part of the city and showed her the church of St. Nicolaaskerk, dating from 1306.

"1306!" gasped Jane.

"Ah, but in the next block is a still older profession than Christianity."

"Can we go there? I mean..."

"Sure." Graham was amused by her interest. "It's a tourist attraction."

Girls posed half-nude in picture windows. Others knitted or painted their nails while awaiting clients. Garish neon signs lit the ancient streets of the red-light district, the Oude Zijds Voorburgwal. Graham held back a chuckle as he watched Jane's face turn an embarrassed pink when they passed the lovely old canal houses and their residents of easy virtue.

They arrived back at the hotel late and left a wake-up call for seven. Jane sank into a chair in their room, sighed and slipped off her shoes. "It's still early in my head."

"I know the feeling." He started massaging her shoulders, loving the feel of her taut muscles under his hands. "Feel good?"

"Sure does." But then she was quiet for a time, finally turning to look up at him. "Graham, we've got to sleep in separate beds tonight."

He felt as if he'd been splashed with cold water. "Why?" he asked, confused.

"I'm on a job. I just don't think it's right. I don't know, it's a feeling I have that I can't shake."

"Janey..."

"I don't want to be distracted."

"Well, sure, okay." Was there something else bothering her? Or perhaps it was just this job. "I'll be awful lonesome."

She gave him a crooked smile and mumbled, "Me, too." Then, after a pause, she asked, "How come they call you Quicksilver?"

He laughed. "Where'd you hear that?"

"Donna."

"Natch. Well, I'll tell you. It's no big secret. My mother called me that when I was a little kid. She never could keep me in her sight. She said I used to ooze under doors. I guess Lew must have let it out in the office."

"Oh." She seemed to be pondering his answer.

He pulled her up from the chair and embraced her gently. She was looking down at the floor. He nibbled at her neck and slid his hands down her hips to her buttocks. She tensed. "Please, don't, Graham," she whispered.

He felt stung. A small anger rocked him. "Can't I even kiss you good-night?" he asked testily.

"Oh, Graham, I'm sorry," she said brokenly, then she put her arms around his neck and covered his lips with hers. It was a long, satisfying kiss, arousing and teasing and loving. When they broke apart he started to ask her again if she was *sure* . . . but he felt her withdraw and gave up.

In uncomfortable silence Graham lay alone in his bed. He could hear Jane's soft breathing and the occasional rustle of bedclothes as she moved. She wasn't asleep, either. He sensed that she wanted him as much as he wanted her, that the empty ache in his belly was reciprocated by one in hers. Why, then, had she turned from him? Why? Damn, it sure was difficult to fall in love.

And he was feeling very guilty about not telling Jane all of his plans, including the so-called contingency plan. Maybe he *should* tell her. That way Jane might give him less of an argument. As it was, Graham still hadn't the slightest notion if she would go along with any of his plans. On the other hand, what could she do to stop him? She was caught between a rock and a hard place, he realized, forced to protect him, unable to stop the ball from rolling.

Damn, he thought, feeling his chest squeeze painfully. If it hadn't been for this diamond job, if there were no thieves, he'd be holding her in his arms at that very moment. And now, even if he did tell her everything, maybe it was too late to smooth over these hard feelings. Would this breach in their relationship be permanent?

He nearly groaned out loud, feeling wounded and sad and alone in his torment. And there she was, lying three feet from him in the darkness, her skin all warm and silken beneath the pretty blue nightgown, the scent of her perfume lifting from between her breasts and wafting the small distance to his nostrils, driving him completely out of his mind.

CHAPTER FOURTEEN

THE BUILDING WAS OLD AND VENERABLE, brick, with tall windows, an imposing portal and an unobtrusive sign that stated it was the Beurs voor Diamanthandel, the Diamond Bourse. It was one of sixteen bourses, or clubs, in the world and the thought of all that glittering wealth inside and her own responsibility made Jane very nervous. She took a deep breath and looked around as Graham signed them in.

Plainclothes guards abounded. Actually they looked like businessmen but Jane recognized them in a flash. She also noticed the electronic surveillance devices that were everywhere.

"This way, *Als 't blieft*, if you please," said a stolid-looking Dutch burgher as he led Graham into a high-ceilinged room, past wooden tables at which sat scores of dealers, in pairs, studying white paper packets of gems with their jewelers' eyeglasses or haggling or shaking hands over transactions.

My God, thought Jane, how many millions of dollars were changing hands at that very moment? The dealers came from everywhere: Europeans in neat suits, orthodox Jews from Antwerp or Tel Aviv or New York in black coats and hats and beards. A babel of voices filled the antique chamber, a clamor comprised of dozens of languages. Bright sunlight flooded the place from the tall, unobstructed windows. Of course, Jane concluded, they all needed natural light to study the stones.

"You okay?" asked Graham as they entered the hallway leading to the high security area and eventually to the vaults.

"Don't be overprotective," Jane whispered back. "I'm fine."

Their companion unlocked a heavy iron grill door, studied the instructions Graham had given him, passed everyone's identifications to a uniformed guard, then ushered Jane and Graham farther into the bowels of the closed area where there were chairs and a table and beyond that, the huge gilded vault door.

Jane took a seat while they waited in the small room. "How much do you think is behind that door?" she whispered to Graham.

"More than we'll see in a lifetime," he replied with a wide grin.

The man returned in a few minutes while a guard reclosed the door to the vault behind him. Then there were papers to be signed by Graham, the counting of the packets to be done, the emptying of them into a wide leather courier belt that Graham had buckled around his waist beneath his sweater and sport coat. Handshakes were dutifully exchanged.

Jane felt a tremor of excitement seize her. She was on the job now. This was what she'd been trained for. And yet she knew that the risk on this delivery was greater than normal. Graham was sure the thieves, with their inside knowledge of this diamond pickup, would try to steal them. He *wanted* them to try. Jane was confident of her ability to protect Graham but the thought of deliberately putting him and herself in danger went against all her common sense and training. And that matter had never been settled between them.

They returned to the front door, accompanied by their guide who said, "*Dank U wel*, thank you," several times in the extra polite Dutch manner before turning them over to the guard posted there. The guard signed them out, phoned for a taxi and handed them back their overnight bags, which they'd checked with him. It was all done efficiently, precisely, automatically. Jane was impressed.

A cab pulled up at the curb and the guard opened the door of the bourse for them. He said, "Goodbye, sir, *dank U wel*," nodded at Jane, saw them out and closed the door behind them.

"Well," said Graham, grinning, "now it begins."

He loved the danger, Jane knew. He absolutely thrived on it. "Wait a minute," she said, scanning the area for anything out of the ordinary, a person loitering, a movement out of place on the street, a vehicle too close to the taxi. Everything looked normal, ordinary, perfectly safe. But, naturally, a crowded city street in broad daylight was an unlikely choice for an ambush. Even amateurs would know better. The thieves might, however, be watching them, waiting for the perfect moment. Still, there was nothing in this Amsterdam street scene that sounded an alarm in Jane's head.

"Okay," she said and followed Graham to the waiting cab. He was taking this all very casually, she saw. Was that merely to put her at ease?

"Schiphol Airport," Graham requested while Jane was busy looking out the back of the cab window, then in front, along the quaint poplar-lined street. She even watched the taxi driver; he *could* be a plant. Every possibility had to be taken into account.

It was five miles to Schiphol Airport, one of the most secure airports in Europe. This leg of the trip constituted the weak point of their journey. Despite heavy traffic, they could be waylaid somewhere along the route. Jane wished now that they'd rented a car so that she could drive. Her evasive driving techniques, she'd bet, were better than their taxi driver's.

"There's the Rijksmuseum." Graham was pointing to a solid, imposingly Dutch building on the right. "Sure wish we had time..."

"Is your door locked?" she asked, leaning across him to check it.

They had to stop for a red light. She glanced around, not exactly nervous, but attuned to every movement near her, on guard, ceaselessly vigilant.

"Hey, take it easy." Graham put a hand on her knee. "Look, there's the Van Gogh Museum. And the Heineken Brewery is not far from here, just to the left."

She ignored him. Craning her head around just as the taxi started up again, she peered out of the back window. Her heart stopped for a split second, then pounded heavily. That man, three, four cars behind them, had a familiar look to him. Had it been only his too-quick maneuver, cutting in front of another car, that had caught her eye? Maybe. But she'd seen something, a jawline, a set of the head under a hatbrim, a glimpse of a familiar movement. Or had she? Was it only her oversensitive imagination? She kept looking out the back window but the car—a nondescript gray sedan—was no longer in view. It was almost as if the driver had realized that she had caught sight of him.

One man, not two?

"Graham," she said quietly, "there could be someone following us. I'm not sure."

"Oh, really?" He turned and looked behind them.

"He's gone now. It could have been, God, I hate to even say it, it could have been the jerk that tried to mug me in Central Park."

Graham watched her carefully. "You sure?"

"*No*, I'm not sure. There was something about the driver I just saw . . . but he had a hat on and I couldn't tell! . . ."

Graham patted her knee. "Good," he said, "I hope they're onto us."

"You're not starting *that* again."

"Jane, nothing's changed. My orders stand." He seemed utterly cool, totally in control, enjoying the hunt, even though he was the quarry.

"I want my objections noted," she said firmly, angrily. "I was not hired to be the cheese in a mousetrap!"

Graham sighed and held her wildly gesturing hand in both of his. "A lovely cheese you make, sweetheart," he murmured.

"How can you . . . how can you," she stammered, "be so casual?"

He shrugged, still holding her hand, raising it to his lips to nibble at her fingers. "It's a job."

Schiphol Airport was crowded. The worst possible scenario for confusion, ambush, attack. And yet Jane could see the many guards, both armed and in plainclothes, that airport security demanded these days. Would anyone dare try for the diamonds under these circumstances? She stayed close behind Graham as he forged his way to the check-in counter; she was coiled tense inside, watching carefully for that one nervous gesture, that one sweat-covered brow. She remembered so plainly Rob Dearborn's lecture on the profile of an attacker. He was a male, usually, between the ages of nineteen and twenty-six, a dogmatic, bitter, confused person who believed fervently that he was right in what he did.

"We have over an hour before we board," Graham was saying. "Lunch! I'm starved."

"No, I couldn't eat a thing."

"Mind if I grab a doughnut or something?"

"No, but I'll have to check out the restaurant."

"Okay," he said with a laugh, "I'll eat on the run and get a stomachache."

But she hardly heard, being too busy watching, her eyes scanning, her muscles ready to react. That man over there, reading a newspaper; was he only hiding behind it? Or that woman pushing a stroller? In practice at ISA Rob had set up a woman with a baby carriage in a park—innocent, perfectly ordinary—but there had been guns under the pink blanket and all the students had been caught red-handed, including Jane.

Graham bought a flaky raspberry pastry. "It's good. Want a bite?"

Jane looked at him blankly.

"This way," he said finally, leading her down a concourse, to their gate, she supposed.

But the concourse quickly turned into a construction site with piles of materials and ripped-up tiles. It was practically deserted.

Jane stopped short.

"Come on, it's a shortcut to our gate."

"It's too dangerous," she said, putting an arm out to hold him back.

"That's *good*, Jane. The thieves are running out of time if they want to steal these diamonds."

"Graham, I can't let you."

"Look, there're a few yards of this mess, then the new concourse." He pulled gently at her arm. "Come on, we're ready for them, Jane. They don't know that. We've got surprise on our side. And there are dozens of security men within calling range. It's perfect for us."

"No." She shook her head vehemently. He was carrying things too far. She sized up the odds if they proceeded farther down the concourse and didn't like them. Hands on hips, she squared off to him. "No," she repeated.

"Damn it, Janey, it's our job!" He tried to push past her.

She had no choice. It was almost as if her body moved of its own volition, smoothly, swiftly, instinctively. Her right hand reached out, found its hold, twisted slightly and Graham was yelping in surprised pain, bent over, neutralized. Whichever way he moved the pain increased, his own weight used as leverage against him.

"Ouch!" he complained. "Come on, Janey, let me go. This is embarrassing. Now, come on, we've got to help Lew!" He tried to wiggle his arm out of her hold. She tightened her grip. He grimaced and stopped in his efforts. "Please, Jane," he attempted.

"You said Lew wanted us to deliberately lure the robbers, not to commit suicide in some deserted—"

But she never finished. Her eye caught a sudden movement. A man was stepping out from behind a pile of construction debris, swiftly followed by another. Her mind saw them, took in their hats and the scarves over their faces and registered threat in a split second.

"Will you let me go *now*?" Graham was asking tightly.

"Very funny," she breathed, dropping his arm instantly.

The two men were big, Jane noted. They wore army surplus fatigue jackets, jeans and longshoremen's caps pulled low. They advanced steadily but warily because Jane and Graham had both whirled to face them, knees bent in ready positions.

"This is it," Graham said out of the corner of his mouth. "I'll take the guy on the right."

Jane could practically feel the sparks of excitement that Graham gave off. *He loves it,* she had time to think, and then the man on the left—her man—pulled a pistol out of his pocket. A blunt, ugly 9-mm pistol.

All her lessons came back to Jane then. She could hear Rob talking: "Get the guy close. If you can reach the gun without moving you have it made. First, you draw his attention some way. That gives you a quarter of a second. You have another quarter of a second before he can pull the trigger. That's a half second. If you can't knock the gun aside in half a second you deserve to fail this course."

Okay, she told herself, *let him come closer.* He did, as if obeying Jane's silent command. He was very close, trying to back them up against a wall, his buddy at his side.

"Hand 'em over," came his muffled voice, pure American in accent.

"Sure, pal," Graham was saying, as if to pacify the man, "I don't want any trouble." Out of the corner of her eye, Jane saw Graham reach inside his jacket. She knew he was up to something. But first, the man with the gun...

The weapon with its black Cyclops eye was pointed at her middle. It was time. Jane faked a cry of fear. "Please!" she yelled, "don't hurt me!" His eyes swung to her, his attention, for that fraction of a second, was total. Her hand, fingers stiffened, shot out and snapped his gun hand aside so fast he had no idea that it was coming until his weapon clattered onto the concrete floor out of his reach.

With satisfaction Jane saw his eyes fill with shock. *Amateurs,* she thought, *Norma was right.* But then she was aware of Graham grappling with the other man, of grunts and thuds, and her man was going for his gun where it lay on the floor. She tripped him expertly and leaped toward where he sprawled on the hard floor.

Suddenly Jane was aware that there were more people on the scene: a woman, blond, scared, carrying a toddler. Two other children holding hands, eyes wide. Oh, Lord, she thought, they'll get hurt!

The gunman scrambled up with surprising agility, grabbed one of the children and held the screaming youngster up in front of him like a shield.

Jane was paralyzed, one eye on the gun on the floor, one on the thief and his hostage. Graham had the second man down on his knees, held securely with an arm lock.

Then everything happened at once. The first man lunged for the gun, his young prisoner kicked him in the shins with drumming heels, the child's mother screamed and threw herself at the thief. Jane tackled him but got tangled up with the hysterical mother. Graham shouted, losing his prisoner in the process; the baby wailed, the first thief swore, the gun was knocked beyond anyone's reach.

And then Jane was holding the baby, the mother was grabbing her two children, Graham was cursing and the two thieves were racing away down the torn-up concourse, around a corner.

"Here!" Jane said, handing the crying baby to Graham. "I'll get them! Call security!"

Graham thrust the baby at its mother. "No," he snapped, "It's too dangerous! They're gone, anyway."

"For God's sakes, Graham, call security!" She tried to pull out of his grasp and it became a tug-of-war.

"Forget it, Jane, forget it this time! You did fine."

"But I can get them!" she cried, incensed.

"Jane, not this time."

They faced each other, panting. Graham's coat sleeve was ripped, his hair mussed.

"How could you? How could you stop me?" She was hopping mad. "It's too late now!"

Graham only said, "See if the kids are okay, Jane."

They were, all three of them, wailing and runny-nosed, while their mother cowered against the wall, white-faced and shaken to the core.

And then there was a whistle and uniformed men were running toward them, and Jane was standing in the middle of the concourse, trembling with reaction and anger, while Graham put a serious businessman's look on his face, one she'd never seen before, and went to meet them.

A half hour later, Graham had somehow managed to make the head of airport security believe that he and Jane were total innocents, merely on vacation, and that the muggers had simply been after his wallet. They left the security office and strode down the long echoing hall back to the main terminal. Jane kept waiting for Graham to explain why he'd lied to the officials but he was uncharacteristically silent.

She finally broached the subject. "Why didn't you tell them about the diamonds, Graham? It would have explained everything."

"I don't want them getting in my way."

"Maybe they can help."

"They'd just foul the whole plan up."

Jane was confused. She walked next to Graham, wondering about many things. First he invited danger, then he appeared to be worried about her safety. He stopped her from doing the precise thing she was hired to do. It was as if he *wanted* the thieves to get away! And then he deliberately lied to the Dutch police.

She glanced up at him but, for once, could read nothing on his handsome features. What, Jane asked herself, did she really know about Graham Smith? He seemed to live on the surface of life, ever moving, as elusive as quicksilver. Norma's warning echoed in her brain: too charming, too carefree. *Watch Graham Smith!*

Jane felt a chill seize her innards, a terrible, tearing doubt. Had Graham's plan gone wrong just now? Could he be planning to steal the diamonds himself?

CHAPTER FIFTEEN

"OKAY, JANE, LET'S get you on that flight to New York now," said Graham.

"You mean, let's get us on the flight," Jane said automatically.

"Just you, Janey," he said carefully.

She stood in the concourse, hands on hips, her face sagging in disbelief. "This is some kind of joke, isn't it?"

His gaze was studiously sober. "I'm afraid not."

"Well, you've lost your marbles, mister. We're both getting on that flight. It's my job to protect you."

"I don't know who's protecting whom," he was quick to answer. "If I hadn't been so darned worried about you, I could have taken care of those thieves myself and they'd be in jail by now."

"Oh, boy, what a lame excuse! It was *you* who wouldn't let me chase them! Oh, if you can't see that, Graham, what's the use of standing here arguing?" Jane sighed. "Now let's get on that plane."

"I'm not going."

"This is no time to make bad jokes."

"It's orders, Jane. Lew said that if we didn't get the crooks by flight time, I was to go it alone."

"You're telling me this is *Lew's* idea?" asked Jane furiously.

"Lew's . . . and mine as well. Don't worry, the diamonds will be perfectly safe."

It occurred to Jane as they stood there facing each other, ignoring the stream of travelers having to step around them, that Graham might very well be planning to rendezvous with the thieves, claim he got robbed—who was to say otherwise?—and split the take three ways. Oh yes, Jane thought darkly, it would be so easy for him to pull it off. Quicksilver. She wished she had the nerve to confront him with his perfidy.

Graham was looking at the time. "Ten minutes, Jane. You have to be on that plane."

What in heaven's name was she supposed to do? Let him—God, how the thought twisted in her stomach—steal the stones himself? Oh damn, *damn*!

He took Jane's arm and began to steer her down the concourse. Her indecision carried her along in silence. What was she going to do?

"I hate for you to be going back alone, Jane. Honest I do. It's a long flight and I know you'll worry.... Wait a minute. Stay right here." He disappeared into a shop and Jane remained rooted to her spot, thinking frantically, knowing that she absolutely couldn't get on that plane and leave him.

An awful image invaded her mind: Graham behind prison bars in a zebra-striped suit, cap and all, and Jane visiting, holding onto the tattered fabric of her love, waiting, waiting all those long years. Then she was angry with herself. Graham was no thief! She was the one who'd gone nuts, who'd listened to a drugged woman's ramblings and taken them to heart. Besides, Graham had just told her that this was Lew's idea. Nevertheless, Lew had not told *her*. And Jane was going to do her job. She was going to stay with Graham and that was that.

But how? He sure wasn't giving an inch.

He came striding out of the shop carrying a plastic sack, a silly grin on his handsome face. What was he up to now?

"Here," he said brightly, "to keep you company, Janey."

She peered down into the bag. "Oh, Graham..."

"I couldn't find one with the right color fur but it's close." He forced the sack on her, put his hands in his pockets and rocked back on his heels.

Jane pulled out the teddy bear and stifled a smile. It *was* awfully cute and was kind of a reddish brown, though certainly not the color of Graham's hair. "Thanks," she said, momentarily relenting, tucking the bear under her arm. She tried again. "Look, Graham, I have no orders from Lew and I just can't go back to New York."

"You'll have to, Jane," he said softly but with absolute resolution. "Or I'll merely sit here and not move until you do."

"You wouldn't."

"I would."

"Graham, can we call Lew right now? I'd feel better asking him."

"It's too early in New York. He's not even awake yet."

"I can't leave you!"

Graham glanced at his watch pointedly. "Five minutes, Jane."

What could she do? He obviously meant it. Indecision tore at her. She needed more time to think.

"Jane..."

"Oh, all right!" She pretended to give in; it was the only way to manage the situation. Let Graham think she was inexperienced and dumb; let him think she'd follow his orders without using her own judgment!

His hand was at her elbow, hurrying her along to the gate. Anger seethed within her, along with a terrible disappointment.

"Now you've got Teddy there to keep you company. I'll see you in a couple of days," said Graham, smiling now.

"If I get in trouble with Lew..."

"I'll take the blame, I promise. There's your gate. Don't worry yourself another minute, Janey. I'm having a ball."

"It's no laughing matter."

"I know. I'm sorry." But he didn't look in the least contrite.

"Just what are you planning?" asked Jane.

"I can't tell you."

"Lew's *orders*?"

"Yes." He put his hand up. "Scout's honor, Janey."

"Are you leaving Amsterdam?"

"Yes."

"But you won't say where to."

"I can't. But I will call the office, Jane, and let them know. As soon as you're back in New York you can find out."

"What do you think I'd do with the information at forty thousand feet over the ocean?"

"Parachute out, of course—" he winked "—to follow me."

She narrowed her eyes at his levity but he ignored her expression, pulled Jane up against his chest and kissed her thoroughly. "I wish we could be together," he murmured. "I'm going to miss you."

For a moment she went weak all over and sagged against him, unable to resist the magnetism of his touch. But it was all wrong; she steeled herself, put her hands on his chest and pushed him away, catching a fleeting look of regret on his face just before he masked it.

The last boarding announcement sounded over the speakers in several languages and Jane stepped back. "Well, goodbye," she said, smiling falsely. "Take good care of yourself and the diamonds."

"I will." He stood there, though, not leaving.

"Well, bye."

"Bye, Jane. Better get on board."

"Um . . . bye." Oh, brother, what was she going to do now? He'd wait there, all right, until the airplane's door was closed. Graham was taking no chances.

Lugging her overnight bag with Teddy still tucked under an arm, Jane boarded and walked toward the back of the plane, her brain working feverishly. There had to be a way to get off without Graham spotting her.

Then she saw it. The food service elevator was still attached to the side of the big jet. If she could somehow ride down on it . . . Oh, how silly. She'd never have the nerve. On the other hand . . .

"Please take your seat, miss," said a stewardess politely.

"I, uh, have to use the lavatory."

The woman frowned. "You'll have to be back in your seat before we taxi, miss."

"Oh, I will," lied Jane.

Ducking into the flight crew's service area was easy, as they were busy checking overhead compartments, seat belts and passing out magazines and pillows. But, oh my, it was going to be a tight squeeze fitting in between those two stainless steel carts. She started to squirm around one of the carriers so she could hide and felt a tug at her leg. Looking down, she discovered a hole in her panty hose the size of a silver dollar. Darn.

What was she thinking! There she was, worrying about a three-dollar pair of hose when she might get caught at any moment! What would she say, what absurd excuse could she come up with? *I was hungry. I hate flying.* Oh, Lord, how embarrassing.

The elevator, which was loaded with the trays of the last flight's leftovers, finally jerked and whined and began its descent to the tarmac.

Heck, this wasn't so bad after all. *Clever,* Jane thought, smiling to herself. Oh, boy, was Graham going to be surprised!

The elevator faltered briefly, causing Jane to reach out for support. Her hand came away from a tray all gooey with red sauce and stringy cheese. Lasagne! Someone's cold, half-eaten meal.

The elevator came to a halt a foot above the ground. The noise outside was deafening, jets pulling in and out of the gates, their engines screaming. She had to find a way back inside somehow. Through the luggage area?

Jane straightened, still hanging onto Teddy, hoisting her bag with sticky fingers. She was stepping onto the tarmac, picturing herself riding up the conveyer belt with the luggage to get inside the terminal when she heard a noise behind her. Spinning around, Jane found four guns aimed at her and four airport security men staring at her without a hint of amusement.

"THE CLOTH YOU REQUESTED for your hand, Miss Manning."

It was the chief of security, the same man who'd interviewed Jane and Graham a short while ago. But this time Jane was the suspect. How humiliating.

She took the damp rag thankfully, grateful for the relatively friendly face of Captain Vermeer. They'd taken her bag, even Teddy, from her immediately, and she had not seen either since. Only these unsmiling, ramrod-straight guards who stood at attention against the sterile white walls of the room in which she'd been sitting—on a hard wooden chair—for hours it seemed. Jane wiped her fingers, thought about removing the spot of red sauce from her skirt but decided not to, and looked up at the captain. "Why are you holding me?" she asked innocently, as if she didn't know that they had taken her belongings to search for a bomb.

"Come, come, now, Miss Manning. You cannot be so naive! You will explain this very stupid thing you have done, please."

Jane did her best, realizing that no matter what she told him she would sound as if she were accusing Graham of stealing the diamonds himself. Why hadn't Graham said he was a courier before? Now he'd really gotten her into trouble!

"I will check this story, naturally," the man finally told her, rising.

"Are you going to call New York?" Jane asked.

"Of course, but it is very early there, I think."

"Will you find out if Mr. Smith checked in at Mercury, please?"

"I shall find out all the facts, miss. And then we shall see what is to be done with you, eh?"

She was allowed to use the bathroom down the hall and one of the guards brought her tea. It was another thirty minutes, however, before Captain Vermeer returned. There was a grim expression on his face.

"What you have done is very serious. And you have caused us much trouble and expense. Do you understand?"

Jane nodded.

"We," he really said, "vee," "have searched your bag and I am afraid the animal is no longer in one piece. Your story has been confirmed by your employer."

"Thank God!"

"Yes. *Dank Gott* you are who you say you are."

"You are going to let me go?"

His eyes pinioned her. "I could hold you, however, for many charges."

"I understand. Really I do. I acted rashly and stupidly."

"Among other things. Go back to your New York, miss, where perhaps such odd behavior is better tolerated. No?"

"Uh, yes." She stood up. "Did they say if Mr. Smith left Amsterdam or where he might have gone?"

"Your Mr. Smith has flown to Bermuda."

"*Bermuda*," breathed Jane, the agony of her suspicions striking her like a blow.

"To London, then Bermuda. I had these flights confirmed. I should not like to find this Mr. Smith sneaking down food elevators, eh?"

Two guards escorted Jane from the room, then handed her the overnight bag and Teddy's sad remains, which she chucked into a trash can. She was angry and humiliated and placed the blame squarely on Graham's shoulders. How dare he put her through such an ordeal!

Bermuda, she mused. Smedley had been going to Bermuda! What was going on here? Jane found a telephone, noticing that she was still being followed by a guard. She could hardly blame them for being cautious. After ten minutes she had Donna on the overseas line. "Graham's gone to Bermuda?" asked Jane.

"That's right. He checked in about an hour ago. What's going on, Jane?" The sound of gum snapping carried across the ocean.

"I'll tell you later. For now, tell Lew that I'm going to follow Graham. I think I know exactly where he is."

"You wanna talk to Lew?"

Jane thought. "No. Just tell him that. Bye, Donna." She hung up quickly in case Lew got on the line and tried to put a stop to her plans. Graham *could* have been telling the truth about Lew's orders although Jane had grave doubts. It was, however, in Graham's favor that he'd checked in with the office. But, of course, he thought she was safely on the plane back to New York.

She had to haggle with the airlines over her unused but marked-up ticket, then she discovered that the only flight available to Bermuda connected through London. And it cost more. She pulled out the brand-new VISA card she'd gotten from her bank in New York and charged the difference. If and when she caught up with Mr. Quicksilver he was damn well going to pay for her ticket!

After a stopover at Heathrow in London, Jane was finally heading west into the setting sun toward Bermuda and hopefully toward some answers to the questions that had been darting through her head ever since she'd talked to Norma.

How could she have fallen for a thief? Jane's judgment had always been sound but now she felt as if her world had somehow tipped and nothing was right anymore. She went over and over the facts. Graham was either truly engaged in an elaborate scheme to lure the thieves or he was in league with them and pulling the wool over everyone's eyes, Lew's included. It didn't seem possible for Graham to be so underhanded and devious—not the man who laughed and teased and touched her with gentle, caring hands, and lived life to the fullest. It couldn't be her handsome man whose strawberry-blond hair caught the light like gold, whose China-blue eyes twinkled with devilry, whose deep voice caressed her ears.

Oh, yeah? thought Jane, sitting bolt upright in her seat and spilling coffee on her sweater. The jerk! Look what he was putting her through! The selfish, cruel, horrible man was engaged in the worst sort of crime. Forget the diamonds, forget all the other goods he'd stolen—to Jane it was far worse that he was deceiving and using his friends.

How could Graham be so crooked?

He's not, her heart shouted, *he's kind and considerate and fiercely loyal.*

Or was that all a facade?

Hour after hour Jane's thoughts vacillated, flip-flopped, drove her half out of her head. She fidgeted in her seat, spilled some soup on her skirt and used the lavatory six times.

"Perhaps you should refrain from more coffee," said the Englishman sitting next to her, the man whose knees she'd bumped every time she passed him on her way to the aisle.

"Sorry," was all Jane could say.

"Hmm. Quite." He rattled his newspaper and turned a shoulder to her.

The Boeing jet touched down on Bermuda at 6:35 p.m. local time. For Jane, however, it was hours later. She was hardly an experienced traveler, and the effects of being bounced from one time zone to another and back again were wearing her thin.

She knew she looked awful. Her hair was stringy and oily. Her makeup had not been touched since early that morning in Amsterdam and her clothes...

Jane glanced down at her stained skirt and rumpled sweater. Real cute. She could change in the ladies' room at the airport into her wool slacks but wool, on Bermuda? So she pulled off her sweater and crammed it into her bag and tried to straighten her white blouse. Of course, she couldn't see that there were rust-colored balls of wool from her "On Special" sweater stuck to the back of her blouse. Nor had she remembered the hole in one leg of her panty hose or the run up the side of the other. And even if she had been mindful of her appearance, Jane's anxiety overshadowed all else.

Now she had a task before her: find the consul general's party. And finding the party did not necessarily mean she'd find Graham there!

Bermuda was paradise in the middle of the Atlantic where British grace mingled with island languor. Jane's taxi sped on the wrong—British—side of the road, across an elevated causeway, along the northern coast toward the capital port city, Hamilton.

The scenery went practically unnoticed. *George,* Jane was thinking. What was his last name? Oh darn, she should have listened better! Some funny name. An animal. George...George...Mondragon! Consul general of Bermuda. Someone would know where his party was, wouldn't they?

The taxi passed beautifully landscaped homes, their stucco exteriors painted in eye-pleasing pastels: pink, cream, violet, blue to match the sparkling water, coral, yellow. Every dwelling had intricate wrought-iron grillwork around the deep-set windows and doors. The profusion of brilliant tropical flowers that glowed in the evening sun finally touched Jane's senses. The plant life was so green, so utterly, overpoweringly verdant, so unlike the dry sparseness of her home that she couldn't help gaping.

Hamilton was a tightly clustered, picturesque town of elegant shops and stucco hotels and international restaurants along winding streets above a colorful harbor where clean white cruise ships nestled alongside private yachts.

The British Consulate was pastel with a surrounding, vine-covered stone wall and a tall white wrought-iron gate. It was, of course, locked at this hour. Jane asked the taxi driver to wait and rang the quaint bell at the gate. No one answered. She stood there, hot and tired and increasingly impatient. Angry tears pricked at her eyelids. "Isn't anybody here?" she mumbled to herself.

How was she going to find Graham? She rang again, waited another minute, shifting from foot to foot. Should she find a phone and see if the consulate had an emergency number? She could always look up George Mondragon in the phone book, she supposed. But the party might not be at his house.

She rang again. Her driver leaned out of his open window and called to her. "They'll all be at the grand affair, miss."

Jane whirled on him. "George Mondragon's party?"

"Sure, miss. The whole island's been buzzing with it for weeks. I took some folks out there already."

Jane closed her eyes and whispered a thank-you. "Can you take me there? Is it far?"

"Hop in. It be about fifteen minutes."

The coastline twisted and dipped, following old stone walls and fertile embankments. The road was so narrow in spots that the cab had to slow to first let other vehicles go by, but more often the taxi driver bullied on past, jockeying for the right of way. The ride was hair-raising but speedy.

The sun was making its lazy low arch in the west, turning the ocean to the color of copper, casting long shadows across the road as they sped on their way.

Why couldn't she be enjoying this new adventure with Graham? How had things gone so wrong? And *what*, wondered Jane for the hundredth time, was she going to do if he wasn't at George Mondragon's? Call Lew at home and tell him the bad news, that Graham had disappeared with the diamonds, she guessed.

Damn you, Graham Smith!

The taxi passed by lavishly foliated hills rising from pink-tinted sandy beaches and estates nestled in junglelike growth. Jane was suddenly struck by the astounding aura of wealth on Bermuda. She was a fish out of water, a cowgirl, duped by Mr. Charm himself, duped and *had*.

What was Graham doing on Bermuda? Luring the thieves, he would no doubt tell her. Hogwash, thought Jane. More than likely he'd come to Bermuda to join forces with Smedley! This little jaunt of his was no coincidence!

It was nearly eight by the time she was deposited at the end of a sandy, palm-lined driveway that led up to a pink villa snuggled into the lush hillside. A beautiful home, an enchanted castle where anything could come true.

She began walking up the drive, her bag slung recklessly over her shoulder, her appearance very much the worse for wear.

There was a gate—wrought iron, wonder of wonders—and a bell. Jane pulled on the cord, peeking through the curlicued grill to see dozens of shining, sporty cars parked in the driveway. Beyond that, off to one side of the house were ladies and gentlemen milling about the lawn, the women in gauzy, glittering formal gowns, their jewelry winking in the gilded evening light; the men in handsome, crisp white dinner jackets.

Jane reached up and slapped at a mosquito that was biting her grimy neck as violin music, haunting and beckoning, sounded from the villa.

Damn you, Graham Smith!

CHAPTER SIXTEEN

GRAHAM GLANCED AT HIS WATCH. Jane must be safely home in her apartment by now, he decided. He felt vastly relieved; he'd telephone her first thing in the morning and reassure her that everything was okay and maybe, he thought grimly, he should bring up the subject of her distrust and clear the air between them before it was too late.

"You look better every time I see you," Eleanor Mondragon was saying. "One of those men who ages so handsomely."

"Why, thank you," replied Graham, forcing precisely the right smile, boyish and flattered. "And you look beautiful tonight. Of course, you always do." She did look quite spectacular, he had to admit: the Grande Dame was dressed in flowing black chiffon, her gray hair wound into an intricate coiffure interlaced with pearls, real pearls. But then it was her husband's final social fling and should be recalled by Bermuda's society for decades.

With his mind still on Jane, Graham sipped on his champagne and viewed the elegant assemblage that spilled from terrace to terrace to the flawless green lawn. Japanese lanterns were strung all around. Uniformed Bermudian waiters and waitresses mingled, carrying silver trays of hors d'oeuvres and drinks. A violinist played lilting tunes next to the splashing tiled fountain.

Eleanor waved to someone across the pool and blew him a kiss. "It was so wonderful to see your mother and father arrive together," she said softly, tapping Graham's sleeve. "We had heard that they separated, dear, and it seemed such a tragic thing for two people who had always been such a close couple."

"It was...*is*...well, I don't exactly know what their status is right now. All I know is that my mother flew in from Canada."

"Oh, they do seem happy," exclaimed Eleanor and Graham followed the direction of her gaze. There was Smedley, up on a terrace, tall and distinguished in his dinner jacket, in a circle of equally distinguished men, arguing happily. British and American politics, no doubt. And over there on the lawn was Renée, radiant in a flowing rose creation, jewels sparkling from her ears and neck, laughing and apparently carefree, engaged in women's talk with several other ladies.

He couldn't help but feel glad, in spite of his concern over his own romantic problems, to see his parents together again, just like in the old days.

"And you, my dear boy, when is some smart young lady going to steal you off the circuit?"

The subject of Jane was on the tip of his tongue when he felt a tap on his shoulder. He turned quickly to see the Mondragon's butler standing behind him, his old face expressionless, his white gloved hands folded properly in front of him.

JANE SAW HIM MATERIALIZE out of the semidarkness as if he were a wraith. So he *was* there! She didn't know if she was relieved or unnerved to see him again. On one hand, a thief didn't let his boss know where he was going; on the other, he could already have handed the stones to an accomplice and be planning to say he'd been robbed.

Jane wiped at a trickle of sweat on her temple and waited impatiently as Graham said something to a man—the butler, she supposed. She wanted to laugh wildly, standing there in the soft hot twilight: the *butler*!

But Graham was approaching, his face a mask of incredulity. "Janey!" he gasped. "What on earth are you doing here?"

He wore an exquisitely tailored white linen dinner jacket, formal black trousers, a ruffled shirt, patent leather shoes. In any other circumstances Jane would have drawn in her breath, spellbound by the handsome picture he made. As it was, she could barely keep her temper under control.

She thrust her face up to the wrought-iron bars. "Did you think I was going to get on that flight and forget about the diamonds? No wonder they call you Quicksilver!"

"But, Janey, I saw you get on that plane. I thought you were in New York!"

"I won't even begin to tell you what I went through to follow you!" She felt ridiculous talking to him through the metal bars as if she were a prisoner. "Will you get that *person* over here to let me in?"

"Uh, sure."

She stalked in and dropped her bag on the ground. "Look, Graham, I'm hot and tired and thirsty. I tracked you down because I have to do my job and now I want to see the diamonds. Are they here?"

"The, uh, diamonds. Ah, yeah, they're here."

"I want to see them. Now."

Graham snapped his mouth shut and seemed to gather himself. "Lord, Janey, you do take a man aback."

"The diamonds."

"They're in George's safe." He looked at her sharply. "You thought I was running off with them. Janey..."

"You're darn right I did."

"You don't trust me," he stated sadly.

"After what you pulled in Amsterdam? No, I don't trust you. That's why I sneaked off the plane you put me on."

"*You what*?"

"Down the food elevator. And then they thought I was a terrorist or something and Captain Vermeer was furious. It was all so horrible."

"Janey, sweetheart, do you mean to say our nice security man in Amsterdam *arrested* you?"

"Only until he got Mercury to vouch for me. And then I had to go to London and . . . you owe me seventy-five dollars for my ticket to get here!"

"But how did you know where I . . . ? Of course, Vermeer called Mercury. Oh, Janey, you should have gone home."

"And let you skip off with the diamonds and ruin Lew's business and make a fool of me and . . . and everyone?"

"I told you—oh, damn it, it wasn't supposed to happen like this. If we didn't get the thieves in Amsterdam I was to go on alone, so they'd be sure and try again."

"Oh, yeah?" She waved an arm toward the lawn. "At a party on *Bermuda*? That's how you'd lure the thieves? Inside a locked gate surrounded by dozens of people?" She eyed him assessingly. "A party where your father just happens to be?"

"Well, sure, that's why I stopped by, to see my folks. Lew knows. It's all approved, Janey."

She folded her arms.

"I told you, we had this contingency plan. . . ."

Could he be telling the truth? Oh, how she wanted to believe him! Her whole mind and heart and body craved his innocence. Please, she prayed silently, let it be the truth.

"Believe me, Janey, everything's under control." He looked at her pleadingly. "Truce?"

She glared at him for another second, then her face crumpled and she felt as if she was going to cry. But that would never do. She was on a job, her biggest, most important assignment to date—Norma's assignment, really—and to be failing so miserably made her feel sick to her stomach. She had to get control of herself. In as level a voice as she could manage, Jane finally said, "Graham, you've got to understand that I want to believe you, that I'm trying to believe you. But either way, I've got my job to think about and I can't let you go running around making me look like a complete fool." Surely he could see things from her point of view.

Tentatively he reached out and patted her back, then trailed a finger up her neck and hooked a lock of damp hair behind her ear. "Everything's going to be fine, really. You did a great job."

She shuddered with the pleasure of his touch. Here she was, trying with every fiber of her being to get back in control and the mere brush of his fingers was sending her straight into that miasma of confusion again. Sudden anger exploded within her and Jane lashed out against him in the only way she could. "And look at you. Look at you! All spiffed up in a...in a dinner jacket! Oh, I suppose you just happened to have it in the zipper compartment of your overnight bag!"

Graham glanced down at himself. "Well, actually, my father brought it along with his stuff."

"Oh, so he knew you were going to be here. And why didn't I know?"

"It was only a possibility. If we'd nabbed those guys in the airport I would have gone straight back to New York with you. Now I'm not in any hurry. This was an alternate route."

"Oh, I see," she said sarcastically. He had an answer for everything. He could be telling the truth. Maybe Lew really *had* told him to send her back. But could she rely on that possibility? Her mind told her no, her heart pleaded with her to trust him. She stood there in the warm, perfumed darkness and felt as if she were going to fly into a million pieces. "Can I see the diamonds, Graham?" she asked, trying to keep her voice level, trying to stave off the misery that would drown her if she let her guard down for an instant.

"I told you, they're—" But he clammed up then. "Okay. I'll go get George to unlock the safe. But really, Jane Manning, you do try a man's soul, my sweet."

"The diamonds, Graham."

Ten minutes later Jane was apologizing to George Mondragon. "I just had to see them, you understand."

"Are you happy now?" Graham asked, leading her out of the den.

"Very."

"Well, now maybe we can get you fixed up and forget about the blasted stones for a little while."

"Fixed up?"

Graham stopped and looked at her. "I assume you want to stick with me, right?"

"Right."

"Well, it would be terribly rude to show up at the Mondragon's big event in that outfit."

It was Jane's turn to look down at herself: creased corduroy skirt, rumpled white blouse, torn panty hose. "Can't we leave? Go somewhere?"

"That would be even ruder. Janey, I just can't, at least not yet. It would look pretty ridiculous—you showing up and hauling me off."

Jane sank down onto a rattan bench and rubbed her forehead with grimy fingers. "Oh, I don't know what to do." She wanted to cry; she wanted Graham to comfort her but she didn't dare weaken. It would be folly to let him touch her or let herself feel anything. What on earth was she to do?

Cautiously Graham sat down next to her. "Poor Janey," he said tenderly. "I would never have put you through this if I'd known you were going to follow me." He touched her hand with gentle fingers but she pulled away.

"Graham, you should know me by now. How could you have thought I'd just let you go?"

"Wishful thinking?" he offered, not very successfully.

Their eyes met and held. Jane felt a deep sorrow grip her. Her love for Graham was tarnished, dirtied. Even if he were innocent, would he ever trust her again?

As if he knew what she was thinking, Graham stroked her cheek. "Come on, sweetheart, let's get you something to wear. My mother will help. And Eleanor. You'll see, you'll feel much better when you're all fixed up. Here I am forgetting that you're probably thirsty and all. I'll get you something. Champagne?"

Jane sighed. "So it's Cinderella and her fairy godmother? Graham, really..."

"You'll be the belle of the ball, Janey."

"And at midnight my gown will turn into rags. Graham, I'm really not in the mood."

He smiled his twinkling, mischievous grin and pulled her up. "And I'm Prince Charming and we get to live happily ever after."

"Do we, Graham?" was all Jane said.

RENÉE AND ELEANOR MONDRAGON stood in front of three dresses that hung on hangers. Their heads were cocked, their brows drawn.

"The yellow," said Eleanor.

"The shoes won't go."

"Perhaps the green then. It's bigger in the waist. And she could wear the white satin slippers..."

"Hmm," said Renée, "now that I see her coloring, maybe the gold. What size shoe do you wear, dear?"

"Mrs. Smith, really, I..." Jane began.

"Now, now. Try these on. We weren't sure of the fit. Pamela is smaller and Bea is bigger."

"Pamela and Bea?"

"My daughters," answered Eleanor graciously.

"Oh."

"She has a lovely figure," said Eleanor, studying Jane as if she were on the auction block.

Renée held up the yellow dress. It was strapless, tucked, with thousands of crystal beads sewn on the bodice. "No, too fussy."

Then there was a taffeta with winglike shoulders. "Overpowering," said Renée, shaking her head.

Eleanor held up another dress. "Try it on, dear," she said.

"Yes," said Renée, studying Jane with her head cocked to one side.

"Yes," agreed Eleanor.

"My gold sandals," mused Renée.

"The clip for her hair," said Eleanor decisively.

"See if my shoes fit," suggested Renée.

They were a touch narrow but Jane, wishing she could crawl into a hole and die, said she didn't mind a bit. "It's only for a few hours, after all."

Eleanor stuck the gold and rhinestone clip in Jane's hair, pulling it back on one side. "Try that."

Jane felt like a mannequin, a ridiculous role for a bodyguard to play. She wanted to laugh and cry at the same time but the two older women were taking their handiwork so seriously, she couldn't insult them.

"Take a look," said Renée triumphantly, pushing Jane toward the mirror.

Jane stared, blinked, then stared again. The gold dress fell from thin straps to the floor, a sleek, metallic, shimmery tube, its curved lines touching her bust and hips in its flow. It was loose yet clinging, terribly simple yet gorgeously complicated. "It's beautiful," she breathed, revolving in front of the mirror.

Graham obviously thought so, too. "Good God, you're an eyeful! How am I going to keep the men off you?" He put a warm hand on her bare back and pulled her closer. "See? I knew you'd feel better."

"Only until midnight," Jane reminded him firmly. "then I turn into a cowgirl again."

The party was in full swing by the time they joined it. Night had fallen and the palm trees swayed softly in the tropical breeze. Frangipani, hibiscus and oleander bushes crowded the emerald lawn and the lighted turquoise pool. Japanese lanterns bathed everyone in a flattering glow. Jane tried to imagine what it would be like to be a real guest at the party, someone who could enjoy the beauty, the music, the gowns and jewels and fine conversation. As it was, she felt both she and Graham were playing a part.

She drank a glass of champagne—too quickly—and smiled and nodded and shook innumerable hands, not remembering a word or a face. And all the time questions and awful, tearing doubts crashed in her head. Graham appeared to be totally in his element, relaxed and debonair, but was he truly as comfortable as he seemed? It could be an act. Jane *hoped* it was an act. But was Graham so caught up in acting that he no longer knew reality from make-believe?

Smedley, looking very handsome in his formal attire, came over to join them. "Have you seen your mother?" he asked Graham.

"Oh, yes, we've seen her. She looks wonderful and she seems to be having a great time."

"You think so? She did perk up quite a bit when I asked her to join me here. Did I do the right thing?"

"Absolutely," put in Jane.

"You better watch out, Dad, or some young attaché will snap her up and you'll be left in the lurch," Graham joked.

"Do you really...? Oh, you're teasing me." Smedley swallowed the last of his champagne. "Perhaps I'd better go find her," he said too casually and wandered off.

There was a midnight buffet set out on the patio. Tables were heaped with seafood salads, caviar, roast beef, fruits of all descriptions, mouth-watering desserts and a luscious six-tiered cake that sported tiny figures of George and Eleanor atop it.

Graham brought Jane a plate piled with samples of everything. They sat beside a pink frangipani bush with the fountain tinkling nearby. A string quartet played a lovely assortment of Mozart and Bach and the sea breeze rustled leaves as background. It should have been idyllic, the fulfillment of any Cinderella's dream, but the props were the only reality in this fairy tale; the prince and Cinderella were false, empty characters, going through the motions, unsure of their next lines or the final act.

The party broke up about four in the morning. The weary revelers left for their homes or hotels or rooms at the Mondragon's huge villa. George and Eleanor said goodbye and thank you hundreds of times. Food and glasses and napkins lay all over the grounds as if Sherman's army had tramped through. One lone party goer was peacefully asleep in his formal attire on an air mattress in the pool.

Smedley and Renée danced obliviously in a corner, totally out of step with the music.

"See you in the morning, Mom," Graham said, tapping her on the shoulder. "The party's over."

Smedley blinked owlishly and looked around. "Who cares," he muttered.

"Good night, *mes chers*," said Renée expansively.

Leading Jane across the littered lawn and into the house, Graham said, "Eleanor told me that you could have the room next to mine." He stopped in front of his door in the dimly lit hallway and took her hands.

Her heart thudded too heavily. It had been a long, long day and she was upset and tired and trying desperately to keep her equilibrium, yet this man's touch still made her heart pound and her knees weak. She looked down. "I'd prefer to stay with you, if you don't mind."

"Janey, ah Janey." He let go of her and shook his head sadly. "I have a feeling that you're on the job."

"I am," she whispered. "Someone here has to remember this is business."

"Business, Janey? Everything between us can be reduced to business?" He didn't sound like the Graham she knew; he sounded older and careworn. "Look, Jane—" he tilted her face up "—can we get everything straightened out when we get back to New York?"

"Oh, Graham." She felt her eyes filling with hot tears. "Oh, how I hope so!"

He opened the door to his room and waited for Jane to enter. She brushed so close to him she could smell the scent of his after-shave. Desire rose within her.

"Well, here we are," he said, attempting levity, trying to regain his normal jauntiness.

Jane could see the two of them reflected in the mirrored closet door—two beautifully dressed people standing close together in an elegantly furnished bedroom. He with hair gleaming golden in the faint light from the bedside lamp, tall and broad shouldered and heartrendingly handsome in his white dinner jacket; she with diamonds sparkling in her hair, her eyes too big, shadowed darkly, her body a column of glimmering golden curves. She hugged at her elbows, feeling empty and cold despite the tropical night air.

What would she do if Graham pulled her into his arms?

CHAPTER SEVENTEEN

JANE KNEW she was asking for trouble by spending the night—no, morning now—in Graham's bedroom. Her body ached with exhaustion, every muscle crying out for rest; her eyes were scratchy and a yawn pressed up from somewhere deep inside her chest. She could see that Graham was subdued as well. He peeled off his dinner jacket, threw it over a chair and started unbuttoning his ruffled shirt.

"For Lord's sake, Janey, relax. I'm not going to bite," he said testily.

"I'd rather be in my own room, believe me," she said with a sigh.

Graham ran a hand through his hair. "Sorry," he mumbled. His shirt was half undone and she could see the fine golden hairs of his chest. "Aw, Jane, don't be mad at me. I can't stand it. Come on over here."

"No," she whispered.

He stared at her silently, his sandy brows drawn together. "I'm not going to let you do this to us," he finally said.

"It may not be entirely up to you, Graham," she answered slowly.

"All right, I'll put all that aside for now, until the job's over. Why don't you at least get undressed? I could use some sleep myself." He yawned widely, the cords in his strong neck stretching.

Jane picked up her overnight bag from the corner where she'd dumped it and went into the bathroom. There was no sense in pushing things by undressing in front of him. Had it only been a few short days ago that she'd been utterly unself-conscious with him, running around his apartment stark naked, laughing, playing hide-and-seek, loving him?

Her filmy blue nightgown was not going to help matters much, she realized, assessing herself in the bathroom mirror. Standing on the cool tile floor, she saw the details of her body beneath the soft nylon. The fabric deepened in color over the hollow of her stomach, lightened and glistened over her breasts and nipples. The material touched her so lightly, yet in her exhausted, keyed-up state, her skin was as sensitive to it as if she had a fever.

Mustering her courage, holding the gold dress carefully over one arm, Jane left the bathroom. Graham was calmly getting into bed, nude. He always slept nude, Jane remembered. His pale, muscular buttocks disappeared under the covers as Jane averted her eyes, flushing with discomfort, unable to banish the images that crowded her mind, images of Graham poised over her, lying beside her, holding her, kissing her....

"Come on, Janey," he said softly and her heart gave a great uncontrollable leap of fear and excitement. Turning her back, she hung the dress carefully in the closet.

"It didn't turn to rags at midnight, did it?" Graham asked drowsily from the bed.

"No, guess I'm just lucky."

"You were beautiful, you were a beautiful Cinderella."

"Thanks," she murmured, putting off the inevitable— getting into bed with Graham.

Finally she padded across the carpet and slipped very carefully into the queen-size bed, as far from him as she could manage.

"Look, Jane, I'm not going to force myself on you. That's not my style," Graham said dryly. "Just go to sleep."

"I'm sort of wound up," she said. "Please turn the light off."

Click. Darkness enshrouded them. Jane lay there stiffly, staring into the night, her heart pounding so hard she was sure Graham could hear it.

His hand moved across the bed, a phantom disembodied entity that came to rest on her hip. Every fiber of Jane's body snapped rigid with expectancy. She tried to find her voice but swallowed instead, her mouth dry and cottony. The word "please" finally crossed her lips, forced up through a constricted throat. She felt on fire suddenly.

"Janey, you'll never get to sleep if you're going to be so tense." His voice came lazily out of the blackness. He rolled over toward her and she was terribly aware of the bed sagging beneath his weight, of the rustle of the bedclothes. "Let me rub your shoulders. You're overtired. You need to relax."

"I'm all right." She didn't sound very convincing.

"You're not. Let me…" His hands touched her neck and began kneading her muscles expertly, warm and strong and knowing, his touch unbelievably pleasurable. He moved down to her shoulders. "Turn your back to me, sweetheart." She did. His fingers found every tired muscle, every spot of tension. She sighed and felt the tautness ebb from her body. She'd let him continue, just for another minute. The sensation was delicious; she felt herself slipping away on a tide of comfort.

"There, that's better," he said quietly, his voice a caress as much as his touch, his fingers massaging, probing, drawing the tightness from her.

She'd stop him in a second, Jane thought, in just another second. But his touch felt so marvelous after her long, dreadful day. So marvelous... She had a moment's realization that she was floating away, her eyes were closing, her body giving up, and then even that faded....

Something was hot on her face. Jane turned her head on the pillow and rolled over with a sigh. Now the heat was on the back of her head. She began to awaken and realized that it was the sun warming her, pouring in through the window and lying in wide swatches of brightness across the bed.

"Mmm," she said, licking her dry lips and stretching her legs. She rolled onto her back and opened her eyes. Graham was standing by the open window, gazing out at the scenery. He looked relaxed, one hand on the casement, the other scratching through sleep-tousled hair that was lit to the color of gold. He was wearing briefs and nothing more. He finally stretched, the corded muscles of his shoulder blades flexing, his flanks long and lean as his arms rose above his head.

He turned away from the light. "Oh, hi," he said, smiling. "Hope I didn't wake you."

Jane averted her gaze and started to sit up. "What time is it?" she asked casually, feeling a slight headache as she moved.

"Around one."

"One! In the afternoon!" She swung out of bed.

"Whoa there. What's the panic?"

"But Graham...the diamonds."

"All is well, my sweet." He moved toward her and she retreated suddenly until the back of her legs bumped into the bed. "Did I ever tell you," he murmured, "that you look beautiful in the morning?"

Then he was standing in front of her, legs apart, reaching up to push her bangs out of her eyes with a gentle hand.

"Don't, please," said Jane.

She wondered how she could want him so desperately in the midst of such doubt. Was it love that allowed for the incongruity of her emotions? Was love really so blindly forgiving?

He lowered his head and kissed her, a soft brush of his lips against hers, warm and provocative. Jane felt her stomach flutter with pleasure even as her mind insisted that she push him away. Graham's arms slipped around her back slowly, soothingly, the way an experienced horseman would handle a skittish colt. He drew Jane toward him until the thin fabric of her nightgown touched the breadth of his chest. His hands moved down her back and spanned her waist, pulling her against him with more urgency. She could feel his hardness then and an ache coiled in her belly.

With every ounce of willpower Jane could gather, she pulled back. Her eyes searched his face as her chest rose and fell too quickly. What was the emotion written in his solemn expression? Was he deceiving her still, using their overpowering attraction as a weapon to confuse her?

Jane stumbled away from him and rushed for the safe haven of the bathroom but his words lingered after her and hung heavily in the air: "You know there's something special between us, Janey."

A half hour later Jane was dressed in clean slacks and blouse, her hair blown dry, her makeup hastily put on. She zipped up her bag, looked around the empty room and then glanced at the golden evening gown still hanging in the open closet. She sighed wistfully and turned to leave.

She found Graham on a sunny breakfast patio, coffee mug in hand, chatting with a few guests who had also slept in.

"Coffee, miss?" asked a maid as Jane stepped onto the patio.

No one was bright-eyed that day. One lady sat in a corner alone, near a tall potted palm, with sunglasses on. Her face was pale. Too much of a good thing, Jane thought wryly.

"We'll be taking off shortly," Graham was saying to his host. "Great party, George." And Jane noticed that of all the people there, Graham was the only one who looked as if he'd gone to bed early with a good book. How did he manage it?

"Are your folks up? I'd like to say goodbye," Jane remarked.

He turned to her nonchalantly. "They already left."

Something was fishy, Jane decided, as their taxi sped toward the airport. It wasn't the diamonds—she'd poked her nose into the belt to reassure herself on that score—and she supposed Smedley and Renée could have risen earlier and not bothered to wait for their son, although it seemed odd, their rushing off like that. And what had happened to Graham's plan to nab the thieves? Had he given up that easily? Did he expect an attempt in the Bermuda airport or perhaps at Kennedy?

"Do you suppose," ventured Jane, "that the thieves followed you to Bermuda?"

"I'm sure they thought of it. If they're not here, they know every move I'm making."

"So your plan is still in effect?"

"Yes, but it would be better if you weren't along."

"Forget it, Mr. Quicksilver, I'm sticking to you like glue."

The argument commenced near the phone in the airport. Graham dialed New York. "Donna?" he said into the receiver while Jane studied faces in the crowd, "it's Graham. Yes, I'm fine.... No, I can give you the message. Tell Lew I'm heading to my dad's place on the Outer Banks—"

"What!" cried Jane, spinning around.

Graham cupped his hand over the receiver. "Quiet, will you? Yes, just for the night," he told Donna. "I'll be arriving back in New York tomorrow... No, Jane and I won't be flying into National...Norfolk, Virginia. Tell Lew. I'm renting a car.... No, no, I'll be fine. It's just that my dad isn't at the beach house and there's a problem there.... You know, the place is really deserted and... Well, never mind, see you late tomorrow. Yeah, bye."

Jane was standing with her feet apart, hands on hips, her jaw thrust forward. "You've really done it now!" she snapped. "The whole office will know every move we're making!"

"Exactly. You know—" his eyes glinted "—you're nose is so cute and freckly when you're mad."

"Oh, stop it! Let me think!"

Short of hog-tying him, there was no way of stopping Graham from pursuing this insanity. Or was it insanity? Maybe it was just a well thought-out scheme to "steal" the diamonds from himself with the help of his father. Why else would they be going to North Carolina? Why else had Smedley left so early that morning? But Graham *did* have the stones—she'd seen them—so how was his father involved?

It was too much for Jane. She slumped sullenly in the plane seat and tried to catch Graham's expression out of the corner of her eye. All he did was turn to her and smile openly and charmingly and pat her hand as the plane lifted into the cloudless blue September sky.

In Norfolk Graham rented a bright red Mustang convertible. "They won't be able to miss us in this number!"

They drove for an hour south to the North Carolina coast, Jane recognizing landmarks along the way: The Chesapeake Crab Company, the Wishart's Hog Farm featuring fresh Virginia ham, the Island Motel with its Triple X films available. Of course, Graham had the top down.

"You realize," said Jane, "that if your thugs *are* following us they could blow either of our heads off with a rifle?"

"It'd be a helluva shot though, wouldn't it?" He looked over at Jane, tipped up his aviator glasses and winked.

"Nothing ever bothers you, does it?"

"Nope. Well, it does bug me that you're doubting my credibility."

Jane fell uncomfortably silent.

There was a long stretch of open country road just before they crossed the bridge to the Outer Banks.

"Well, well," said Graham, his head tilted to look in the rearview mirror.

"What is it?"

"That car. Back there behind the camper. He's been moving up fast and was ready to pass the motor home but then pulled back into his lane."

"You think he spotted us and fell back?"

"Could be."

If this was a farce, Jane thought, it certainly was an elaborate one.

By the time Graham pulled into the sandy driveway leading to his dad's house, the car that was following them—that was *maybe* following them, Jane corrected herself—had disappeared. Not that it couldn't have been a quarter of a mile back up the road. How difficult would it be to spot a shiny red Mustang in Smedley's driveway?

At first Jane didn't notice that the elder Smith's car wasn't there. But when Graham tilted a pot beside the garage and produced a house key, she asked curiously, "Where is your dad, anyway?"

"Maybe he and Mom stopped at the Island Motel," he said humorously.

"That's ridiculous." Jane took her small bag from Graham and put it in the guest room. "So what now?" she asked when she returned to the living room. "Do we just sit and wait or would you rather go for a walk on the beach and leave the diamonds here, with the door unlocked, of course."

Graham patted the belt under his shirt. "We sit and wait."

Jane sank miserably onto the couch, keeping an ear tuned to Graham's movements and musing on the frailty of love and trust.

Graham. He *was* a daredevil. And she loved that part of him, cherished the adventurous spark that had never left him. But that trait of his had a dark side as well, one that might easily get him into trouble, such as now, when he imagined he was outsmarting them all—challenging, daring, seeking that singular thrill.

Could he be as guilty as he looked to her? Wouldn't stealing the diamonds and getting away with it be the ultimate dare, like shaking his fist at the world and walking away victorious?

Oh, he was capable of doing anything he pleased, Jane knew. The question remained: was he capable of a criminal act?

Just then there was the sound of a car in the driveway. Graham came out from the kitchen where he'd been rattling around in cupboards. "Don't tell me that's Dad." He strode to the window.

"It must be," Jane replied, following him.

Renée was there as well, swinging her legs out of the car gracefully, waiting for Smedley to unload the trunk.

"I never expected Dad today," Graham muttered, "much less Mom. I thought he was going to put her on a plane to Montreal." Graham dropped the curtain and turned to Jane, shaking his head in disbelief.

"Oh, here you are!" Renée exclaimed as she swept into the house. "I thought you were headed home to New York, *mon cher*." She gave Graham a kiss on the cheek. "And Jane, too." Renée stood looking at the two of them, then shrugged. "So we are all here. How lovely."

"You're staying?" asked Graham tentatively.

"Perhaps. We shall see." Renée smiled charmingly, in a manner reminiscent of Graham's.

But her son was frowning, a hand rubbing the afternoon stubble on his chin. "Where's Dad, anyway?"

"Fetching the dogs from the neighbor's."

"I, uh, thought you were going to Montreal," Graham said carefully.

"Oh, I *was*. But then I said to myself, why not spend some time at the beach? And the boat. You know, I have not been out on the boat in so long," Renée said nonchalantly, but Jane read between the lines and realized that what Renée meant was, "I wanted to spend some more time with Smedley and see how our tentative truce works out."

A moment later the dogs bounded in, jumping and barking and leaping, knocking the sliding screen door half off its track.

"Settle down!" yelled Smedley, huffing up the steps behind them.

"Hi, Dad," said Graham.

"Oh, you're here already," said Smedley.

"And so are you," replied Graham elliptically.

"I will freshen up," Renée was saying gaily, "and then we'll see what there is for dinner." And she disappeared down the hall.

"I *tried* to get her to go to Montreal," Smedley said in a stage whisper, "but you know your *mother*."

"What are we going to do now?" asked Graham. "I don't want her around tonight."

"Your father knows...?" put in Jane.

"Of course," replied Graham distractedly.

"I tried," said Smedley again.

"The boat," said Graham decisively. "You get her on that boat tonight, Dad."

"What if she won't go?"

"She'll go if you ask her nicely. And I mean *nicely*. Hearts and flowers and all that."

"I don't know if she'll listen."

"She'll listen, don't worry. She went to Bermuda with you, didn't she?"

"So," said Renée, bustling back in, "now for dinner."

"Wait a sec, Renée," said Smedley, catching a silent directive from Graham. "Why don't we go out on the boat tonight?"

"Tonight? But..."

Smedley looked down at his feet, and Jane could have sworn she saw him scuff a toe as if he were an embarrassed schoolboy. "We can fish and cook dinner there. All by ourselves. You know you love the ocean at night." He glanced up to see how she was taking it.

"Why, Smedley..." Renée said, for once nonplussed.

"Then we can, uh, sit on the deck and watch the moon." His voice wavered on the last phrase but he plunged bravely on. "And talk about things."

"Mom, really, I think it's a great idea to go out on the boat," urged Graham. "A great idea! And soon, too, before it gets dark. Don't you think so, Dad?"

"Oh...oh, yes, sure, before dark. Renée, shall we get ready?"

"Well, I don't know. I have to pack, you realize. I cannot *go* just like that." And she snapped her fingers.

Graham rolled his eyes.

"And I wish to talk to you, Smedley, alone." Her back as straight and stiff as a ramrod, Renée disappeared out onto the deck. Smedley followed, looking pained.

Graham sank into a chair and rubbed the bridge of his nose. "The best laid plans of mice and men..."

"What if they don't go out on the boat?"

"I'll make them go to a motel."

"You really think..." began Jane.

"Yes, damn it, I think this house is *not* going to be the safest place for a second honeymoon tonight!" he snapped.

"And I'm supposed to go along with you, whatever crazy thing you plan to do?" Jane retorted angrily.

He put up a hand to silence her. "Yes, and let's drop the subject. I'm positive everything will be cleared up by tomorrow and, boy, you better give me one huge apology, lady, and I mean *huge*."

Jane was about to say that she hoped she could when the raised voices of Graham's parents filtered into the house.

"Is this some kind of plot?" Renée was asking. "I'm not stupid, you know, and I know my son and his mad notions!"

"I would merely like your company, Renée," said Smedley.

"After a year?" came her sharp query.

"Yes, damn it, after a year."

"Don't you talk to me like that!"

"Then, for Lord's sake, Renée, come out on the boat with me!" shouted Smedley.

"You really want me to?" she asked, suddenly sounding vulnerable.

"Yes, damn it!"

"Sh! The children will hear!" warned Renée.

When his parents came in, Graham was studiously occupied reading a magazine and Jane was busy getting herself a soda from the refrigerator.

"Graham," said his father, "your mother and I are taking the boat out before it gets dark."

"Terrific!" said Graham innocently.

"Will you please go pack," Smedley said to his wife, none too gently. "And for God's sake, Renée, just a small bag!"

Renée said over her shoulder, "I shall bring whatever I require. It might be a trunkful, *mon cher*."

A half hour later, the dogs yelping in the drive and scratching the paint on the car with their jumping, the couple was ready to leave. Renée had not taken along a trunk, Jane noted, but a bag that would have sufficed most people for two weeks.

Smedley swore as he put the case in the trunk of the car and pinched a finger when he closed it. Renée ignored him, waving and blowing them both kisses.

"Be good!" she called. "Please, *mes enfants*."

Jane smiled dutifully and waved back, thinking these two were going to make this reconciliation work yet.

"They're off at last," stated Graham, standing there with his hands in his pockets, the setting sun catching his hair and setting it aflame.

A pirate, Jane thought. He would always, no matter the outcome of their night, be her buccaneer.

"Well—" he turned back toward the house and grinned at her "—we're all alone now, Janey."

CHAPTER EIGHTEEN

JANE UNWRAPPED A FROZEN PIZZA and crammed the empty box into the trash can. "What I really can't figure out," she said to Graham casually, "is why you're so all-fire sure the thieves will make a try tonight." *There, that was put calmly,* she thought, proud of her control.

It *could* be true, after all, that he was actually being honest with her. Paying lip service to his story wouldn't hurt. No matter what, though, she planned to watch his scheme unfold and be ready to foil any attempt of his to make off with the stones.

Graham was busy turning on the oven, opening and closing cupboard doors, mumbling about the missing pizza pan.

"Well?" she said.

"Oh. The thieves have to try. Can you think of a better setup than this? A deserted house, nighttime, no witnesses..."

"But *us*," Jane reminded him.

"I meant there are no witnesses in the area, no one to notice them or their car." He put the pizza on a cookie sheet and stuck it into the oven. "Remember, no one's seen their faces yet. No one can identify them."

Jane frowned. "I know there's something familiar about one of them. It makes me so mad that I can't put a finger on it but everything happened so fast in Amsterdam. But

I'm sure...there was something—that man in Central Park that day..."

"Don't worry, we'll find out soon enough, Janey."

"I don't know how you can be so sure."

"Call it experience or a gut feeling or intuition." Graham chucked her under the chin. "Now come on and help me put the dogs away. With those two buffoons loose no one would get within a mile of this place."

Jane followed Graham out to the deck where he whistled for the dogs. They came eventually, galloping up from the beach, tongues flapping, stubby black tails wagging. Heckle jumped up, sandy paws square on Graham's chest, and almost knocked him over. He laughed and pressed the dog down.

"Someone should take those dogs in hand," grumbled Jane. "They're the most ill-behaved, useless mutts I've ever seen."

"They're enthusiastic," corrected Graham. "My mother gave them to Dad for Christmas one year and he'll never get rid of them, believe me."

Finally Heckle and Jeckle were locked safely away in the guest bedroom with bowls of dog food and water, which they were lapping up and spattering the floor with when Jane last saw them.

"Now what?" she asked.

"We eat the pizza."

"I mean what do we do about setting the trap?" Jane asked impatiently.

"We act natural, as if we don't have a care in the world. We eat, we go to bed—together—and we turn the lights off and leave the doors carefully unlocked."

"Then we lie there and wait."

"Yes," Graham said. "Together. With hours to waste."

Jane checked the oven, turning her back on him. "What if we fall asleep? And where will the diamonds be?"

He patted his waist. "I'll take the belt off and leave it on the dresser."

"Do you think they're watching us now?" asked Jane uneasily.

Graham shrugged. "Probably. I certainly would if I were them."

Jane shuddered. *Was* he one of them?

"Aw, Janey, don't be nervous," Graham said, misinterpreting her tremor. "You could see they were absolute amateurs. You and I can take care of them without so much as a broken fingernail."

She turned, leaning back against the kitchen counter, and studied his face. Could he be desperate beneath that easy facade? Could Smedley be involved in this, too? After that blatantly coincidental meeting in Bermuda, Jane had to consider that possibility. Was Smedley planning on receiving the "stolen" diamonds and splitting them later with the two mystery men and Graham? Or was Smedley going to sneak back and help steal the diamonds himself? Did he need money? Renée must receive an allowance from him and she did have *very* expensive tastes...

Jane thought about what Graham had just said. He was right; she and Graham could take the two thugs—if they were working together on the same side. "Boy, I hope so," was all she replied.

They took their sloppy pieces of pizza out onto the floodlit deck and watched the ships' lights slide across the black satin water.

"It's beautiful," Jane said with a sigh. "I wish I could enjoy it more. Just the thought of somebody out there watching us makes my skin crawl."

"It is too bad," Graham agreed.

"You mean it makes you nervous, too?" Jane asked hopefully.

"Well, no, I mean it's too bad you aren't enjoying yourself."

"Oh."

"You know," Graham said after a while, "I miss those two galumphing brutes. Things aren't right without them spraying sand all over and bringing me rotten fish heads."

The night breeze carried sea odors on it: salt water and seaweed and wet sand. It was getting seasonably cool out. Soon a person would need a sweater, Jane thought.

"It's hurricane season," Graham said unexpectedly.

"Sure doesn't seem like it," mused Jane.

"It can change in an hour. But nothing's headed our way right now, don't worry."

"Nothing but trouble."

Graham was fiddling with something at his waist.

"What are you doing?"

"I'm taking this damn belt off. It makes me sweat." He pulled it out from under his shirt and gave a sigh of relief. "And if they're watching us this'll give them even more incentive."

Jane sat up straight. "Put that somewhere safe!" she whispered.

"Not too safe, Janey. They have to think they can get at it. You don't hide the cheese in a mousetrap—you load the trap with the biggest, juiciest piece you can find."

"I hate this! I'm a bodyguard, not a mousetrap!"

Graham tossed the diamond belt carelessly on the patio table and leaned over Jane. "If you're upset, I'll drive you to a motel or even the Norfolk airport. You know I would have preferred to do this alone. I don't want anything to happen to you, sweetheart." His voice reflected his concern; he was worried about her peace of mind. She had to believe he cared.

"Oh, no, I'm staying," she said. "After all this, I'm sticking with you to the end."

He ran a finger along her jawline. "I was afraid that's what you'd say. It's that stubborn streak of yours, Janey. But then I wouldn't want you without it, would I?" He straightened. "Time for bed," he said briskly. "Let's retire and await developments. I'd just as soon get it all over with."

"So would I," Jane said fervently.

Halfway to Graham's bedroom, she froze in horror then whirled on him. "The diamonds!" she cried. "You left them on the deck!"

"So I did," he said unconcernedly. "I'll get them."

But Jane pushed past him, raced out through the door and pounced on the belt where it still lay on the table. "Thank heavens!" she breathed. She felt the small, hard shapes inside the belt with her fingers, just to make sure. The diamonds were there.

"Sorry," said Graham behind her. He sounded sheepish. "That was dumb."

"Inexcusable," Jane said between clenched teeth. "Unless you *want* the thieves to get them!"

He hesitated a moment, as if there was something he wanted to say but then shook his head and repeated, "Sorry."

"This is Lew's business," Jane said, shaking the belt in his face. "And my job. And Norma's and Peter's and Donna's and everybody else's jobs! These diamonds are precious for a lot of reasons!"

But Graham just turned away and went back toward his bedroom without responding. Jane was filled with disappointment and pain. She wanted to run after him and shake him and pummel him and scream at him: *Why, Graham, why? What are you doing? Tell me, confide in me. We can fix it somehow. Bow out before it's too late. If our love means anything to you, please, make this come out right!*

But she couldn't. Her only hope lay in keeping quiet, in going along with his game, in being totally ready to react to whatever happened. "Never give your opponent a hint of what's in your mind," Rob Dearborn had taught. "That way you always have the edge."

Abruptly Jane realized that she was all alone on the floodlit deck, surrounded by black ocean and empty sand dunes. The sea oats waved in a night breeze, their dark, spindly shadows reaching toward her. Her mind played a nasty trick on her and she believed, for a moment, that someone really was out there, waiting and watching. She shivered, hurried inside, slid the screen door shut and stood in the living room, her heart pattering like the tattoo of horses' hoofs on a race track.

Graham was already in bed, still fully dressed, propped up with a *Gentleman's Quarterly*. "Want the lights off?" he asked pleasantly.

"Yes." Jane noted the diamond belt on the dresser. How would they come for it? Through a window? Would they create a diversion and hope Jane and Graham left the diamonds unguarded?

"Tired?" He looked at her over the magazine.

"Yes. No. I couldn't sleep a wink."

"Well, we have to turn the lights off eventually. If you want to get some sleep, you can. I'm used to staying up."

She glanced at him sharply. Oh sure, he'd love that! Jane peacefully, conveniently asleep when the diamonds disappeared!

"Come on, sweetheart, it's warm and comfy in here."

Gingerly she slipped her shoes off and slid into bed next to him, leaving as much space between them as possible. It was only last night that they'd been in the Mondragon's guest room and she'd gotten into bed with him there, as well. This was getting ridiculous. If Rick Como had been sent on this job, would Jane have had to share a bed with him? Or was this all Graham's doing?

"Lights out," Graham said as he snapped off the lamp.

The bedroom was plunged into darkness. Jane felt her heart constrict. Would the thieves come soon? She lay there stiffly, listening, straining to hear in the blackness. When Graham's hand touched her clenched fist she gasped.

"Hey, it's only me. Relax. They'll wait a good long time before they try anything. They'll want us to be asleep." He pried her fingers away from her palm. "You can't lay there like Chuck Norris all night."

Jane saw a glimmer of humor in the situation. She tried to relax.

"That's better," came Graham's disembodied voice. His hand played with her fingers. "You want to talk?"

"Talk about what?"

"Anything. You start."

"I can't think of anything." What Jane wanted to talk about was not idle chatter. "You first."

"Hmm, let's see." He was silent for a while. "Do you want funny stories or life history or philosophy?"

"Funny stories." Jane settled herself more comfortably, one ear cocked for trouble. It was going to be a long night.

"Did I ever tell you about the time my roommates stole my clothes and left me naked in the girls' dorm...?"

It was a funny story. Jane laughed and found herself feeling easier about everything. Graham had a way of making the best of a situation. He was a nice person to be around and he took the edge off unpleasant circumstances. He made life fun.

The night ticked on. Once Jane heard a loud thump and sat bolt upright. "Shh!" There was another thump.

"It's the dogs," Graham said.

But Jane had to get up and tiptoe down the hall to listen at the guest room door. There was another thump, then the slurping of water and a long whining yawn. Yes, it had been the dogs.

"Your feet are cold," Graham said when she climbed back into bed.

"How do you know?"

"I can tell. Should I warm them up for you?"

"No." Jane felt a sudden irrational spurt of fear. If he touched her she was lost. "Talk some more."

He was lying on his back, an arm behind his head, one leg crossed over the other. She could see his profile now that her eyes were used to the dark. A flood of images piled one upon the other in her mind, a photo album of mental snapshots. Graham naked, poised over her, making love to her. Graham on the *Renée*, fluid and efficient, fearless in the storm. Graham at the hospital, enfolding her in his arms, comforting her after Norma had been shot. In his apartment in New York cooking. At the top of the Empire State Building. At the ranch in Rifle in Jared's jeans and boots...

"You know, I'm not so young anymore. Thirty-three," he said in a pensive tone.

"The venerable old age of thirty-three."

"Now don't tease, I'm trying to be serious. You see," he said then hesitated, "I think I...fell in love with you, Janey, way back that first day in Rifle."

Jane lay frozen, unable to breathe. Did he mean it? Her suspicion wove ugly threads into the fabric of Graham's words. Was he only trying to put her off guard?

His hand reached across the blanket to take hers. She felt the warmth of his grasp and something within her melted.

"A man shouldn't be alone. Or a woman. I'd hate to grow old alone. I guess my parents' separation affected me more than I thought. I'm awful glad they're trying to get together again. I imagined them alone, my dad here and Mom in Montreal. Lonely and getting older. It hit me. It's time, Janey. I want to settle down. I want to marry you."

Silence filled the room to bursting. What could she say? She wanted to kiss him, to whisper, "Yes, I'll marry you. I love you," but she couldn't. Her awful suspicions had to be quieted first.

What a dreadful mess.

"Janey?"

She licked her lips and tried her voice. "Yes?"

"You're shocked."

"Yes, no. I don't know."

"Well, will you?"

"What?"

"Marry me?"

"Oh God, Graham, I'll have to, uh, think about it. This is really a big decision."

"You love me, don't you?"

Her answer was instant and truthful. "Yes, I love you."

"Well, then, that's all I need to know. Take your time, Janey, and let me know when you're ready. Hey, I know this is a lousy time to ask you. You're all tense and tired and worried about the diamonds." He squeezed her hand. "Trust me. Nothing will happen to them."

Trust me, he said. Oh, how she wished she could throw herself at him and cry, "Yes! Let's get married right now!"

But first she had to trust him. "I'm sorry, Graham. It's just that I have to get used to the idea." Horrible, trite words lifted from some bad Gothic novel. She was a liar. She'd been thinking about marrying Graham since the first day she'd met him.

"Sure, sure, scary, isn't it? A whole life together? Kids. Babies crying and all those little problems. Fights and doing the dishes and the flu and getting old together. But I love you, Janey, and we'll be a wonderful couple."

He was right. They were meant for each other. Graham couldn't be a thief, not her handsome, dashing, fun-loving buccaneer, her romantic hero, not Graham.

A second later he was telling her about how he hated kids' toys in the living room. "We'd need a family room, don't you think? City or suburbs? And we'd go to the ranch in the summers. Your dad can teach the kids how to ride. And my dad can teach them how to sail..." He leaned over and brushed her cheek with his lips. Her heart squeezed with love and pain. "You want to go into the other room and get some rest?"

"No," she said quickly. "I'm fine."

She must have dozed off a while because she found herself jerking awake. But Graham only told her to go back to sleep and patted her hand again. Instead she half sat up, pounded the pillow behind her into a hard ball and dug her fingernails into her palms. *No sleeping,* she told herself. To pass the time she imagined a life in which she was Graham's wife. They'd go on wonderful vacations, everywhere in the world. They'd ride and sail and have fascinating friends. Around every corner would be an adventure. And they'd love each other so much. She could work part-time when they had children; she'd be at home waiting for him when he got back from his assignments.

She was lost in the brightly colored fairy tale of Graham and her and two amazingly beautiful children on a picnic in a delightful sylvan setting when she became aware of Graham stiffening beside her. Simultaneously, down the hall, the dogs began to bark and throw themselves against the guest room door.

Jane found herself on her feet, every muscle alert. "Where are they?"

Graham was beside her in the darkness. "In the living room," he whispered grimly. "Let's go."

"Get the diamonds," she said quickly, then she edged out into the hall. The lack of light would hinder the thieves more than her and Graham, who knew the layout of the house, and the dogs' barking would cover the sound of their movements.

"Careful, Janey," came Graham's quiet voice. "I'll try to get around behind them. They must have come in—" But his words were cut off by a splintering crash, and before Jane realized that Heckle and Jeckle had broken through the door she saw their fleeting shadows dart into the living room.

Instantly there was pandemonium: furniture overturned, thumps, cries of fright, dogs growling and yelping.

"The light!" Jane cried, "I'll get the light." She edged around the wall toward the switch. A voice was cursing in the darkness, a familiar voice. *Who was it?* She reached the light, readied herself for movement and snapped the lamp on.

A tableau of chaos met her eyes when they adjusted to the sudden brightness. Graham was moving between the two men and the sliding doors, the dogs were leaping about, chairs were knocked over, lamps broken. The thieves stood stock-still in the center of the room and Jane immediately recognized the faces, but then things moved so fast that she didn't have time to put names to them.

The two men started edging toward the open door to the deck. Graham said something and stood in their path. Jane was on her way to grab one of them while Graham took the other. The first thief tried to push past Graham. A dog streaked through the air after the man, slamming into Graham's shoulder, knocking him sprawling into the fireplace. There was a thud and Graham lay motionless. The thief stopped, snatched the diamond belt from where it had fallen out of Graham's hand, flashed a look of utter fear and hate at Jane, then fled out the door. His companion hurried after him.

Chase them or see to Graham? Jane's mind screamed. The dogs were at full cry down the beach after the two men. She kneeled by Graham, terrified, but he was already trying to sit up. Thank God, he was all right.

He looked dazed and there was blood on his forehead. "Go after them," he croaked. "Janey, get them. I'm okay."

She had time for a split second of relief, then she was out the door, following the uproar Heckle and Jeckle were making. A pink mother-of-pearl light washed the sky behind the ocean. Dawn. The night was over. She could see deep footsteps in the sand then smaller dog prints overlaying them. She couldn't let those men get away. They had the diamonds! This shouldn't have happened! It was those dogs, those damn, misbehaved dogs!

It was difficult running in the loose sand, frustrating, like the awful slowness of a nightmare. She pushed herself, panting, and the sounds grew closer. Just beyond the next dune she spotted several dark struggling figures in the quickening light.

One dog had a man by a trouser leg, snarling and pulling, while the man tried to kick at him. The other dog was playing tug-of-war with something in the second man's hand, his legs braced as he tugged and growled and shook his head. My God, it was the diamond belt!

Jane ran up and without stopping knocked the first man down with a roundhouse kick. Jeckle let go of the man's pant leg and cocked his head at Jane in question, sniffed at the fallen form curiously then stood guard over him. The second man—it was Frank Hansen, she realized, finally putting name and face together—was panicked, terrified of Heckle but not letting go of the belt. He gave a mighty yank and Heckle released it with a yelp; Frank flew backward to land in the sand, the belt flying out of his hands. Jane leaped on him and got him in a joint lock.

"The police are on the way," she said panting, praying Graham *had* phoned them. But at least she had the two men—Frank and his friend, Harve—and she wasn't about to let either one get away, no matter what!

Crouching there in the pale light, her heart pounding like mad with triumph and nervousness and anxiety, Jane wondered how long she'd have to keep these men under control.

Was Graham all right? Had he called the police yet?

Heckle was busy with something down by the waterline. The belt. He was tossing it about, worrying it as if it were one of his raggedy toys. "Heckle!" she called. "Come!" He stopped and looked at her, undecided. The first rays of the sun were spilling across the ocean, reaching toward Jane over the tips of the waves. "Come, Heckle!" she called again.

The dog started toward her, growling and flinging the belt. She took her eyes from her prisoners for a split second and yelled at him. "Dumb dog! Come, Heckle!"

He galloped toward her, still shaking the belt, and with horror, Jane saw the gems tumbling from a tear in the fabric and Heckle was gaily shaking more out. They glittered and winked as they arched up into the pink sunlight then fell to the wet sand.

Jane couldn't move and, oh Lord, the tidal surge was sucking the stones out into the ocean and the stupid dog wouldn't stop cavorting and miserably, horribly, Jane had to watch the foam carry ten million dollars in diamonds out into the Graveyard of the Atlantic.

CHAPTER NINETEEN

THE DIAMOND CAUGHT THE LIGHT and shot blue fire. Jane moved her hand so that everyone could see it better.

"Well, when's the big day?" asked James, the brother closest in age to Jane, a joker, a teaser, as open as the Colorado sky.

Jane turned in the circle of Graham's arm and tilted her head up to him. "Well, we thought we'd leave it up to Daddy. We want to have the wedding here, don't we, Graham?"

Tom Manning rubbed the gray stubble on his chin thoughtfully. "Is this gonna be a big shindig or something we can handle?"

"Small," said Jane promptly. "Renée and Smedley will want to come, of course. And all of us and..." She was counting on her fingers and looked up, surprised. "That's not so small."

"How 'bout Thanksgiving?" Tom peered at Graham. "You ready, boy?"

Graham laughed. "Yes, sir, Mr. Manning, I'm as ready as I'll ever be!"

"Brave fella." Tom nodded in admiration.

"You got guts, mister," Jared said, slapping Graham on the back.

"Think you're up to a bachelor party?" asked John.

Graham cleared his throat. "You men really are going to have to take it easy on a city slicker like me," he said humbly.

"Quit shufflin' your feet," ribbed James. "Jane told us about you. You're puttin' us on."

They all laughed. Jane was thrilled that everyone seemed to be getting along so well. She'd been nervous as she and Graham drove up the long dirt road to the ranch, and a little choked up at the memories that came rushing back at her. But Graham had put a hand over hers and she'd known he understood and that he'd always be there for her.

There she was, a woman who was all grown up, had gone out into the world and succeeded. A woman who was coming home with the man she was going to marry. It was all a little overwhelming and emotional but she had her anchor, Graham, so she would never be adrift.

There was a big dinner waiting for the Manning clan, a homecoming celebration. Trish, Joe's wife, was setting the table with John's fiancée. Little Joey, fat-cheeked and content, was being passed around from burly arm to burly arm.

"Boy, has he grown," said Jane.

"He's gonna be a big boy," said Tom proudly.

There were two extra places at the table, Jane noticed. "Who's coming?" she asked curiously.

"Rob Dearborn and his wife," said James. "We thought he'd like to hear all about your job."

Jane was ecstatic. "Oh, Graham, you'll be able to meet them! Isn't that great?"

"Wonderful," Graham said wryly. "Maybe he can give me a few pointers on how to get out of that arm lock you got me into in Amsterdam."

"She put you in an arm lock?" asked Tom suspiciously.

"Was that to make you marry her?" asked Jared, hooting with laughter.

Jane snapped something rude to her brother.

"It's a long story." Graham grinned at Jane.

"I think we better hear it," said Joe. "Sounds interesting."

"Oh, it's interesting, all right," replied Graham.

Rob Dearborn and his wife arrived shortly. His smile was reserved, his manner as quiet as usual. He gave Jane a warm handshake and turned to Graham as Jane introduced them. "Good to meet you. I'd like to talk to you sometime...."

His wife smiled apologetically and pulled on his arm. "Later, dear."

"You folks going on a honeymoon?" asked John.

"Well, we'd like to sail the *Renée*," began Jane. "That's Graham's father's boat."

"I thought Renée was Graham's father's *wife*," said Tom, puzzled.

"She is. The boat's named *Renée*, but we're having a little trouble reserving her—the boat, that is."

"My parents don't want to get off her," Graham explained. "They're on about their fifth honeymoon by now."

"Hey, we'll have to go see this boat of yours," said Jared. "I've never been on anything but a rowboat."

Jane pictured the Manning men crewing the *Renée*. "You'd all sink her," she groaned.

"Dinner," called Trish.

The conversation around the big dining table was animated, the Manning men interrupting one another loudly and frequently, the women talking across broad chests about the coming wedding. Tom Manning stood at the head of the table and carved the roast and looked content while Graham took the inevitable teasing in stride in spite of Jane's retorts—"Stop that Jared," and, "That's cruel, John!" and, "Not at the dinner table, Joe." More than once her face turned the color of ripe apples.

"Are you going to give up your job then?" asked Trish.

"Oh, heavens, no," Jane was quick to reply. She put a forkful of potatoes down and looked around the table. "Lew, my boss, was thinking of selling Mercury. We may buy it."

"You and Graham?" asked Tom.

Jane glanced at her father. "Yes. Graham thinks we make a good team."

"You can't deny it, Janey, we *do* make a good team," remarked Graham, taking her hand and smiling proudly at her. "The best ever."

Jane looked down at her plate, embarrassed and thrilled, adoring Graham, loving and ruing her position in the spotlight.

"What about children? I mean," said her father, "you'll be a married woman."

"When we decide it's time for a little one—" Graham looked at Jane "—well, I guess we'll work that out, too."

"Sounds like a tall order," Tom said.

"Daddy," chided Jane, "don't be old-fashioned."

"Umph," came a sound from her father's chest and a debate over working married women sprang up hot and heavy around the table.

"Is it always like this?" asked Graham of Trish Manning.

"Every time we all sit down to a meal together." She shrugged and smiled. "You'll get used to it."

"I hope so."

"Tell us about this arm-lock thing," said Joe, wisely changing the subject. "You've got our curiosity ticking."

"Go on, you tell them," Graham urged. "They'd never believe me."

Jane took a deep breath. Where to begin? With Amsterdam or even further back, with the mugging in the park, or Norma?

"Well," she said, "Mercury Courier was having trouble..." She went on to tell them about the thefts, Lew's suspicion that they were inside jobs, Norma's shooting.

"My Lord," her father thundered, "and you're telling me this work isn't dangerous?"

Rob and Graham spent a good five minutes calming him down.

"Do you want to hear the story or don't you?" Jane finally asked.

"All right," muttered Tom, "get on with it."

She explained about Amsterdam and the theft attempt at the airport, including the infamous arm lock Graham couldn't break. Her brothers nodded, having been the subjects more than once of Jane's arm locks—in practice, of course.

"So that move we practiced worked well against the man with the gun?" Rob wanted to know.

"Perfectly," Jane replied. "He didn't have a chance to pull the trigger."

"Go *on*," said James.

"Okay, so the two guys got away at the airport and..." She told them, shamefaced, about her suspicion that Graham was trying to steal the diamonds, about her chasing him to Bermuda, carefully leaving out her near-arrest by Captain Vermeer—that was *too* embarrassing—and about the party.

"What did you wear to the party?" asked Trish, wide-eyed.

The men mumbled scornfully as Jane started to describe the gold dress.

"Janey, my love," said Graham, leaning close, "I think you'd better get on with the action."

She told them about the beach house and how they'd set a trap for the thieves. "But the dogs ruined everything."

"The dogs?" John asked.

"Heckle and Jeckle. Smedley's two Dobermans."

"Dobermans, you mean, watchdogs?"

"Well . . ." said Graham.

"Dumb mutts," said Jane. "Crazy dogs." She told them about the chaotic confrontation in the house, Graham getting knocked out and the chase down the beach.

"And I was staggering around in the house trying to remember my own name," said Graham. "It only took me a little while, though, and then I called the police and went looking for my bodyguard." He shook his head and chuckled, remembering. "I'll never forget the sight. There was one man on the sand out cold and the other afraid to move because of Jane and the dogs and my sweet little Janey, jumping up and down, mad as a hatter, watching the diamonds wash out to sea."

"So who were the thieves?" asked Jared.

"Frank was Donna's boyfriend and Harve was his partner. See, Donna was the receptionist at Mercury." And Jane had to describe that whole part of the story, about how Frank had known every move the couriers made because of Donna's penchant for gossip. "And Harve was the man who tried to mug me in Central Park that morning. I knew one of the thieves in Amsterdam looked familiar. It was driving me crazy because I couldn't remember—"

"*You got mugged?*" Tom Manning rose from his chair and hovered over the table again.

"He tried," said Jane. "Rob, that roundhouse kick took him right out, worked beautifully."

Tom sank back silently, shaking his head.

"The *diamonds*, Jane, what happened to the diamonds?" asked John. "Did you get them back?"

Jane exchanged a glance with Graham, who looked down modestly, hiding a grin. "You tell them, Jane."

"No, it was your idea," said Jane.

"Come on, squirt," shouted James, "tell us!"

"There weren't diamonds, they were rhinestones," said Jane. "Glass."

"You mean you went through all that to deliver *rhinestones*?" Jared demanded.

"I exchanged the real ones on Bermuda with my dad. We'd planned it a few days before with Lew's approval," explained Graham.

"So what I saw in the safe there," Jane told them, "were rhinestones. Then Smedley delivered the real ones to New York the next morning and was back on the Outer Banks before dark."

"A sleight of hand," mused Rob. "Very clever."

"Very transparent," said Graham, "but it worked. The real diamonds were never really in any danger except for a short time in Amsterdam and Jane and I always had the edge."

"But," she said, "Lew didn't want anyone to know about the switch."

"And rightly so," put in Rob. "The fewer who know a plan, the more likely it is to work."

"I sure was mad, though," reflected Jane.

"And all along poor Janey thought *I* was stealing them myself," said Graham.

"That's dreadful." Trish shook her head.

"Oh, it was." Jane turned to her sister-in-law. "From now on, though, it's all on the up and up between us. No more tricks. Graham—" she swung around and caught his eye "—promised. Didn't you, dear?"

"You bet, my sweet," he hastened to say.

Dessert was hot apple pie à la mode. Jane ate a fair portion then settled back in her seat, her arms folded across her stomach. "I do feel sorry for Donna," she told them. "The poor girl had lousy judgment."

"This Frank sounds like a real winner," said Rob.

"Well, it's history now," said Graham, serving himself a second helping of the pie. "They go to trial next month and the D.A. thinks they'll each get twenty years. It would have been life, or worse, if Norma hadn't made it."

"Will she be all right?" asked Rob's wife.

Jane nodded. "She'll be back on the job by Christmas. She's even promised to brush up on her karate."

"It will serve her better than any weapon," said Rob with assurance.

"I think," Jane mused, "that her mistake in judging Graham hurt her more than the bullet."

"But she apologized," said Graham. "She's a real lady."

"And as for Donna," Jane went on, "they aren't prosecuting her because she didn't know a thing about what was going on. She did get fired, though. And I don't blame Lew one bit. It will be a good lesson for her. Heck, she's already got a new spot in Macy's. Accounting department."

"What about your apartment?" asked her father. "Seems like you just moved in. And your landlady, what's her name?"

"Lily," said Jane. "No problem. Lew hired a new receptionist and she's desperate for a place. She'll even buy all my pots and sheets and everything." Jane stopped and glanced over at Graham. "Everything but Pard."

Tom Manning looked bewildered. "Can't says ol' Pard was ever for sale."

Jane had to explain. Even after her explanation of the huge stuffed horse the Manning clan looked vaguely perplexed.

After dinner Jane and Graham announced that they were taking a walk, all the while trying hard to disregard the knowing smiles directed their way. A brilliant canopy of stars spread overhead as they headed toward the barn, arms wrapped around each other. The air was sharp and cold, and snow had dusted the hard ground.

"That's quite a clan you've got there," Graham said in an amused tone of voice.

"Think you can handle 'em, pardner?" she replied, laughing.

"As long as they don't get the shotguns out."

"Graham, you aren't really mad at me, are you? I mean because I thought you were stealing the diamonds?"

He tipped her chin up. "You were doing your job, Janey. I admit it, I looked guilty. I wanted to tell you a hundred times but Lew—"

"I know, he made you promise not to tell me."

"Listen, if it had gone on another minute, I'd have told you, Lew or no Lew."

She snuggled up against him. "Okay, just so there are no more secrets between us."

"Never again," Graham swore. "It's too much trouble keeping a secret from you." He smiled down at her. "Come on, let's go see my ol' buddy, Pard."

"Your *buddy*?"

"Sure, after all, we were pretty close there for a while."

Jane laughed. "For a little while, anyway."

They walked to the barn, holding each other close. Graham's lips brushed hers. "Cold," he murmured, "but I bet I can heat them up."

The barn was warm and dark and echoing, filled with the smell of animals and hay and leather, a familiar, welcoming odor to Jane. She flicked on the light and blinked in its brightness. A whinny came from a stall down the line and Graham tugged on Jane's sleeve. "There's Pard." They stopped at the horse's stall and Jane held her hand out.

"Come here, boy, that's it. Remember your old *buddy* here, Graham?" Pard chewed affectionately at her glove.

"I'll tell you something, Janey," said Graham as he put an arm around her shoulder. "I'm new at this love business but I honestly believe that marriage has to be able to survive a crisis. Lots of them probably."

"Like your folks."

"Yes, like them."

"I love you very, very much, Graham Smith," said Jane.

"And I love you," he whispered, taking her into his arms. Then he looked over at Pard. "Think the old boy'll be jealous?"

"Never mind," murmured Jane, pulling his head down.

It was several minutes later when they broke apart. Jane leaned back in Graham's arms and studied his face, his beloved, familiar face. His eyes were laughing, full of fun, shining like steel in the light.

"Who says you can't catch Quicksilver?" breathed Jane lovingly.

Pard lifted his head and gave a long, satisfied whinny.

Harlequin Superromance

COMING NEXT MONTH

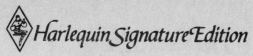

Penny Jordan

Stronger Than Yearning

He was the man of her dreams!

The same dark hair, the same mocking eyes; it was as if the Regency rake of the portrait, the seducer of Jenna's dream, had come to life. Jenna, believing the last of the Deverils dead, was determined to buy the great old Yorkshire Hall—to claim it for her daughter, Lucy, and put to rest some of the painful memories of Lucy's birth. She had no way of knowing that a direct descendant of the black sheep Deveril even existed—or that James Allingham and his own powerful yearnings would disrupt her plan entirely.

Penny Jordan's first Harlequin Signature Edition *Love's Choices* was an outstanding success. Penny Jordan has written more than 40 best-selling titles—more than 4 million copies sold.

Now, be sure to buy her latest bestseller, *Stronger Than Yearning*. Available wherever paperbacks are sold—in October.

What the press says about Harlequin romance fiction…

"When it comes to romantic novels…
Harlequin is the indisputable king."
—*New York Times*

"…always with an upbeat, happy ending."
—*San Francisco Chronicle*

"Women have come to trust these
stories about contemporary people,
set in exciting foreign places."
—*Best Sellers*, New York

"The most popular reading matter of
American women today."
—*Detroit News*

"…a work of art."
—*Globe & Mail*, Toronto

An enticing new historical romance!

Spring Will Come

SHERRY DeBorde

It was 1852, and the steamy South was in its last hours of gentility. Camille Braxton Beaufort went searching for the one man she knew she could trust, and under his protection had her first lesson in love....

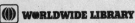
SPR-1